THE
CHANNELER

Book One of The Wind Lord's Gambit

William H.
Kline IV

For the Months,
and the Years.

Cover designed by Chris Daemon

This book is a work of fiction. Names, characters, places, and incidents either are products of the author's imagination or are used fictitiously. Any resemblance to actual persons, living or dead, events, or locales is entirely coincidental.

William H. Kline IV

Printed in the United States of America

First Printing: Dec 2018
Amazon Kindle Direct Publishing

ISBN-978 1790702 879

Books by William H Kline IV

The Wind Lord's Gambit
The Channeler
The Guardian
The Blood Mage
The Mage Knight (coming soon)

CHAPTER ONE

People several generations ago talk about remembering where they were and what they were doing during the Kennedy assassination. People of the next-younger generation say the same thing about the attacks of September 11th. But people of this generation, every single one of them, can remember without a doubt what they were doing when the power commonly called 'magic' returned to the world. Despite, or maybe because of, all the chaos and calamity that took place afterword, that one moment remains locked in the memory of all humanity.

For Tommy Nelson, the day was notable because he didn't have to go to school for a whole week.

None of the aftermath really affected Tommy at all. When people experienced a new kind of power, saw strange, new things, and went insane from it all, Tommy didn't care. No one that Tommy knew lashed out in a torrent of power and burned their family alive or destroyed an entire building. When the inevitable government crackdown happened and squads of trained men came to Tommy's school looking for "mages", it just meant that Tommy got out of class for the afternoon while they ran the tests. Sure, several of Tommy's classmates were escorted out of the building, never to be seen again, but what did that matter? All it meant to Tommy was a shorter line at lunch, and he wasn't very good friends with any of them, anyway. Not really.

Today was not such a lucky day for Tommy, he reflected, as he sat in class and let the teacher's words wash over him. The subject was math, and the teacher, Mr. Miller, was droning on about the many uses of some theorem that he'd introduced to the class last week, and Tommy suppressed a brief but intense urge to stand up in the middle of class and shout at Mr. Miller that, yes, they'd gotten it already, and could they please move on?

For Tommy, that was the worst part of school: the repetition. It sometimes seemed like the goal was not to teach him things, which he loved, but to make him surrender an arbitrary amount of his time for no good purpose, which was something that he simply could not stand.

With a heavy sigh, Tommy looked longingly at his backpack sitting on the floor. There were two comic books and a science fiction novel in there, any of which he'd much rather be reading. But he'd been caught reading in class several times before and had gotten in a lot of trouble for it. The first few times, the teacher gave Tommy detention and made him stay after school. At first, Tommy was anxious about that, but he came to realize that detention was just a good excuse to sit and read for an hour, so it stopped bothering him. However, that made Mr. Miller even angrier, and he'd put Tommy into in-school suspension. In-school suspension was even better than detention – in suspension, Tommy didn't have to go to class at all, and instead got to sit in a quiet room and read for an entire day, with no teachers, parents, friends, or anyone else to bother him.   Mr. Miller had also called Tommy's parents, though, and they didn't see his suspension for the godsend that it was. His dad was particularly angry with him and told him that if he got suspended for even one more day, his dad would take all his books and throw them in the fireplace. That got Tommy's attention really quickly; he knew that his father would make good on his promise, because once when Tommy had accidentally broken his dad's favorite coffee mug, his dad made Tommy bring him one of his favorite toys, and then he broke it in front of him. Dad said it was to teach him a lesson and to show him what it was like to have something that he cared about be broken by someone else for no reason, but Tommy secretly thought it was to get back at him. Tommy *loved* his dad, but he didn't really *like* his dad.

The bell rang and startled Tommy out of his reverie. He looked around, blinking for a moment as his fellow students gathered up their notebooks and papers and started to file out of the room. He'd been daydreaming again, of course – yet another problem that Mr. Miller was always harping on him about – but at least this time it was the bell that caught him out and not Mr. Miller calling on him to answer a question that he hadn't been paying attention to.

Tommy slid his math textbook and his notebook (the only notes he'd taken were some three-dimensional cube drawings that he liked to do and a comic strip that he called 'The Doodles') into his backpack, being careful not to crush the comic books inside. He stood, slinging the backpack over his shoulder, and walked past Mr. Miller, who was carefully erasing the chalkboard and paying no mind to a grateful Tommy, who was in no mood to listen to another one of the teacher's lectures about "being successful" and "making something of himself".

One of the school bullies, a football jock named Mikey (but whom everyone called "Poochie" for some strange reason that Tommy didn't understand) threw a shoulder into Tommy and caused him to stumble as he walked out into the hallway, but

3

Tommy ignored both him and the ensuing laughter and walked away, hoping today wouldn't be one of those days where the bullies decided to follow him. He wasn't in the mood for dealing with the stupidity of bullies today, either. In fact, all he really wanted to do was get home, plunk down on his bed, and read for awhile. Fortunately, one of the super geeks walked by going the other direction, and the bullies turned their attention on the hapless boy, allowing Tommy to escape.

Tommy didn't bother to visit his locker – he didn't intend to do any of the homework he'd been assigned during the day, anyway, and all the books he really wanted were already in his backpack – and instead slipped out of the school ahead of the rush. Forgoing the sidewalk, Tommy vaulted over the guard rail and half-ran, half-slid down the steep embankment and into the woods on the other side. There was a path of sorts back here – several of them, actually – that Tommy called the Druggie Trails, because all the druggie kids came out here to smoke. The druggies might tease him a little, but in general they left him alone, and that was preferable to running into Poochie or one of his equally Neanderthal cronies outside of the protection of the school. Tommy liked going home through the woods, anyway. It was quiet and peaceful and gave him some time alone with his thoughts. Plus, the winding paths always kind of reminded him of some secret trail through hidden lands, where he could pass undetected by the people of the town.

The trail wound itself out by the old railroad tracks, and instead of crossing them and following the street home, which was the more direct route, Tommy decided to walk along the tracks for awhile. They ran kind of toward his home, and he was much less likely to run into other people back here. Tommy's mother had always yelled at him for playing near railroad tracks (it seemed like the town was infested with them), but these tracks were old and rusted. Tommy knew that it was safe – no train had been on these tracks for some time, and none was likely to in the near future. Heck, a construction crew had even torn up this very same set of tracks much farther along, down where they crossed the canal. "How could a train even come down the tracks when they aren't complete any longer?" he had asked his mother, but she didn't even seem to hear him, and had ranted on and on about how many thousands of children were killed every year by trains.

As he made his way down the railroad tracks, sometimes balancing and walking up on the tracks, other times stepping from wooden tie to tie (but never, ever stepping down on the stones below), Tommy started to daydream again. He imagined himself being revealed as the last living heir to some foreign ruler, and how wonderful it would be to be suddenly vested with near infinite wealth and power. It was a common daydream for Tommy, and he was right in the middle of the part where Poochie got down on his knees and begged him for forgiveness right there in the middle of the school cafeteria when he realized that he'd gone way too far down the tracks and missed his turn.

Tommy hastily looked around. He'd never been to this part of the tracks before. He must have gone a mile or more past the street that would take him to his house, and he wasn't really sure how he'd gotten that far. Worse, it was getting late, and the sun had gone down behind the trees that surrounded the tracks, leaving Tommy in deep, dark shadow. He felt a sudden surge of panic and an urge to flee, to run into the woods, to be anywhere but right there on those rusted railroad tracks. The urge was so intense that Tommy missed his step onto the next railroad tie and stepped down onto the rough rocks between the ties. The rocks shifted unexpectedly, and Tommy twisted his ankle and fell to the ground with a shout of pain.

He rolled onto his back and lay there for a few moments,

clutching at his throbbing ankle and hissing in agony. He just realized that he'd scratched both his arms, as well, and a few drops of blood ran down his arm and dripped off his elbow onto his backpack.

"Damnit, damnit, damnit," Tommy shouted. His mom would have a long lecture for him about using profanity if she'd ever heard, but no one was close enough to hear, and in any case, Tommy was past caring. His ankle was throbbing, he was covered in black, soot-like dirt from the rocks that surrounded the rails, and the blood from his arm had stained both his backpack and one of his favorite shirts. A girl had once told him he looked nice in that shirt, so he wore it every chance he got, even though it was faded and slightly stained. Now, it was ruined for good.

"Damn it!" Tommy yelled one more time, as he used the rails to help himself stand up and gingerly put some weight on the ankle. He gasped at the pain, but the ankle held his weight, so it probably wasn't broken. "Just twisted, then," he muttered to himself, looking around. He was in a real stew, now. It was fairly dark out and rapidly getting darker, and he'd have to be very careful to avoid turning his ankle again. Tommy realized he was in for a long, painful walk home.

He turned for home and had just taken his first few ginger steps and was beginning to think about what his mother would say to him for getting home so late when he saw a man standing by the edge of the forest. The man had long, oily hair and needed a shave. He was overweight, and his belly bulged at his black t-shirt and pushed out over his stained jeans. The t-shirt the man wore was badly stained and bore a picture of an anthropomorphic pig dressed like a policeman and riding, most absurdly, on a moose. "Canadian Bacon", the legend below the picture said, and Tommy thought that it was a pretty stupid shirt to wear – it wasn't funny, and in fact barely made sense at all.

The man's skin was bad, and he had an almost greasy look to him. Tommy took an involuntary step backwards, away from the man, and almost fell down again as his ankle sang with pain. The smile that he flashed at Tommy was almost a leer, and Tommy would have run if he'd been able to.

"Hurt yourself, did you?" the man said, licking his lips.

"I'm ok, I just want to go home," Tommy replied.

"You are bleeding. Do you live close by?"

"Not far, I'll be fine. I just need to get home; my mom is expecting me."

The man took a step toward Tommy and ran his tongue over his lips again. "No one lives out this far," he said. "No one but me. Here, let me help you." The man took another step and reached out toward Tommy, who shook his head and took another step backwards.

"No thanks, Mister. I'm fine, really," Tommy replied, but the man kept advancing on him, stopping only when Tommy bent down and picked up a rock, cocking his arm to throw. "Leave me alone! You stay back!" he screeched, his voice cracking.

The man stopped, then, and stood regarding Tommy with a puzzled look on his face before replying, "That's not very nice! What are you going to do, throw that rock at me?"

Suddenly, Tommy felt incredibly foolish. Filthy, bruised, and bleeding, here he was threatening some random stranger with a rock? Tommy blushed and dropped his arm to his side, abashed. "I... I'm sorry, Mister. I don't know what I was thinking. I guess you just startled me, that's all."

Suddenly, the man's friendly demeanor evaporated as he got a huge, wicked grin on his face and a cruel look in his eyes. He raised his hands to chest height and looked down at them, muttering some words under his breath. A dark cloud formed there, like a thick fog of oily, black smoke. He looked up at Tommy and threw his hands out at him, as if he were pushing the cloud toward Tommy. The cloud of smoke flew at Tommy's head faster than he would have thought possible. Tommy had time to shout "Mage!" before the smoke enveloped his head.

The thick smoke wrapped around Tommy's face, choking him and cutting off his breathing. He tried to shout but could only hack and gag, his lungs refusing to cooperate. He tore at the cloud with his hands, trying to somehow tear it off, but it was no good – his hands passed through the cloud like it wasn't there, not even disturbing it in the slightest. Trying to breath only caused his lungs to spasm more, and he tried to cough but couldn't. Tommy started to see stars before his eyes as he looked down at one of the rail ties, and he realized that he'd fallen down to his knees. Tommy's chest got tighter and tighter, and he felt himself fall forward, but the cloud stayed wrapped around his head.

As blackness washed over Tommy, he could hear the greasy man laughing.

CHAPTER TWO

Tommy could still remember when they took his friend Stephen away. That wasn't his real name – Stephen was Vietnamese and his parents called him "Bao", but when he started school, he changed his name to something easier for Americans to say (and spell). Stephen wasn't a good friend of Tommy's, but he *was* a friend, and they got together sometimes to play video games and such. Sometimes, they'd even trade video games for a while, if they both had something the other wanted to play.

Tommy sometimes dreamed of Stephen going away. He was dreaming of him, now, only somehow it was himself that the men were taking away... or maybe he was dreaming that he was Stephen, in that confusing way that dreams can be multiple things.

Tommy dreamed that he was in the line for inspection. They'd been called out of their class (his teacher that year, Mrs. Houck, had been annoyed at the interruption and had been very rude to the men that came) and filed into the gymnasium, where they were divided into several lines to stand against the bleachers, which were folded in for storage. Tommy had never actually seen the bleachers unfolded – they seemed to stay like that all the time – but he'd asked one day what they were and the gym teacher had told him.

A dozen Army men walked up and down the line, keeping a close on eye the students. At least, Tommy thought they were Army men. They wore camouflage clothes and carried rifles like the Army men did in his video games. Gradually, Tommy approached the front of the line. He was glad to be getting near the front - he was tired of standing, and he was starting to get really bored. He hoped if he could get back to class before most of the other students, he could grab a few minutes to peek at the comic books he had in his bag.

Finally, it was the turn of the student in front of him - Tommy didn't know the boy because he was in a different grade than Tommy, but he'd seen him around the playground. The boy stepped up to a folding table, where a young man sat surrounded by more Army men. Tommy finally got a clear look at the man behind the table. He looked young - much younger than Tommy's parents - but he had a deep sadness in his eyes, and his face looked worn and down. Tommy saw heavy metal clasps on the man's forearms, wrists, neck, and ankles, all attached to thick metal chains that clanked and rasped every time he moved. The man held his hands out toward the boy in front of him, close to the boy but not actually touching. Tommy heard a buzzing sound, like a large bee flying by, and then it was over - the man shook his head without speaking, and the Army guys motioned the boy aside.

Then it was Tommy's turn. He stepped up to the man. It wasn't sadness in his eyes, Tommy decided. It was hopelessness. It was the look of someone who had no reason to live and was just going through the motions of life. When the man held his hands out toward Tommy, he heard the buzzing again. Only this time, it was much, much louder. It was so loud it sounded like a large bee was inside his ears, and it only got louder - soon it was like a thousand bees had taken up residence inside his skull, and Tommy clutched his hands to his head and shrieked in pain.

The buzzing vanished as quickly as it started. The man behind the desk smiled sadly at Tommy. The Army men were already moving around the desk toward him, and Tommy panicked. He turned and tried to run, only to bump right into another soldier who had moved up behind him. The soldier had a snarl on his face and a mean look in his eyes, and when Tommy tried to pull away from him, the soldier cocked his fist back and hit Tommy square in the nose.

Dream-Tommy fell backwards on his butt and started to cry. Blood was gushing from his nose, but when he tried to put his hand to his face to staunch the flow, the soldiers fell on him. They tackled his arms and legs and pinned him to the ground. He tried to argue with them, to tell them he'd be good, to tell them they were making a mistake, but all that came out was a shriek and some blubbering. Tommy saw one of the soldiers pull a set of chains out of a bag. They looked like the ones the young man was wearing, only much smaller, with shorter chains. Quickly and efficiently the soldiers snapped the chains around Tommy's arms, legs, and neck. Only once he was completely bound up did the soldiers get off his arms and legs and let him move.

Tommy tried to stand up, but the chains were too short and wouldn't let him. The blood from his nose was running back into his throat and choking him, and Tommy kept sputtering and gagging. He could see his fellow students - some of them staring at him in horror, others pointedly looking away. At least no one was laughing at him, though. Tommy squirmed on the floor, scared and horrified, but he felt like he'd die if everyone started laughing at him. A soldier approached Tommy and slipped a dusty hood over his face, and as darkness surrounded him, Tommy woke from the dream.

He didn't wake at home in his bed, though. He was confused and bewildered - it wasn't him that the Army guys had trussed up and taken away - it was Stephen. Yet he was tied, arms, legs, and neck, just like in the dream. Instead of the gymnasium floor he was lashed to a large wooden table. His nose and throat were dry, and his tongue felt like it was made of sand paper, and he coughed and gagged, reminding him of how he had been choking on his own blood in the dream. He thrashed and pulled on the ropes that bound him - they weren't chains, like in the dream, but were instead a rough, stiff, and scratchy rope that hurt his skin. The rope reminded Tommy of his mother's clothes line - thick, grey, and stiffened by years out in the wind, rain, snow, and sun.

When Tommy thrashed, the greasy man stood up from where'd he'd been sitting near the end of the table. He had a thick finger marking the page of a comic book - one of the ones that had been in Tommy's backpack - but when he saw that Tommy was awake, he laid the comic book face down on his chair, open to the page. Tommy tried to yell but could only gag - he always went to great lengths to keep his comic books in good condition, and he would never, ever even consider laying one open like that. It damaged the spine of the book and wrinkled the pages.

The man walked over to where Tommy lay bound. He cocked his head to the side and smiled his greasy little smile. "Ah, awake at last," he said, "I realize it would have been nicer to finish while you were asleep, but it's so much more delicious awake".

Some saliva had returned to Tommy's mouth, and he managed to reply, "F-Finish what?"

"Oh, don't you worry about that," the greasy man smiled again. "It'll all be over soon."

The confusion of the dream was fading, and Tommy got even more afraid and started to cry. "I want my Mommy. I wanna go home," he wept.

That just made the greasy man smile all the wider. "I'm afraid that's not on the schedule for tonight." He pantomimed pulling out a clipboard, flipping through pages, and running his finger down a page. "Nope, no going home on the agenda tonight. At least, not for you. Me... well, I'm already home." He made an expansive gesture with his arm, and Tommy, still scared and crying, took note of his surroundings for the first time.

He was in what appeared to be a one-room building, judging by the grimy windows in three of the walls. There was a filthy, stained, and sagging couch against one wall, next to a refrigerator that appeared to have seen better days. A blanket and pillow on the couch testified that it also doubled as a bed. A washing machine and a clothes dryer were against the other wall, but all the relevant wires and hoses were disconnected and laying across the top of the machines. The third wall was hung with a variety of garden tools – shovels, rakes, trowels, hedge trimmers, and the like, all of which were covered with cobwebs and badly rusted. The chair in which the greasy man had been sitting sat against that wall, beneath and between the tools. The large table to which he was tied dominated the room and left little room on the sides to move around. A bare light bulb dangled from the ceiling on a wire and illuminated the whole place, although the dust and dirt that coated the bulb gave the light a sallow cast. The whole place looking like nothing so much as an old storage shed that had been converted half-heartedly to living quarters.

The greasy man approached the head of the table where Tommy lay lashed down. Tommy whimpered and tried to pull away, but the stiff ropes cut into his skin painfully and the rope around his neck threatened to choke him, so after a few seconds of struggle he subsided into weeping and soft pleading. The man came to the side of the table and held his hand out palm down, several feet above Tommy's chest. "Don't worry," he said, "this won't hurt me at all." He then bowed his head and started to chant under his breath in a language that Tommy didn't recognize. For several long moments nothing happened. Tommy was just starting to think that maybe the mage was just trying to scare him when suddenly a nest of thick, grey tendrils sprouted from the man's hand. They started out short, but very quickly started to grow longer and descend toward Tommy, who started to shriek and plead with the man to please, please let him go.

Tommy tried to shrink away as the grey, ropey tendrils got close to his body, but he was unable to get away. When the first one touched the skin of his neck, it stiffened and bored into him, and Tommy felt an intense coldness, colder than he'd ever felt before. He screamed with the pain and terror of it, and his screams increased in volume as more of the things attached themselves to his chest, his forehead, even his lips. When two tendrils lashed out and attached themselves to Tommy's eyes, he screamed again as his vision vanished. He could feel the coldness spreading from each of the tendrils, pulling at the warmth of his body, pulling at his life, tugging at his very soul.

Without warning, Tommy heard a huge crash and splintering of wood. It sounded like a car had just rammed the side of the shack, and Tommy felt small splinters of wood rain down on his body. There was another large thump, and the tendrils tore away from Tommy with a ripping that was almost, but not quite, audible. The pain was the most intense Tommy had ever felt in his short life. Once, on a dare, Tommy had stuck his tongue to a frozen metal fence post. His tongue has stuck to the post, and when Tommy pulled away the skin tore away painfully. This felt a thousand times worse than that day – it felt as if the skin on Tommy's soul had been torn away, leaving his spirit raw and bleeding like his tongue had been on the day with the fence post. The pain was too much for Tommy to even scream, and he writhed on the table and made feeble attempts to breath.

With the second thump and accompanying pain, Tommy's vision had begun to return, and he saw that the greasy man had been knocked across the room, where he had sprawled across the floor. The wall with the garden tools had completely disintegrated, and there was a huge, gaping hole that covered most of the part of the wall where a grimy window once was. A man strode out of the cool night air, through the hole in the wall, and into the shack. He was tall, so much so that he had to duck slightly to step through the hole. He seemed to be the exact opposite of the greasy man – he had long blonde hair held back in a ponytail, and he was clean-cut and as lean as the greasy man was portly. This man wore jeans and a nice button down shirt, and although his face was twisted in a snarl of rage, Tommy thought that the man radiated a calmness that he'd never experienced before, as if just by being nearby, the man made his pain and terror somewhat lessened.

"Jordan, you wretch," the man bellowed. "I warned you I'd be coming for you if you continued this foul practice!"

The greasy man, meanwhile, had picked himself up off the floor. His cheek was bleeding where a flying shard of wood had scratched it open, and he no longer looked scary, only sad and pathetic. He stood before the blonde man and dry washed his hands. "Micah..." he began, "Such a pleasant... SURPRISE!" he finished with a shout, punctuating the word by throwing both of his hands toward the blonde man like he had to Tommy earlier that day.

Tommy wanted to shout a word of warning as another inky-black cloud flew toward the blonde man, but the man simply raised one hand and swatted the thing away like an insect. It vanished the minute his hand touched it, and Tommy wondered why that hadn't worked for him.

15

The blonde man took another step forward, and the greasy man held his hand forward, palm out. More of the black snaky tendrils shot out from the greasy man's palm, straight for the other man, but the blonde man simply swatted those aside, and they vanished as well.

The blonde man didn't move a muscle, but suddenly a large ball of fire streaked forward from thin air and struck Jordan in the chest. The impact knocked the greasy man back against the wall, and Tommy heard a sickening crack when his head hit the wooden wall. The greasy man's body flopped down to the couch, and it looked almost like he was sleeping were his neck not bent at an impossible angle and his hair and clothes on fire.

Tommy could only lay and stare in shock as the blonde man stepped over and touched the ropes binding him. Each rope parted beneath the man's touch as if it had been sliced by the sharpest of blades. Once Tommy was free, the blonde man gently helped him into a sitting position. By then, the fire had spread from the greasy man's clothing to the couch and part of the wall, and it was spreading rapidly.

"Fire..." was all Tommy could manage to gasp. The man looked over at the spreading blaze.

"This is a foul place. Let it burn," the man replied. Then he turned his gaze to regard Tommy. "My name is... well, it's not my real name, of course, but you can call me Micah."

"You're a mage," Tommy said. The realization had just struck him, and along with it, surprise. Mages were supposed to be dark, twisted, and evil, like the greasy man, yet this man was anything but.

Micah gave Tommy a sad smile and helped him off the table

and to his feet. "Yes, I am," the man said. Stars swam before Tommy's eyes when his feet hit the floor, and a wave of extreme dizziness took him. He felt the man's hands on his chest, lifting him as he blacked out, and the man's words followed Tommy down into darkness. "...and so are you."

CHAPTER THREE

Tommy awoke on a small cot in a pool of sunlight. The light seemed extremely bright and felt like it was stabbing into his brain, so Tommy pinched his eyes shut for a moment. "*A mage. That man said I was a mage,*" he thought to himself, remembering the night before. The only things Tommy knew about mages were the things he had learned in school – that mages were all wicked and dangerous because they used their powers to disrupt the peace of society. The only good mages were the ones that had agreed to work for the government. Those mages all wore chains that limited and restrained their abilities, so that they could only use their powers for the benefit of all. Mostly, it seemed that what they did was help the government track down and capture other mages, although Tommy could remember hearing occasional news stories about large battles between government mages and rogue mages.

That's how it had been, back in the beginning - mages using their powers to kill and steal, or even to try to take control of an area. Tommy remembered hearing about one insane mage who had actually taken control of the White House and declared himself President for life... until he fell asleep in his chair that same night and was killed by the Secret Service agents. He'd heard that there was a town in California that had been totally destroyed when two mages had both laid claim to the area and used their powers to fight over it. They kept fighting long after the thing they were fighting over had been totally ruined, and they were only stopped when a third mage had stepped in and put an end to both of them. It had always seemed that the only thing mages ever did was hurt people. Tommy had never understood why mages would choose to be like that – why couldn't they just be like everyone else? Surely there was no reason that they had to use their power, so why couldn't they ignore it and be normal?

From everything Tommy had heard, it seemed like most mages were like the greasy man last night – wicked people who got what they deserved. That the man Micah had helped him – saved him, actually – and was both kind and gentle had been a shock to Tommy.

Tommy opened his eyes again. His head still hurt, and his body was sore, particularly the ankle that he had twisted last night (could it really have been just last night? It seemed to be ages ago), but he found that he could stand the brightness, and he looked around. He was in a small, dusty room with a rough wooden floor. A row of long, narrow windows were high off the ground on one of the walls, and they were thoroughly coated in dust and dirt. In fact, the entire room looked like it had not been cleaned in years. There was a small wooden box against one of the walls, and the only other furnishings were two flimsy-looking cots – the one that he was laying on, and another on which Micah the mage sat watching him.

"Good morning," the man said. "I have to imagine that you feel a good deal like crap."

Tommy forced himself into a sitting position, and his head swam for a moment. He tried to nod, but it made his head hurt more, so he replied, "Yeah."

"Have you heard adults talk about hangovers? What you are feeling right now, that's kind of what it feels like."

Tommy boggled at that. His dad had gone out with his friends a few times and gotten a hangover the next day, and once his mom and dad had sat up late drinking wine. The next day *both* of them had hangover headaches. If this was what people felt when they went out drinking, Tommy was amazed that they were willing to do it. He was absolutely certain that, without a doubt, he never wanted to feel this way again. He shook his head in amazement, then groaned when the movement sent slivers of pain into his skull.

The man gave him a sympathetic look, and then said, "So, you may not remember, but I introduced myself last night. I'm Micah, and you are...?"

Tommy remembered the man's name and thought it sounded somewhat familiar, but he couldn't place where or why, so rather than be rude, he replied, "Thomas. Tommy, really. Everyone calls me Tommy. Like the gun."

Micah seemed surprised. "Like the gun?" he asked. "Why would you put it like that? Why not... like the inventor of the light bulb?"

Tommy blushed furiously. "Well... uh... you see... when I was little, I got into a bunch of green apples and ate them all. I was up all night on the toilet, and my dad said my butt was going off like a machine gun, so he started calling me Tommy Gun." Tommy suddenly wondered why he was telling this stranger about his butt, and he blushed again, but Micah only slapped his knee and laughed.

"Tommy Gun!" Micah chortled. "That's a great story,

Tommy. You shouldn't be embarrassed about it. Everyone does silly things when they are young."

Tommy couldn't help but grin back at the man, but he was still feeling a little lost and out of sorts, so he asked, "Say, Mister..."

"Micah," the man interrupted.

"Uh, ok. Say, uh... Micah, ummm... where am I?"

"We're in a safe room. It's a kind of place for mages to hide. If you must know, we're in a warehouse in a town not far from your home."

The mention of home had Tommy bolting to his feet. "Home!" he exclaimed. "My parents will be worried sick!" Tommy took a step, intending to head toward the door, only when he looked around, he realized that there was no door. He stopped, completely confused, and said, "How...?"

Micah grinned at him and said, "How did we get in here? The door to this room was walled up a long, long time ago. I doubt that even the owner of the building even knows that this room exists. There's no way in or out, except by magic. That's how we got in here, and that's how we'll get out." Tommy stared at him, and he must have looked afraid, because Micah added, "Don't worry; I'll take you out, when it's time. First, however, you and I need to talk for awhile. Don't be afraid. We're just going to talk, nothing else."

"Magic," Tommy said. "You said I was a mage. Last night, before I passed out. But I'm not, and I don't want to be. I've been through the tests at school."

Micah smiled his sad smile again. "Jordan was an evil

man, Tommy, and bringing you into our struggle without your consent was not the least of his misdeeds. But he did it, it's done, and neither you nor I can change that, now."

Tommy furrowed his brow. "That greasy man made me a mage?"

Micah sighed. "No, not really. Not like you are thinking. He was actually trying to steal that part of you that makes you a mage, to take it and use it to make himself stronger. Since I interrupted him, all he succeeding in doing - besides giving you that terrible headache - is awakening a part of you that had lain dormant." He let out another heavy sigh. "You see, Tommy, the real truth is that almost everybody is what you call a 'mage'. Nearly every human being on this planet has the ability to learn to control magic of some sort. It's just that some of us, people like me, have the ability awaken in them all on its own. Those are the people that the government tests find. Others have it forced on them through circumstances – sometimes things like an illness or a car accident can trigger it. The tests will find those people, too, but only after the power has awakened in them. That's why you get tested at school every year. But usually, if someone makes it to adulthood without awakening the power, then it won't happen on its own or by accident, and they have to be painstakingly taught to use it." Micah looked genuinely sympathetic. "I'm sorry, Tommy, but you are in that second group. Now that it's been awakened in you, you can't go back. You *are* a mage."

Tommy sat down heavily on the dusty floor of the room as the sun's rays filtered in through the filthy window panes. "But what... I mean, how do you know? I don't feel any different. Besides the hangover, I mean."

Micah shifted on the cot for a moment and looked at him intently. "Tell me, Tommy... Do you know what a sunset sounds like?"

Tommy blinked several times and stared at Micah for a long moment. The question, of course, was completely ludicrous – how could a sunset have a sound? Except that, as Tommy thought about it, he realized he DID know what a sunset sounds like. "That's stupid-" Tommy began, but the mage was staring intently at him, and Tommy realized that the man had known the answer before he'd asked the question. Somehow, this mage understood that Tommy would know the answer to a question he'd never even thought to ask.

Tommy considered lying and denying it, anyway, for a moment, but he realized he wouldn't be able to hide it from Micah, so instead he said, "I think it's kind of like... a roaring, or a rushing... or maybe a chime sound, like one of those metal things musicians use to make a certain note?" Tommy scratched his head in confusion. Why was it so hard to put a label on the sound?

"A tuning fork? I suppose it can be like that, in some ways," the mage said, a queer sort of half-smile on his face. "It is all those things, and none of them at all, of course. Because, as you realized when I first asked the question, a sunset doesn't actually make a sound. No video camera or recorder would register a thing. The sound is only there for those who are sensitive to it, Tommy. For those who can *hear*. Because what you are hearing is a change in the energies of the world; the bright, frenetic energy of the day giving way to the calm, peaceful strength of the night. That is the sound you think you hear but can't quite put a name to, and if you asked someone who isn't sensitive to those energies, who can't hear the sound... well, they'd probably think you were crazy and send you to a psychologist." Micah flashed a wry grin at him. "But I assure you, you are as sane as anybody."

Tommy thought on this for several moments. Could it be

true? It didn't seem possible. The prospect seemed both terrible and horrifying. "I don't want any of that," Tommy said. "I just want to go home to my parents."

"If you decide you really want to go home, I won't stop you. I'll even take you there myself. But... Tommy, I don't think it's a good idea."

"What? Why not?" Tommy asked, puzzled.

"Think about it. You didn't come home last night. Your parents are surely worried about you, and without a doubt they called the police."

Tommy's stomach clenched, and he felt like he was going to throw up. Here he was sitting and talking while his parents were worried to death! "They must be so scared, I should get home to them, tell them everything is okay."

"And where are you going to tell them you've been, Tommy?"

The question seemed obtuse to Tommy. "I'll tell them a mage grabbed me, but that I got away. I won't tell them about you."

Micah sighed. "Do you think they are stupid, Tommy? They know there is no way you are going to get away from a mage without help. At the very least, they are going to wonder what interest a mage would have had in you. The minute you mention that, the very second they suspect that you've had dealings with someone who uses magic, they are going to whisk you off to be tested... and you *will* fail the test."

Tommy shook his head. "I'll tell them I don't want to be a mage. I'll tell them I don't know how to do any magic, and I'll promise to never learn."

That seemed to upset Micah. "Tommy, use your head. Do you think they care? When you've seen friends at school get dragged off in chains, did the men dragging them away listen to them? They won't even give you a chance to tell them anything, and they wouldn't care if you did. They'll clap you in chains and haul you off to prison. You'll go away, and none of your friends or your family will ever see you again."

Tommy got scared and started to cry again. Everything the mage was saying was true, and he knew it, but he didn't want to admit it. It was too scary, too terrible to be possible.

Micah got down off the cot and sat cross-legged on the floor next to Tommy. "A lot of people think badly of mages. They wonder why we have to use our powers, why we can't be content with normal lives like everyone else. The truth is, Tommy, that most of us would love to live normal lives. We'd like nothing more than to put this all behind us and be just like everyone else. But the government has forced this upon us. They want to chain us and cage us, take away our lives and our freedoms and everything that we love, just because of what we are. People like you and me... normal lives are denied to us, Tommy. We can't even refuse to use our powers – we can't have normal jobs and normal homes, so we have to use our powers just to survive."

"So it's true, then." Tommy said. "What they say about mages. That you all steal and kill."

Micah shook his head emphatically. "Absolutely not. There are other ways to put food on the table than stealing, and usually, mages only kill each other, and only when we must, like I had to do with Jordan last night. I won't lie to you, Tommy. I actively work against the government that would imprison me, and I have a group of cohorts, both mages and not, that support me in that endeavor. I have destroyed their prisons, and I have freed the people they have captured. But let me be very clear on one thing: I am in no way asking you to help with all of that. If, when you are older and more experienced, you decide that you want to be a part of our movement... well, we'll talk about it, then. What I *am* asking you to do is to come away with me. I'll give you a new home. I'll give you new friends and family. And I will teach you to use and control the gift that you have."

"What if I go home and don't say anything about mages? What if I just say I ran away, but decided to come back?"

"That might work, for a little while, assuming that the police believed you. They might decide to test you just to be sure, and it is entirely likely that they might link you to Jordan when they find him – a suspected mage that burned to death near your school. But even if they don't, how long would it last? How long before you they performed a random test at your school, or before you walked too close to another mage like Jordan who can sense your ability?" Micah gave Tommy that same sad smile he seemed fond of. "I'm sorry, Tommy, but there is no other way. If you go home, you end up in prison or worse, and I can't promise that I'll be able to be there to save you a second time. If you go with me... well, you get your life and your freedom, eventually, after you learn some things. You may even get to see your family again someday. That's all I can offer you, but it's better than the alternatives."

Tommy hung his head in his hands and wept. He sobbed huge, hitching sobs and sputtered when his nose started to run. He bawled until there were no more tears left. Micah let him cry the whole time, without speaking a word or attempting to comfort him. Finally, what seemed like hours later, Tommy looked up at the older man and said simply, "Okay."

"Okay, what?" Micah asked.

"Okay," Tommy replied. "I'll come with you."

CHAPTER FOUR

Micah reflected on the early days of the Return. He wasn't really sure if magic had ever truly been gone, or if people had just forgotten how to tap into it. He didn't know, and he didn't think anyone ever would. All that truly mattered was that it was here, now, and had to be dealt with.

When people spoke of the days following the Return, they usually talked about government officials, law enforcement officers, and other community leaders struggling to retain some semblance of control in a world turned upside down. People sympathized with the harsh treatment that the world's governments handed mages, under the thin justification that it was the only way to keep civilization from tumbling into anarchy. The police tried to arrest mages who broke the law, but how could you arrest someone who could melt handcuffs or explode a hole in the wall of a prison cell? Knowing that they'd be completely unable to restrain dangerous and volatile mages, governments resorted to a "shoot first" mentality. Many mages were killed, and those that remained responded in the only way they could – they met violence with violence and began using their powers to actively target anyone they deemed as a threat.

Some mages sided with the government, of course. Micah himself had tried to be one of those, although he had an innate distrust of the government. He tried to work against the violent mages, to help and protect police officers, and to consult and advise government officials whenever possible.

What nobody mentioned, of course, was that it was no picnic for the mages, either. Labeled as pariah by most of their fellow citizens, many mages soon found themselves alone in the world, betrayed by friends, family, and lovers. Micah remembered a single mother who was a mage and was turned in by her own children, who then ended up in a foster home because there was no one to raise them.

But even worse than that was learning how to deal with and even use the powers they had discovered. There was no one to instruct them, no one to tell them what was and was not possible. The structured classes that the few mage schools offered these days would have been a godsend back then, but even now they were still learning, experimenting, and discovering. Even now, men and women were still getting injured or even dying trying to learn more about the power they'd been given. But the problems of today were nothing compared to the days following the Return. Some men and women simply went insane from the new stresses on their senses. They heard things that shouldn't be audible and failed to cope with the changes. Others committed suicide rather than face the backlash from their friends and families. Many, many others tried to race too fast and too far and expended their very life's energies trying to do the impossible.

In fact, sometimes Micah thought that it was only the extremely high mortality rate among mages that allowed the governments to get a handle on the situation in the first place. That, of course, and the discovery that the mineral tungsten seemed to inhibit and block an individual's access to magic. Micah wished he knew who discovered that, so he could thank the man or woman with a fist to the face. At first, it was the tungsten injections that attempted to "cure" mages but instead left them thrashing in seizures until they mercifully passed into a coma and died. Then, it became tungsten bullets and, later, tungsten powder sprays to render a mage "inert" for capture. The fact that the bullets often killed the hapless mages long before the tungsten could enter their system seemed to be conveniently missed by advocates of their use. By comparison, the tungsten infused prison cells and tungsten bindings of today were extraordinarily humane. China, being the world's foremost producer of tungsten, was consequently the first major government to bring it's "mage problem" under control and to restore some sense of normalcy, but the other major world powers soon fell into step, as well.

"Whatcha thinkin' about?" Tommy asked, breaking Micah out of his reverie.

Micah shook his head. "Nothing important. Just the old days, when I was new to magic, like you."

"It wasn't *that* long ago," Tommy replied. "It was before I started high school, but still not that long ago."

Micah favored Tommy with a sad but wry grin. "Sometimes, it feels like ages ago, Tommy. So much has changed."

Tommy sat in the booth across from Micah, gobbling french fries. The older man had such a pensive look on his face that Tommy had been worried. "Did someone help you, like you are helping me?"

"No. There was nobody to help me. I had to figure it out myself."

"Was it hard?" Tommy asked around a mouthful of fries. He had missed dinner last night and breakfast this morning and found that he was ravenous.

Micah couldn't help but chuckle. "Yes, it was very hard. It still is very hard, as you will soon discover."

"When do we start?" Tommy asked.

Micah smiled at the boy, amazed at the resilience of youth. The boy had had his world turned upside down in less than twenty-four hours, and here he was, anxious to start learning. "The next class doesn't begin for a few more days," Micah answered. "We'll spend a day or two together, then I'll give you a day or two to get settled in."

Tommy frowned, puzzled. "Class? What class? Aren't you going to teach me?"

"Maybe sometimes, but probably not very often. I'm very busy, Tommy, and I don't often have time to teach anymore. But not to worry, I'll be taking you to my school. You'll have classes there just like your old school, only some of them will teach you how to use your new gifts. You'll have classmates, friends, and teachers, just like in a normal school."

Tommy had a panicked look on his face. "You aren't going to abandon me, are you?"

Micah reached across the table and patted Tommy on the back of the hand. "No, Tommy, I won't abandon you. I'll check in on you from time to time, and you can always come see if me if you need to. Don't be afraid. It'll be fun, I promise."

A scowl crossed Tommy's face. "I hate school. It's so *boring*."

That caused Micah to laugh. "Never fear about that, my

little friend. This won't be like normal school, I can tell you that much. For one thing, you aren't stuck learning at the pace of your classmates. When you prove that you've learned all there is to learn in one class, you move on to the next whether your classmates are ready to move or not."

The thought intrigued Tommy. "Like skipping a grade? Moving up with older kids?"

Micah nodded to him. "Yes, although you'll find that you'll often be in classes with people of all ages. Sometimes, you might be learning the same thing as an old grandfather. Other times, you might be with children much younger than you. It all depends on how fast you learn."

"Oh," said Tommy. He felt like he needed some time to digest that concept, but it did sound better than his old school. He reached into his basket of fries, only to find that he'd eaten them all. "Could I have some more fries, please?" he asked.

Micah nodded to him and rose to his feet. "Of course. I figured you'd be hungry. Wait here and I'll go get you some more. In the meantime... think about what you want to do for the next couple days."

"Do?" Tommy asked. "What do you mean?"

Micah put his hands on the table and leaned in close to Tommy. "I won't lie to you, Tommy. Once you start learning, you aren't going to be allowed to stop. Not for a while, at least. It's far too dangerous, both for yourself and for others. For a while, you are going to be on a tight, regimented schedule. You won't be permitted to leave a fairly small section of the facility. But for you, that part will be over quickly, I think. You'll soon move up and be granted more privileges." Micah stood and stretched his arms.

"So, think about what you want to do before you start."

"What *can* we do?" Tommy asked as Micah headed toward the counter to order more fries.

The man grinned at Tommy over his shoulder. "Just about anything you want."

Tommy sat and thought about that while Micah was at the counter ordering more food. When he and Micah had left the door-less warehouse room, Micah had taken his hand and... stepped. They didn't move, but there was a brief moment of vertigo, and then they were somewhere else. Suddenly, they were outside in a parking lot, next to this fast food restaurant. Micah told him that they weren't even in the same state anymore, and Tommy had goggled. He'd asked Micah if he would learn how to do that, and Micah had said that it was incredibly difficult to do, but that he felt confident that Tommy would one day be able to manage the feat. Tommy had gotten excited at that; it certainly hadn't *looked* difficult when Micah had done it, but if he could learn to move around like Micah did, it would be a tremendous gift indeed.

By the time Micah returned with the fries, Tommy had a couple of ideas. When the man sat down, Tommy asked him, "Micah, what is your real name?"

The smile disappeared from Micah's face. "I'm sorry Tommy, but I can't tell you that."

"Why not? Aren't I one of you, now?" Tommy asked.

Micah sighed. "Yes, you are, after a fashion. But one thing you have to understand, Tommy, is that the government's mage hunters are actively looking for me. I've foiled their plans too many times, and they bear me a deep grudge. They would like nothing more than to track down my old friends and family and use them to try to get at me. My family doesn't deserve that. They haven't done anything wrong, they haven't committed any crimes, and they don't deserve to be imprisoned or tortured just because they happened to once have known me."

A hurt look crossed Tommy's face. "I'd never tell them. I'd never tell anyone."

Micah's voice suddenly took on a very sympathetic tone. "I know you wouldn't, Tommy. That's why you are here, right now. But the only way to keep a secret safe is to tell no one. What happens if, God forbid, some day you get captured by the mage hunters? They would do whatever it took to get you to tell, and although you are a strong boy, they would eventually break you down. Or... heck, you and I may have a falling out, some day." Micah shook his head. "It's nothing against you, but I just can't tell you. My family doesn't deserve that."

Tommy thought about that for a few moments and decided that it didn't matter. He wouldn't want someone hurting his parents because of him. If the man wanted to keep his secrets, Tommy decided that he should let him. Instead, Tommy asked, "Can we go anywhere? Anywhere at all?"

The grin returned to the older man's face. "Well, just about anywhere. Within reason, that is. If you wanted to go to the bottom of the ocean, that might be a problem – we could go there, but we'd quickly drown or be crushed by the pressure. We probably couldn't go visit the Oval Office in the White House without being arrested or worse. But if it's not overly dangerous, I'll take you there."

Tommy smiled at the thought of them popping in on the President. Boy, wouldn't that cause some waves? He hadn't thought of things like the bottom of the ocean or the oval office, however. He had other ideas and said "I've always wanted to see the pyramids."

But Micah shook his head. "Sorry Charlie. No can do, there. The pyramids are in Egypt, Egypt is in Africa, and in case you hadn't heard, Africa is a war zone. Some dark mages have taken control of much of the continent. Men much like the greasy man, Jordan, that you met, only much, *much* more dangerous. The only way we can go to Africa is if we're prepared to fight, and I couldn't guarantee your safety. Maybe someday, once you've learned a little bit. Then I'll take you to Africa."

Tommy was disappointed, but he did understand. He'd heard the news stories about the strife in Africa, and he remembered being grateful that there was a wide ocean between him and the troubles. It was a letdown, but Tommy had some other ideas, too. "Could we go see Stonehenge, then? Or the Grand Canyon? Or maybe even Disneyland?"

Micah grinned broadly. "That's a tall order right there. You'd better finish your fries quickly. It sounds like we've got a couple of full days ahead of us."

CHAPTER FIVE

Micah had refused to take Tommy to Egypt, saying it was a desolate and embattled place, but as Tommy dreamed, he saw it as it was before – old, ancient, and although somewhat battered by the years, still strong and majestic. To Tommy's dream-self, the area practically thrummed with power and mystery, and he walked around the pyramids and marveled at their beauty.

In his dream, Tommy saw the past unfold exactly like the stories Micah had told to him. He saw the emergence of the anti-mage organizations in other countries, and how mages because hunted and persecuted for the misdeeds of others. He saw the good mages who stood up for what was right and fought with the government against their brethren, helping them hunt down and drive out or destroy the dark mages who used their powers to steal, kill, and dominate. In Tommy's dreams, these dark mages were all wicked, cruel, and looked surprisingly like the greasy man who had tried to hurt him. Tommy saw the dark mages flee to Africa. He watched as the continent, which, to his young mind, had always been a wild, dangerous, and uncivilized place become increasingly unsettled.

Then, Tommy saw the governments of the world turn on the good mages who had helped them. Now that the dark mages had been mostly brought to heel in most of the civilized world, governments no longer had need of the mages who had helped them. The very same people who had been crucial to the survival of order suddenly became the biggest threat, and the fear and suspicion which clouded any who dared to use magic turned on to those brave men and women. Tommy saw the mages and their families get hunted down and killed or imprisoned for no other reason than who they were and what they could do.

Just like Micah had said, Tommy watched as these "good" mages packed up their families and fled to Africa, as well. Only, when they got there, their dark brethren remembered them. The dark mages remembered who had helped the governments hunt them down. They remembered being driven out, fleeing for their lives, and it caused them to hate. A great war ensued between the dark mages and the new arrivals. Titanic battles ripped across the surface of the country, setting whole towns afire and leveling cities. Tommy's dream-self wept bitter tears as he watched the beautiful pyramids and architecture crumble under the onslaught until only barely recognizable piles of stones remained.

The battle was brief, however. The dark mages had been on the continent for months and had had time to establish themselves. They had homes and bases of operations. They had truces and alliances. The newcomers had none of that and were encumbered by the remains of their families. Some of the good mages surrendered and became slaves to the dark men and women they had once hunted. Others felt the betrayal of their home countries too strongly and joined the dark mages, succumbing to fear and hate and trying to carve out a piece of the ravaged continent for themselves. But the rest of the refugees, the large majority of them, were slaughtered. It made Tommy sad to see the brave men and women die. He felt that they deserved better, that someone should have stood up for them or helped them, somehow.

The dream fell apart suddenly as the sound of a door opening woke Tommy from a sound sleep. He sat upright in his bed and looked around in confusion. The last few days had been a whirlwind of new places and exotic sights, and at first, he couldn't remember where he was. Then it came to him – he was in his dorm room at Micah's school. The room was small and rectangular, and was dominated by four beds and four wardrobes, one at the foot of each bed. The room had no other occupants when Tommy had arrived, so he had tried out all the beds and chosen the one that he thought was most comfortable. The walls were cold, smooth stone – all the walls here seemed to be made of stone – and had no windows, so the only light came from the only other furniture in the room, which was two shaded floor lamps in the corners. The setting was wholly austere, and the room as a whole was smaller than Tommy's room at home.

The thought brought Tommy a twinge of regret, and he thought to himself, "I have to stop thinking like that. This is home now."

Tommy turned and looked at the door to the room. Another boy his age was struggling with an over-large suitcase, which was stuck in the door. Tommy stood up and moved to help the boy. He pulled on the leading edge of the case, which slid in easily, and the boy came stumbling in after it.

"Uh, thanks." The boy said, sticking out his hand. "I'm Ryan."

Tommy shook the boy's hand and introduced himself. "I'm Thomas, but everyone calls me Tommy."

Ryan started to say something, but at that moment was shoved from behind by someone outside the door, and he stumbled and fell against Tommy. Tommy lost his balance, and the two boys sprawled to the ground in a tangle of limbs. The rest of the shover's body followed his hand through the door, revealing a slightly older boy with a military style duffle bag thrown over his shoulder. Tommy disengaged himself from Ryan and stood up, dusting himself off. He scowled at the newcomer, who had thrown his bag on one of the beds, as Ryan stood and finished dragging his large suitcase to a different bed on the other side of the tiny room.

The shover turned and put his hands on his hips and looked down at the two other boys. "I'm James L. Thorton, the Third," the older boy said with a haughty tone in his voice. "Of the Long Island Thortons, of course."

Tommy didn't know what the Long Island Thortons were, but he took an instant dislike to the larger boy. He wore faded but fashionable blue jeans, and a t-shirt that made Tommy's throat constrict. It was a black shirt and bore a picture of a pig dressed like a policeman and riding a moose. Tommy knew that it would bear the legend "Canadian Bacon" before he even saw it. He wanted to scream and run, but there was nowhere to go – the big boy was still standing in the doorway – so instead he said, "It's not nice to push people."

"Awww, come on," said James L. Thorton of the Long Island Thortons, gesturing toward Ryan, who was still struggling with his suitcase. "He's been holding us up since we got on the bus."

"Bus?" asked Tommy, confused. There hadn't been any roads leading up to the school, and he hadn't seen any vehicles of any sort once he got here. In fact, the lack of cars in such a large place was rather notable.

"Yeah," said James. "You stupid or something? The bus,

you know? How we got to the portal?"

Tommy shook his head. "I didn't ride on any busses. A man named Micah brought me here." Tommy looked at both of the other boys in confusion. Both of their mouths were agape with astonishment, and they were looking at Tommy with open amazement. "What?" asked Tommy.

Then, James burst out laughing and turned his back on Tommy. "Okay, okay, you got me," James chuckled, shaking his head. "That's a good joke, man."

Tommy was totally confused by that, but even more so by the younger boy's reaction. "That was a mean joke to play," Ryan scowled. "You should be ashamed of yourself." Ryan turned his back on Tommy, too, and resumed trying to lift his suitcase up onto his bed.

"But... but, I... I mean, it wasn't-" Tommy stammered, but he was immediately cut off by the door opening again.

A middle-aged man poked his head through the door. He was almost completely bald except for a thin ring of hair that ran from one ear, across the back of his head, and to the other ear. He was very thin, almost to the point of being gaunt, and he reminded Tommy of nothing so much as a hawk. The man peered around the room through thick, horn-framed glasses, his mouth tight with either disapproval or impatience, Tommy couldn't decide. The man stared at them each intently for several long moments, while the boys all stared back, almost afraid to move. Finally, the man spoke.

"Very well, then. I'm Chancellor Duvey. You boys will come with me so I can show you around the school."

Tommy started to leave the room, but James hadn't

moved and was in his way, so he stopped.

"What's a Chancellor do?" asked James, his voice full of belligerence.

The older man's lips compressed even further, but he spoke without annoyance in his voice, merely adopting an instructional tone of voice. "Chancellor means that I'm in charge of running the school, much like a principal. Did schools have principals where you come from?" The Chancellor hardly waited for the boys to nod. "Yes? Then you'll understand that I'm a very busy man and you must come along quickly." With that, he turned and left the room without giving the boys time to answer. James merely shrugged and followed him out. Ryan paused to throw another dirty look Tommy's way, then he too headed for the door. Tommy sighed and followed the other two boys.

Once the boys were outside in the hallway, the chancellor set off at a brisk pace and began to speak.

"Your schedules will be ready for you when you return to your rooms. Since you boys are close in age, you will likely have similar schedules. However, there will be areas where you differ, of course, both due to your aptitudes and level of education." Tommy frowned at that. Micah had told him that he would be allowed to progress at his own pace, so he had assumed that there would be some kind of test to determine how far along he was. Tommy had always scored very highly on all the English exams they had taken at school, and had been very proud of his skill level in that area, although his math levels tended to fall behind his classmates and was a source of embarrassment to him. The chancellor had not stopped talking, however. "Breakfast for initiates is served from seven until eight every morning," he said, pausing briefly to look significantly at the boys. "Then classes begin promptly at eight. Lunch is at noon, dinner is at five, and classes end at eight in the evening." Tommy's mouth dropped open, and the other two boys groaned in dismay. Twelve hours of school? Tommy wondered what he'd gotten himself into. The chancellor heard the groan, and stopped to regard the boys, his hands on his hips.

"Yes, it makes for some long days. However, we've found it best to keep initiates busy. It keeps you out of trouble. You will have a less rigorous schedule once you graduate and become novices. *If* you graduate and become novices, that is." The tone of the chancellor's voice made it clear that he thought their chances of graduating were slim indeed, but he paused only a moment before continuing. "From eight until ten every night is your personal time. You can use it to study or just relax, although initiates that lay about quickly find themselves falling behind their classmates."

Tommy raised his hand at that, but the chancellor continued before acknowledging him. "Lights out is enforced at ten every night, and I will not stand for initiates that bring or make their own lights and disturb their roommates. Yes... Mister Nelson, is it?" asked the chancellor, clearly both annoyed by the interruption but pleased at Tommy's courtesy.

"We can read, right? During personal time, I mean?" Tommy asked.

The chancellor chuckled in reply. "You may read, of course. In fact, I highly encourage it. However, so long as you are an initiate here, you will only have books that are supplied to you by the school. Once you graduate to novices, you can have your own books for information or pleasure, but you'll be much too busy to read anything extracurricular for a while." Again, the man's tone made it obvious that he thought that might be a very long while indeed.

Before he could continue, however, James blurted out "What about weekends?"

The chancellor favored James with a grim smile. "Weekends? We don't have weekends at the school. Classes for initiates and novices take place seven days a week. And you would do well, mister Thorton, to learn some courtesy from your classmates."

James scowled at Tommy, as though the rebuke were somehow his fault, but the chancellor had already turned and resumed walking down the hall at his brisk pace. The other two boys paused to glare at Tommy one more time before following, while Tommy trailed behind, biting his lip in consternation. Micah had said nothing about school twelve hours a day, seven days a week. He'd said that Tommy would be very busy when they got to the school, and had told him to enjoy the little vacation they'd taken, but nowhere had he mentioned the inhumane hours they'd be keeping. The amount of school combined with the seeming scorn of his two classmates had Tommy seriously wishing he'd never made the snap decision to come with Micah, and he found himself wondering if they'd allow him to leave if he asked nicely.

Tommy was interrupted out of his thoughts by their arrival in a narrow, elongated room. A series of long tables dominated the room with benches down either side, with a cafeteria-style serving area on the far end of the room. Both the benches and the serving area were completely empty, but there was space for maybe thirty or forty people to sit at the table at once. The chancellor paused briefly to explain that this was where they'd be taking their meals before he whisked them off out another door.

The next hour was filled with a whirlwind of locations. Tommy saw classrooms both large and small. Some of them looked like the classrooms he was accustomed to back in school, complete with desks and a chalkboard, while others were simply small square rooms with mats on the floor. None of the rooms had windows, and however they were furnished, all of them were made of the same smooth, grey stone. Tommy was shown a large gymnasium-type room, and told it would be their physical fitness and martial training room. He groaned again at that – gym was his least favorite class, next to math, although he had to admit that the martial training sounded interesting, and he wondered if they'd be taught karate. He had always wanted to go to karate class when he was younger, but his parents always said they couldn't afford it, so it was something that he'd never gotten to try. Tommy got thoroughly turned around about halfway through the tour, and he wondered how any of them would find their way through the warren of passages and classrooms. Finally, they came to the most impressive stop on the tour, and as they stepped into the room, Tommy's jaw dropped in awe.

CHAPTER SIX

he boys had stepped into a massive round chamber, at least a hundred feet across. The large room was dominated by an immense, semi-opaque crystal that seemed to jut out of the floor. Its jagged points almost reached the ceiling forty feet above them, and Tommy got the impression that the room, and maybe even the entire structure of the school, had been built around it. The crystal had a deep bluish tint to it, but it glowed from within with a soft, silvery light, and Tommy could see many smaller lights moving deep within the structure of the thing. A waist-high, wide railing surrounded the thing, and it reminded Tommy of the communions rails he had seen around the altar one time when his grandmother had dragged him to church. Arranged outside the railing was a series of padded floor mats and padded benches that alternated and ran the entire circumference of the room. There were several people either kneeling on the mats or sitting on the benches, all dressed differently but staring intently at the crystal. They didn't even look up when Tommy and his group entered the room, but continued to stare, and the chancellor turned to speak to them.

"This is the channeling room. It is here that you'll pay your dues... your 'tuition', as it were, for your food and shelter and the training you'll receive while at this academy. Every single person here spends at least some time every week channeling

45

magical energy into the large crystal you see here. The crystal stores the energy, and then it is used by powerful spells cast by the senior mages to do things like turn the generators that provide electricity, keep our school hidden from outsiders, and the like." The chancellor had the droning tone of a teacher delivering a lecture, but Tommy didn't mind. He was enraptured by the whole scene. "Occasionally," the chancellor continued, "it will even be used by the senior mages to perform services for outsiders – for a large fee, of course – so that we can obtain world currencies to purchase the things we cannot produce ourselves. As initiates, you won't be required to channel much energy, but as your skills grow, so will the requirements. Personally, I also think that channeling is very good practice for students, as well. It will teach you to handle more and more magical energy and will increase your tolerance for using magic without fatigue. Once you graduate to novices, you will also be able to channel energy to obtain goods and services from the school. If, for example, you wish to purchase books as Mister Nelson had asked."

The chancellor seemed about to continue with his lecture when James opened his mouth and took a breath, about to speak. After an instant and a caustic glance at Tommy, though, James thought better of it and raised his hand instead. The chancellor paused in what he was about to say and nodded to James.

"I don't have to do any of this. My father already paid my tuition," James said to the chancellor.

"Every single-", the chancellor began, but a familiar voice from behind Tommy cut him off.

"Your father paid your entry into this school, nothing more," Micah said, stepping into the room behind them. The chancellor quieted immediately, took a step backwards, and bowed at the waist to Micah as he entered.

James apparently couldn't decide if he should be angry at or awed by Micah. Still, he persisted, and began "But, my father-" before Micah cut him off again.

"Your father has no influence here, Jimmy. You'd better get used to that right now. The fee he paid to us was to accept you into the school so that you might have the best help and training available." Micah jabbed a finger at James. "It is for this very reason that I was reluctant to bring you into the school. Students who have a sense of entitlement do very poorly, here, and I have my doubts about you. Your father's generous donation to our cause has secured you a place in our school, but do not think that it has guaranteed your success. You will attend classes like everyone else, you will earn your way like everyone else, and, if you should choose to break our rules, you will be expelled like anyone else." Micah stared at James for a long moment. The young man had visibly wilted under the lecture, and he stood with his head down, looking crushed.

After a long moment, Micah's face lost its serious cast, and he turned and clapped Tommy companionably on the shoulder. "Tommy!" he exclaimed. "I trust you are finding your accommodations acceptable?"

Tommy smiled up at Micah, pleased to see a familiar face. He was still fairly worried about the long school days with no weekend breaks, and although he didn't want to seem like a cry baby in front of Micah, he couldn't feel particularly enthusiastic about it, either, so he replied "It's okay... I guess."

"You guess?" Micah frowned. "What's the problem, Tommy?"

"Well, I dunno. The room is kind of small, but I don't really mind. I guess I'm just a little scared about so much schoolwork."

It was then that Tommy noticed the two other boys and the chancellor. James was staring at Tommy with complete and total amazement on his face, as if Tommy had suddenly sprouted a second head. Ryan's face, however, was a mask of fury. The smaller boy was glaring at Tommy with pure, unadulterated rage, and Tommy almost wanted to take a step back from him. Even Chancellor Duvey was scowling at Tommy, a thoroughly scandalized look on his face.

Micah appeared to not notice any of it, however, and instead he gave a chuckle. "Yes, Tommy, I understand. Every new initiate coming in has the same concerns, I assure you. However, we've found that a tight schedule is necessary, at least in the beginning, in order to teach you things quickly enough in order to avoid accidents. Plus, it helps keep you out of trouble while you are still adapting to our lifestyle." Micah gave Tommy a knowing wink.

"Accidents?" was all Tommy could think to say.

The lighthearted smile never left Micah's face, and his tone remained carefree, as well, but the topic was serious. "I won't lie to you boys. Starting out is a dangerous time for you. It's very easy to slip up and hurt yourself or others. At times, it may feel like trying to hold a slippery eel that is trying to bite you. But it gets easier, I promise you, and I think you'll find that you are having so much fun that you don't mind the tough schedule." His tone suddenly got more serious, then, and he continued, "But I must caution you, all of you, to be careful about following our rules. It can be tempting to take the easy route and delve into forbidden areas. I'd sooner destroy you myself than have you fall into that sort of thing." He favored all of them with a significant look. James was still gawking at Tommy, and Ryan was still glowering, so Tommy nodded as if he understood. Micah apparently took that as the confirmation he was waiting for, and he smiled again. "Good luck, then and welcome to you all."

With that, Micah walked over to the giant crystal, pausing only to exchange a few quiet words with a man who was getting up from one of the benches. Micah seated himself cross-legged on one of the mats, stared into the crystal for a moment, and then closed his eyes.

The chancellor motioned for the boys to leave the room, so they did. Once outside, he glowered at them. "Mister Nelson, you've got a lot of nerve talking to the High Archmage like... like he was one of your schoolyard pals. Next time you speak to him, you will address him as 'Sir' or 'My Lord'." He turned on James. "And you, Mister Thorton. I'd like to assure you again that you'll receive no special treatment during what will more than likely be your very short stay with us. Is that understood? By ALL of you?" The boys looked at the ground, abashed, and nodded their assent. "Very well, then. Come along, we have more to see. We'll finish up here, you'll have dinner, and then you'll return to your rooms to place your things in order before lights out." With that, he set off again and left the boys to trail behind.

The rest of the trip was fairly mundane. They saw a laundry where they could drop of their clothes for cleaning (a convenience for which Tommy was extremely grateful – his parents had made him help with the laundry, and Tommy had always hated it), a medical clinic they could visit if they got injured or were feeling sick, a quiet room that smelled of incense for peaceful meditation (Tommy couldn't see why he would ever need to use that, but there were several people in the room when they visited), and even a barber where they could obtain a haircut should they have a need. The final stop on the tour was a brief visit to the lavatory facilities, which were just down the hall from

Tommy's room; there were showers and toilets and the usual sorts of things Tommy had come to expect.

After the tour, the chancellor took them back to the dining hall for dinner. They all got trays of food, and the chancellor sat to eat with them. The food was splendid – Tommy had expected disgusting food, like in his school cafeteria, but it was way better than even the meals his mother had made. He ate fried chicken with mashed potatoes, green beans, and even a small piece of pumpkin pie for dessert. Although Tommy had normally been a diffident eater, he found himself gobbling the food. Although the hall was fairly crowded, it was very subdued and quiet – totally unlike the cafeteria at Tommy's school. At first, it was nice to have a bit of quiet for eating, but after a while the persistent silence started to unnerve him. By the end of the meal, James was shifting in his seat and looking around nervously, as well, but just sat and sullenly picked at his food, while the chancellor ate methodically and in total silence.

As Tommy looked around, he had expected the room to be full of other kids his age. He was very wrong, however. Some of the children were his age, and a few were even younger, but many of the other people eating in the room were full grown adults. Tommy even saw a couple men who looked old enough to be his grandfather! He made a mental note to ask about that should the opportunity arise. As the other people in the room finished eating, they rose one by one, returned their dishes to the kitchen, and silently filed out of the room.

Finally, the chancellor finished, gazed at each of them in turn, and stood, motioning for them to follow. He led them back to their room, told them he would be there to guide them to their morning classes, bid them good night, and left.

The boys went to their respective bed. James and Ryan

began unpacking. Tommy found a stack of new clothes on his bed. A note on the top simply said, "Enjoy, M.", so Tommy figured it was a gift from Micah. Mostly, it was jeans and t-shirts, but there were a few fashionable button-down shirts, as well as underwear, pajamas, and other assorted clothes. Everything was clean, new, and neatly folded. Tommy was relieved – he'd been wearing the same clothes for several days, and he had been wondering what he was going to do when it came time to wash them. He picked the clothes up and put them in his wardrobe, arranging them so he could find what he wanted. Tommy took off his old clothes, which were admittedly a little stinky, and put on a pair of the pajamas. In doing so, Tommy discovered a sealed envelope at the bottom of the stack. The pajamas fit well, so Tommy laid down on his bed and inspected the envelope. It was addressed to him, so he cracked the seal and opened it.

Before he could review the contents, however, James spoke up. "So, you really DID know the High Archmage, then?"

Tommy had to look up to be sure James was talking to him. "You mean Micah? He's the one who brought me here."

James shook his head and grinned. "That is so cool, man. I'm jealous. So what's he like? He seems pretty mean to me." James was clearly still smarting from the lecture he'd gotten earlier.

"He's nice. He was very kind to me. He saved my life" was all Tommy could think to respond. Although he had spent a couple days with Micah, he didn't really feel like he knew the man at all.

Tommy was saved from further response by Ryan, who interjected with an angry "Great. I'm stuck with TWO spoiled, pretentious jerks." With that, Ryan flopped down on his bed and made a show of opening his own envelope. James shook his head and went back to unpacking, leaving Tommy to investigate his envelope.

Inside was a weekly schedule, showing Tommy where he was expected to be and what classes he'd be having at what times. As he looked it over, Tommy couldn't suppress a groan.

His first class of the day, every day, was Mathematics.

CHAPTER SEVEN

Tommy's face hit the ground a fraction of a second before the rest of his body, and his breath went out with an "Oooof" sound. Tommy knew he should get up, but his body refused to obey, so he decided to just lay there for a moment. The mat he'd landed on was somewhat soft, at least, but it had that old sweat and antiseptic smell that gym mats always get, and Tommy couldn't help but wonder briefly if he really wanted to have his face pressed against it. It reminded Tommy of the time they'd done wrestling in gym class at school, when he'd spend the entire period with his face pressed against either the stinky gym mats or the even smellier bodies of his classmates.

"Get up," Ryan taunted him.

Tommy groaned and wished fervently and not for the first time that he was back in Math class, but he began picking himself up off the floor. His whole body felt bruised, and he moved like an old man, slowly and with great stiffness. His wish to be back in math class wasn't facetious, either – he had had a genuinely interesting time in Math that morning and was looking forward to the next day's class. It wasn't all "lecture and homework" here. Tommy worked at his own pace, investigated things that were interesting to him, and spent time with the instructors one-on-one. He'd left the class feeling like the intense school schedule might be positively tolerable.

Until it came time for his current class, that is. Listed on his schedule as physical fitness, the class was something more akin to physical defense than anything else. The instructor, a tall, thin man who introduced himself as Lord Kalish and who wore loose robes that reminded Tommy of an Arab, had told the class that he was going to assess their skills. He had taken pairs of padded wooden swords off the walls and passed them out, and then paired them up two by two. Some heavy padded gloves, shin and elbow pads, and a heavy foam helmet came out of a large box in the corner of the room and rounded out the equipment. Lord Kalish had then instructed them to try to hit each other with the swords. Tommy had gotten paired with Ryan, given that they were of an age and a fairly similar build, although Tommy was taller and heavier than the lithe Ryan. Tommy had expected that this would give him an advantage over the smaller boy, but he had quickly been disabused of this notion. Not only had he not managed to hit Ryan even once, but he had never even gotten close. Every time he swung the sword, Ryan seemed to anticipate the stroke and either blocked it or moved out of the way to strike Tommy soundly on the head or chest. Tommy had lost count of the number of times he'd been hit, and this last one had been a particularly heavy blow to the head that had sent him reeling to the ground.

Tommy had finally gained his feet and was about to raise his weapon against another of Ryan's brutal attacks when Lord Kalish clapped his hands twice loudly. "Gather here, everyone," the man called in an accent Tommy couldn't quite place – it seemed to be a cross between several different accents and made Lord Kalish sound foreign and exotic. Tommy was incredibly grateful for the interlude, but Ryan just shot him an angry scowl and turned away. Both boys headed over to the gathering, Ryan walking with his back stiff and Tommy limping slightly and dragging his padded weapon on the ground.

When all the boys had gathered around Lord Kalish, the instructor asked, "Do you know why is it that we study to learn the sword?"

Several of the boys shrugged and glanced at one another, but Ryan's hand shot into the air. Lord Kalish acknowledged him with a polite nod.

"So that we can defend ourselves in close combat, when there isn't time to use magic," Ryan said with pride and confidence in his voice.

"Hrm. Well, perhaps that is one reason. Perhaps. But a mage of any significant skill does not have such a problem. With practice, it will take you no time at all to use your magic, and you will find that a short distance will make things easier, not harder." This made Tommy remember Micah's encounter with the greasy man – both men had used magic at a very short range, and seemed to have no problem with it.

One of the other student's spoke up. "So, if magic is easier closer, why use a sword? Why not use a gun? We should be learning guns."

Tommy had to nod with respect at that. It hadn't occurred to him previously, but having it pointed out, he couldn't help but wonder why they would learn a weapon that became obsolete hundreds of years ago. Tommy half-expected Lord Kalish to be angry at being so questioned, but the man simply smiled and spread his hands in a gesture of wonder, saying "Why indeed! That is the question I ask you. Very well, you do not know. Lord Kalish will tell you. The answer is that, as you learn to use magic, you will learn to protect yourself, protect your body. A weapon that is held in your hand is as easy to protect as the rest of your body. True, a gun is held in your hand, and if you wish to strike an opponent with the gun, then it is a fine choice." Several students chuckled at that, but Lord Kalish did not pause. "To be effective as a weapon, the gun must shoot a bullet, yes? And when the bullet leaves the gun, it leaves your hand. Now, the bullet is in the air between you and your opponent. It is as easy for him to work his magic on the bullet as it is for you to try to stop him. He could stop the bullet, perhaps turn it aside, or perhaps even turn it against you. Lord Kalish would be very embarrassed to be required to tell your parents that you were killed with your own bullet, yes?" Again, the class chuckled, and Lord Kalish paused for a moment to let the laughter subside before continuing. "It is also true that policemen and soldiers will use guns, so many mages spend much practice in defeating them. In fact, there is a saying among my people; 'Do not hurl the arrow which will return against you'. You should remember this always." Lord Kalish hefted his own practice sword and held it up for the class to see. "But a sword... an opponent will find it very difficult to use against you. He will find this as difficult as he would find using your own body against you, simply because you hold the sword in your hand. So! You require a weapon to use when your magic is not available or is busy with other things, yes? " Lord Kalish raised the blade of his sword, and then briefly but quickly spun it around his body. "The sword is the perfect weapon. It is elegant. It is useful. And when Lord Kalish is done training you, it will be deadly."

The man paused for a moment to give his words time to sink in. "You know that those who master the use of magic are named as mages. Those few mages who master the sword as well are named 'Knights'. An elegant title for mastery of an elegant weapon, yes? Any of you might be called knight someday, if you have the fire in your belly for it. But listen to Lord Kalish - talent does not matter.   The strength of your arm does not matter. The age of your body does not matter. No man gains the title of knight except for one path – practice. If you wish to be named knight, you must practice, practice, and practice."

Lord Kalish stopped and looked around at the eager young eyes staring up at him. He could see the wonder in their eyes, and the desire, yet he suppressed a sigh. Most, if not all, of the boys would quickly give up their pursuit of titles when they learned how much work was required. Lord Kalish had seen it many times before in many other classes, but he did not want to discourage the boys on their first day, so he simply stated, "Now is the time for bathing. You are stinky boys and Lord Kalish will teach you no more today."

Tommy hurried off with the rest of the boys. In school he had always been wary of showering with the other boys in gym class, but today he quickly stripped off his clothes as he listened to the other boys chatter about how they were going to practice every day and become knights. Ryan was among the loudest of the bragging boys, and he commented often that women were attracted to men who were called 'Sir'. Tommy didn't know if he had the dedication to practice with the sword every day, particularly if it was going to be anything like today. What he did know was that a nice, hot shower would feel wonderful on his aching body. In this, at least, Tommy was very, very right.

CHAPTER EIGHT

After physical fitness, Tommy's schedule said it was time for lunch. Although he was ravenous, he had lingered overlong in the shower, letting the warm water cascade over his aching back and limbs. As he stepped into the lunch hall, Tommy quickly realized the error of his ways. Most of the large tables were already filled with other students, and there was no room for him to join the few classmates that he knew – Ryan, James, and several other boys from his classes were all gathered around a single table, and it was obvious that there wasn't even enough room for the boys that were already there, much less one more. There was also a steady stream of other students flowing into the room. Tommy shook his head to clear it and hurried over to the line at the kitchen.

The food seemed well made, if simple. There were slices of meatloaf with a mushroom gravy over them, some macaroni and cheese, and a mixture of peas and carrots that Tommy tried to refuse and was told in no uncertain terms that he was required to eat, all served on a sectioned plate that Tommy carried on a tray, just like he had in the cafeteria back at his regular school. Tommy was frustrated by the peas and carrots, since he hated vegetables and always refused to eat them, but when Tommy went to get a drink, his heart sunk further still – his choice in beverages seemed to be limited to either milk or water. A cafeteria worker walked by and Tommy stopped her to ask where he might get a soda pop.

The worker gave him a sympàthetic smile. "Nowhere, honey. The school doesn't think pop is healthy for children, so you won't find it anywhere." She patted him on the head and then walked away. Tommy was simply too flabbergasted to take umbrage at the pat. No soda? Tommy shook his head and wondered again at what he'd gotten himself into. He contented himself with taking a glass of milk and settled down at one of the few remaining empty tables.

He'd been sitting alone for several minutes, feeling completely pathetic, depressed, and sorry for himself when a young girl just about his own age set her tray down across from him.

"Do you mind if I sit here?" she asked as she plunked her lunch tray on the table and sat down anyway, even before Tommy had a chance to reply. Because she was already sitting, Tommy couldn't think of anything to say. He felt stupid inviting her to sit when she already was, so he swallowed a mouthful of meatloaf and said, "Uhh...."

"I'm Mae. Like the month, but with an 'E' at the end. Instead of a 'Y', I mean. M-A-E. It was my grandmother's name." She stood up to extend her hand out across the table toward Tommy and added "You are one of the first-years, aren't you? Just started?"

Tommy stood to take her hand and shake it gently. The skin of her hand felt soft and cool under his, and Tommy was painfully aware that he was sweating. He fervently hoped his hand didn't feel clammy to her, and he managed to reply, "Uhh... yeah. I just started. Today is my first day. I'm Thomas. Tommy, I mean. Everyone calls me Tommy."

As they both returned to their seats, Tommy took his first real look at Mae. She was pretty, in a plain sort of way, with long, curly chestnut colored hair that stretched down past her shoulders in extensive, looping ringlets. Her face was round, with brown eyes so dark they looked almost black peeking out from behind thick glasses. Her glasses were black ovals with little wing-like things that stuck out at the corners, and they reminded Tommy of glasses his old crazy Aunt Mary used to wear. She had a small mouth, a petite but pointy nose, and ruddy cheeks that formed tiny little dimples when she smiled. She looked like the kind of girl that got teased a lot at Tommy's old school. In short, Tommy thought she was beautiful.

Mae continued talking, however, and Tommy was so stunned that he almost missed her saying "I'm on my second year, so I'm a year ahead of you. I remember what it was like, though. Starting out, I mean. It seems really scary, but you'll get used to it. I wouldn't go back to my old school for ANYTHING." She smiled at Tommy again and began eating her lunch.

Tommy, on the other hand, couldn't think of anything to say. He'd never been much of a lady's man at his old school, and being confronted by this stunning beauty, here, unexpectedly, was too much for his brain to process. He contented himself with filling his mouth with food – at least it prevented him from having to say something and let him avoid saying something that Mae would find stupid or lame.

Fortunately, Mae didn't seem to have any problem with Tommy's silence. She easily filled the conversation void, talking in between shoveling her lunch into her mouth. Tommy wondered if she could even taste the food, she was gobbling it so fast. "You're the new boy, right?" Mae asked. Seeing the confusion on Tommy's face, she added, "New to magic, I mean. You used to be a mundane. A normal person, I mean. They don't like us to use that word. 'Mundane'. They don't like us to say 'normal person', either. The teachers claim we are all normal people. But you know what I mean, right? I mean, you can't say 'a person who doesn't use magic' all the time, right? That seems like a lot to say all the time."

Tommy blinked slowly under the onslaught of conversation. He could tell from Mae's pause that she was waiting for a response, but it took him a few minutes to sort through her sentences and figure out what exactly he was supposed to respond to. When he finally wheedled it out, he was confused. "Uhhh... yeah," he replied, "I'm new to the whole magic... thing. How did you know?" Tommy was slightly suspicious – was there some sort of mark on him that he couldn't see? Or was Mae using her magic to read his mind?

Mae grinned. "There are very few secrets around here. You'll see, everyone talks to everyone, and since we don't really leave the school much at all, there's not all that much to talk about. Plus, everyone knows who the applicants are each year. Some people train and study for years in hopes of getting an invitation to join the school, but there are only so many spots each year, so most people have to apply for several years before being accepted. Someone new, like you, is always worth talking about. Everyone wants to know who you are and what you'll be like."

"Oh. I'm... uhhh... Just me, really. I'm no one special. I didn't even really want to come here."

Mae giggled at him, and it made Tommy's heart flutter a little. "No one special? The word is that you arrived with the Archmage Micah, unannounced and unplanned, without even an invite. They say that he saved your life, and that you pledged your life to him in return. Do you think he'd do all that for somebody who isn't special?"

Tommy frowned. "I never pledged nothing. Micah saved me, but I didn't have any place else to go. I didn't want to go to jail." Tommy felt a sudden wave of sadness pass over him. He blinked quickly several times to keep from crying. "I never even got to say goodbye to my mom and dad."

Mae frowned, somewhat put off by the somber turn of the conversation, but she persisted. "I'm sorry. There are some other students like that here. One of my good friends came to the school the same way, but he's a year older and has a different schedule than I do. He eats lunch with the apprentices, not us novices. Maybe I can introduce you some time? I'm sure you would get along great!"

Although still feeling depressed, it was hard for Tommy to ignore Mae's enthusiasm. Her personality was simply so bubbly that it was difficult to stay in a bad mood. He was just about to reply when someone clapped him hard on the shoulder, and instead he let out an involuntary yelp of pain. Tommy turned to see that it was Ryan who had assaulted him so.

"Come on, buddy," Ryan said gruffly. "We've got Introduction to Magic in two minutes. This is going to be an awesome class; you can play kissy face later."

Tommy blushed furiously. He most certainly had NOT been playing kissy face with Mae, and he was mortified that Ryan had let on that he really, really wanted to. Mae appeared not to notice, however, because she was nodding furiously.

"You should go! That was my favorite class in first year! It's so interesting! That's why we're all here, after all. To learn about magic, right?" Mae made a shooing gesture at Tommy, but she was smiling as she did it. "Go! Go! I'll see you at dinner!"

Abashed, Tommy picked up his tray and followed Ryan to the drop-off. He turned once to look at Mae, and she smiled and shooed him again. Tommy smiled back, then the impact of what had happened hit him. He'd talked to a pretty girl! And she wanted to talk to him again! Today! Moreover, she had totally ignored Ryan's comments about playing kissy face. Suddenly, Tommy felt like he had something to look forward to. Dinner couldn't come soon enough.

Ryan, however, was shaking his head as Tommy dumped his trash in the bin and placed his dishes in the wash rack. "Man, you just have all the luck, don't you?" Ryan smirked.

For the first time in days, Tommy felt like he couldn't come up with an argument against him.

CHAPTER NINE

The instructor for Tommy's next class was Micah himself. The man nodded slightly to Tommy as he entered the room, which looked to Tommy like any other classroom in any other school he'd ever seen, complete with an overhead projector and whiteboard. Tommy felt a kind of excitement at seeing Micah there, and he eschewed his normal back of the class policy and took a desk a couple rows from the front. James took the seat right next to Tommy, and Ryan sat immediately behind James.

After a few minutes, when it was apparent that all the students had arrived and taken their seats, Micah waved one hand at the door and it slammed itself shut. Several of the students looked around at one another, unsure of how to react to the sudden surprise.

"Most of you know who I am," Micah began. "For those who don't, my name is Micah and I am the head of this school." James looked over at Tommy and grinned broadly, and Tommy couldn't help but to grin back.

Micah continued, "Your normal instructor, Professor Corbet, had a personal issue and could not be here today. I am filling in for him. Although it is a rare thing that I teach classes these days, you will see me often as your progress in your educational journey. For one thing, any student wishing to advance to the next level must undergo a test and pass an interview with myself or one of my senior leaders. I also personally run all outings and field trips that leave the school, so you will hopefully see me then, too."

Here, Micah's face got much darker and foreboding. "One reason I do NOT want to have to see you is because you broke the rules," he scowled. "Our rules are few, but they are very important and are in place for a very good reason. I take them extremely seriously, and I have little sympathy for anyone who breaks the rules no matter what their reason may be. Those who break the rules quickly find themselves banished from the school," Micah paused, fixing the class with an intense stare. "Or worse," he finished with a finality that say little but implied a great deal.

Abruptly, Micah's demeanor changed. He shed the rough and dark expression like he would shed a coat and became the friendly and open person that Tommy had come to know. "I think I've said enough about that, of course. So, why don't we continue? First, let me explain the rules."

Several students in the class opened notebooks and got pencils at the ready, so Tommy did the same. He'd always been an indifferent note taker in school – he always started out the school year with good intentions, but after a few weeks he lost his focus, and after the first couple of months he usually stopped taking notes entirely, preferring instead to doodle in his notebook. But this was something totally new, something he knew absolutely nothing about. He felt at a disadvantage, since the other students seemed to already know a great deal about the school and about magic, so he was determined to take good notes.

"The first rule," Micah began, "Is that you will not use magic on or against your fellow students or instructors, nor on any of the staff or anyone else who inhabits this school, except under controlled circumstances when directed by your instructors. Many students get tempted to play pranks on each other using magic. I simply will not tolerate it, so don't do it. Don't even THINK about doing it. Is that clear?"

A young girl that Tommy had never met raised her hand from the back of the class. Micah acknowledged her with a simple "Yes?"

"What about to help someone," the girl asked. "Like if someone is hurt, or something."

Micah shook his head. "A good question, but the answer is still no. At some point, you may become skilled enough that we would permit you to help someone in need. But for now, you are forbidden from even making the attempt. Although there is a slim chance that you might succeed, it is far more likely that you could cause irreparable harm to your patient, yourself, or both. Is that clear?" Silence around the classroom indicated that it was, and Tommy made sure to write a firm 'No Exceptions!' in his notebook.

"Good. The second rule, then, is that you shall never use magic to break any laws of the outside world. This means no stealing, no trespassing, and no injuring, hurting, or coercing of other people. I think this is fairly clear. If it was against the rules for you to do it before you became a mage, then it is against the rules for you to do it after. Any questions?" Again, a few moments of silence confirmed that there were no questions.

"Finally," Micah continued, "But most importantly, you will not practice any kind of dark or black magic." Micah paused and regarded the room. Tommy looked back at him expectantly, since he had no idea what it was that the man was talking about. "You are all so quiet. Can anyone in the class tell me what I mean by black magic?"

Micah's eyes scanned the room before locking with Tommy's eyes. Tommy felt his pulse quicken and the sweat start to form on his arms and neck. "Oh god," he thought to himself, "Please, please don't ask me. I don't know the answer. I don't know anything at all. You know I don't know the answer, why would you pick on me...?"

Then Micah, with his eyes never straying from Tommy's, said, "Yes, Ryan? You have an answer?" and Tommy felt relief wash over him. He saw the corners of Micah's mouth twitch up, for just a moment. If he hadn't been staring straight at the man he would have missed it, but there was a sparkle in Micah's eyes that said 'Gotcha!', and Tommy could almost see that he was laughing on the inside. Tommy's jaw almost dropped in surprise – the man had been having fun with him!

"Dark magic is evil things, like summoning or necromancy." Ryan beamed with pride at his answer.

Micah nodded to him. "Yes, very true. I want to be clear, though. 'Evil' can be a bad word to use. If I were to hurt an innocent person using only, say, fire magic, then that would be an evil thing to do, but it would not be 'black magic'. Does that make sense?" Micah paused and looked at the class. Several of the students nodded, including Tommy, so he continued. "Summoning and Necromancy are indeed the two main types of black magic."

Micah's voice took on a lecturing tone again. "So, let's talk about the lesser of the two evils, as it were. You called it 'summoning', but that is something of a misnomer. There really is no 'summoning', except perhaps in the blackest of rites, and perhaps not even then." Tommy hoped things would get clearer –

he stared at his notepad, unsure about what he should even write down. Fortunately, Micah continued. "The proper name for this type of magic is 'conjuration', and it goes something like this: If you infuse enough magical energy into an inanimate object, you can cause it to become animate and follow whatever orders you program into it."

Micah looked around the room and saw open confusion on most of the student's faces. He sighed, and began again. "Think of it like a computer. You need to provide power into the computer, in the form of electricity, and you need to give the computer instructions, in the form of a program. Conjuration, then, is building a type of computer out of just about anything, using magical energy instead of electricity." Comprehension dawned on several faces, so Micah asked, "Can anyone tell me what problem this presents that we label it dark magic?"

Ryan's hand was the first in the air, but Micah nodded across the room to a girl who looked to be several years Tommy's junior. "Yes... Mary?"

The girl in question smiled and stated simply, "Computers are stupid."

The glass giggled, but Micah smiled at Mary. "In a nutshell, yes. Think about a computer. It can do simple things fairly easily, but doing anything remotely complex requires a lot of programming." Micah spread his hands out to his side, parallel to the ground. "Take the floor, for example. If I wanted to program something to clean the floor, I'd have to teach it what was dirt and what was not – I wouldn't want it to strip the varnish off the wood. I'd also need to teach it how to move around your desks, when it needs to stop, what it should do with the dirt it collects, and so on. The more instructions I need to give the computer, the more power it needs. In this case, it would be quite a lot of energy." Suddenly, a stiff breeze blew along the floor of the room. Micah brought his hands together, and all the dust and dirt on the floor was swept by the breeze into a small ball of dirt that dropped quickly onto Micah's open palm. "All to accomplish something that is much more easily done another way."

A couple of the students clapped at the demonstration, and Tommy couldn't help but grin with respect at the man's showmanship.

"So, here's the problem. In order to conjure something that is useful, you need to use an immense amount of power. When you use that much power in a conjuration, it becomes quite dangerous; Any little flaw in the programming could have disastrous results. Let me tell you a story." Micah sat down on the edge of the desk at the front of the room and took on a more conversational tone. "Years ago, we had a conjurer in our midst. He was a young boy, but slightly older than most of you. He was ambitious, and he was actually quite good at conjuration, even though it was already a forbidden practice in our school. This young man decided to make a conjuration to take care of some of his chores. He built the conjuration – the 'program', if you will – and it actually worked. However, the conjuration was so complex it needed a lot of energy. A constant flow of energy, actually, and this young man did not want to sit and continually provide magical power to the thing. After all, what good is it to have a conjuration do his chores if he has to be there to supervise? So, he added a program to the thing so that it could seek out and gather its own magical power, and he turned it loose. But where was the biggest available source of power? Well, it was from the student himself. His conjuration leapt upon him and attacked him. It began to rapidly drain magical energy out of him, leaving him with nothing to defend himself. When there was no more magical energy to drain, the thing didn't stop. It kept drawing on him until it

69

devoured his very life force. The poor student was found on the floor, cold and dead."

Micah paused to let his words sink in to the class. Tommy swallowed a lump in his throat, and wondered what he'd gotten himself into. But Micah wasn't finished. "Even worse, after the student was gone, his conjuration lived on. It went on to attack and injure several other students before it was destroyed. It was only a matter of luck that no one else was killed." Micah stood, his story clearly concluded. "So. My message to you is, don't try it. Not even once, not even to see what you can do, not even to see what it's like. There will be no appeal for anyone who is caught practicing conjuration; expulsion will be immediate and irrevocable."

This time, Micah did not pause to ask for questions. "But far, far worse," he continued, "is what is known as Necromancy – the magic of death. Necromancers steal life and energy from other people in order to strengthen themselves. I'm sure I don't need to tell you that it's wrong to take someone else's life for your own selfish use. If you needed to be told that, you wouldn't be sitting in this class. But I want you to understand just how dangerous this type of magic is. When a necromancer steals life from someone, he absorbs that person's strength... but also their weaknesses, as well. Fear and hatred. Sicknesses of the body and the mind. Necromancers take pieces of these things and absorb them into their own being. For this reason, necromancers inevitably end up alone, so consumed with the fears they have absorbed that they cannot stand to have others around. Their bodies decay around them from the poisons they absorb, but they hang on to life, powered by their stolen strengths." Micah shook his head. "It is a horrible life with a terrible ending. But although we pity necromancers, we also do not give them any mercy." Micah held his hand up, clenched into a fist, and his face was clenched into a grimace. "Any mage in this academy will destroy anyone found practicing necromancy. Without mercy, without a trial. And mark my words – more than likely, someone in this very room will be tempted to try it, despite my warnings. Someone always does, and that someone always gets caught. *Always*."

The class sat silent for several minutes, and Micah let them as he looked around the room, meeting each student's eyes one at a time. Some students quickly looked away in fear or embarrassment, others held his gaze. Nowhere did Micah see the telltale signs of defiance that meant a student was already considering the darker paths, so after a few minutes he clapped his hands. "Well!" he began, and several students jumped at the sudden noise. "Let's begin the fun part, shall we?"

CHAPTER TEN

Tommy's feet wanted to skip along the ground as he headed to dinner, but his mind was too tired to let them. He was really looking forward to getting the chance to talk to Mae again (Although, he admitted to himself, he didn't really get to do much talking last time), but the "fun part" that Micah had talked about turned out to be incredibly difficult. Micah had started teaching them to use magic, and the exercises he led them through were very frustrating. They were supposed to be learning how to get in touch with the magic that Micah claimed was all around them. He had explained to them that they could only hope to use magic when they were very calm, relaxed, and at peace, so he led them through a series of calming mental and physical exercises. Tommy was still really sore from the drubbing he had taken in physical fitness, and he found it hard to relax while stretching his aching muscles. Still, he did manage to get in the right frame of mind. Or, at least, he thought he did. Once they were calm, Micah had instructed them to reach out with their minds and touch the magic floating around them. But Tommy found that trying to "'reach out" like that took a great deal of effort, and it ruined his state of calm, so he had to repeat the entire process all over again. Tommy thought he could almost feel something out there, when he was at his most calm. Something that was distant and scattered, yet massive at the same time, like a giant thunderhead just on the horizon. Tommy didn't feel too bad about his failing to reach out – all the other students, Ryan included, had similar problems and every one of them failed to attain the state that Micah had asked of them.   After all, Ryan seemed to know everything about magic, sword fighting, the school, and even the teachers and prominent leaders at the school. If he couldn't do it, then how could anyone expect Tommy to succeed?

Tommy's mind wandered as he stumbled along. He was still anxious to see Mae, but he was just so incredibly tired. Tommy pushed through the double doors that led to the dining hall... and stumbled out into the cool night air. He shook his head and blinked several times, wondering where he was and how he had gotten there. Obviously in his fatigue, he'd taken a wrong turn, but he wasn't sure where or how to get back to someplace he recognized.

Looking around, Tommy found himself in a vast, broad courtyard, illuminated from above by the stars and the almost full moon, which seemed unusually crisp and clear. Above and behind him, a mountain rose almost unimaginably high.   In the bright moonlight, Tommy could make out windows and casements up most of the height, and an occasional balcony actually protruded from the side. The mountain was larger than Tommy could have possibly imagined, and he wondered if the school filled it entirely. As Tommy continued to stare, he realized that the mountain extended to both his left and his right, and the top of it was wreathed in a coating of snow that almost glowed in the ephemeral light. Most of the school had been built directly into the mountain, with the outdoor areas in a kind of box canyon between cliffs, Tommy realized, and as he looked across the courtyard, he saw a large, thick wall stretch across the entire mouth of the canyon. It was distant – at least a quarter mile away – and Tommy guessed that it would have to be almost a hundred feet high. Within the wall, Tommy saw many other structures, all of them stone. Most of the buildings looked like squat stone houses, but there were many larger ones as well, some of them so big as to resemble a warehouse. Tommy also saw what he thought was several fields of wheat and corn, and maybe some other crops, as well – although the courtyard was well lit, it was still dark out and difficult to discern.

It was then that Tommy realized that the majority of the light wasn't coming from the moon after all. The shadows told him much of it was coming from something he couldn't see. He stepped around a corner and gasped at what he saw.

There was a long, round building. It had a long, arched roof that came down to meet the ground. The roof was constructed of some kind of alabaster stone and broken by a series of large stone arch supports, spaced every twenty feet or so, and made of a much darker stone than the roof. Between every arched support was a large, gothic window made of some kind of frosted glass, and each was lit from within by a soft glow that was very reminiscent of moon light, yet much, much brighter. At the front of the building was a large double door, made of a dark wood and polished to a glowing sheen. Something about the place – perhaps the architecture – reminded Tommy of a church, and he felt like he could almost hear a soft thrumming sound, deep and strong and just below hearing, coming from the building. "What IS it?" Tommy asked himself in a whisper.

"Don't you know? That's the Hall of the Paladins," a voice said from right behind Tommy, who let out a yelp and jumped into the air in surprise.

Tommy spun around and found behind him a young man, perhaps twenty years old, with long brown hair and very bad acne. Tommy put his hand out to lean against the wall for a minute, trying to calm his racing heart. "You... You scared the life out of me," Tommy gasped between breaths.

The young man looked down at him. "You aren't supposed to be out here."

Tommy nodded in acknowledgment. "I know. I got lost looking for the cafeteria." His heart was still pounding with the adrenaline of being startled.

"Oh," said the young man, "yes, that happens with novices. Ok, follow me, I'll take you back. Come on," and with that, he turned, opened the door that Tommy had come through, and entered the building. Tommy stared after him for a moment, then trotted for a few steps to catch up, dodging around the closing door without touching it.

"What's a Paladin?" asked Tommy when he caught up with the man, who was walking at a brisk pace.

The man didn't slow but gave Tommy a clear sidelong glance. "You must be new here. A Paladin is someone who specializes in white magic. But they don't tell you much about it unless you take some kind of oath, and you can only take the oath when you become a Mage-Knight."

"Oh," was all Tommy could say. The man seemed to take it as an indication of his understanding, even though Tommy felt like he didn't really understand at all. It sounded to him like some sort of secret society, within the already secret society that was the school.

"Here we are, the novice dining hall" the young man said, gesturing to a set of double doors. He then turned, and, without preamble, returned the way he came.

Tommy stared after him for a few minutes, then

shrugged and pushed through the doors into the dining hall. Immediately, a wave of sensations washed over him. The warmth of the room, the smells of food, and the murmur of conversation hit him, and Tommy realized that he was ravenous. As he walked to the serving area to get his food, he spied Mae sitting with a couple other students at the same table they'd eaten lunch at. She saw him, bounced in her seat, and waved, and Tommy couldn't help but grin.

Tommy picked up his food – there was no line since he was late, although some of the food looked slightly dried out, like it had been sitting under a heat lamp for a while. There was a generous helping of chicken in some kind of cream sauce over noodles, steamed carrots, and a small brownie for dessert. Tommy decided that it wasn't particularly dazzling fare, but it was hot and smelled good, and his stomach was growling at the prospect. A tall glass of milk rounded out his tray, since there was still no soda available, and Tommy headed over to the table. He stepped up next to Mae, and barely managed to set his tray on the table before he dropped it in utter shock.

There, sitting across the table, was his old friend Stephen, whose real name was Bao, and who had been taken away by the army men at Tommy's school a couple years ago. Tommy couldn't have been more surprised – he had tried not to think of Stephen since he'd been taken away, and except for the recent nightmare he'd had while the greasy man had held him captive, Tommy had not given Stephen much thought. He certainly never expected to see the other boy again. People who got taken away for using magic were *never* seen again.

Stephen was grinning up at him with that same old goofy grin he used to wear, clearly getting a great deal of enjoyment out of Tommy's surprise.

"Stephen, this is..." Mae started to say, but Stephen interrupted her.

"Hi, Tommy! It's good to see you again," Stephen said, standing slightly and extending his hand across the table towards Tommy.

Tommy shook Stephen's hand and returned his infectious grin. But before Tommy could ask how Stephen came to be here, they both noticed Mae looking rapidly back and forth between them. "You two know each other?" Mae asked.

Stephen nodded. "Tom and I used to be friends. We went to elementary school together, back before the return of the magic."

Tommy finally got his surprise under control, released Stephen's hand, and sat down at the table. "How...? I mean, the last time I saw you..." Tommy trailed off. He didn't want to embarrass Stephen by discussing the state in which they'd last seen each other.

Stephen grinned at Tommy. "From what I've heard, I got here almost the same way you did." Stephen looked to his left and right to include the rest of the table. "I was one of the unfortunate kids who failed the magic testing at school," he began, and the others at the table nodded sympathetically. "They beat me, slapped the chains on me, and hauled me off to a big white van. They tossed me in the back without even a word and drove off. I won't lie to you guys – I was scared out of my mind. All I could think of was how my mom and dad were going to worry when I didn't get home from school – and what they would think when they heard what had happened to me."

Tommy felt an irrational surge of jealousy as Mae put her

hand on Stephen's shoulder, but Stephen merely favored her with a brief smile and continued with his story.

"The guy driving the van was obviously in a hurry – He was driving really fast, and I could hear the tires squealing when he went around turns, but I couldn't really move. I do know he seemed to hit every single bump in the road, because I got bounced around so much I started to get dizzy. Then we hit a particularly hard bump, and I knocked my head hard against the side of the van. I shook my head and the hood came right off, and after I blinked a few times I realized that it wasn't a bump – the van was actually flipped over on its side, and I was lying along the wall. The back doors had come open, one of them actually coming off the hinges, and standing there in the door was a man. My eyes weren't adjusted to the light, yet, and with the sun behind him, he almost seemed to glow."

"Now, you have to understand... All this had happened so quickly. I was scared out of my wits, I was beat up, and I was confused. So, I did what any normal person would have done in this situation." Stephen paused and favored them all with a wry grin. "I screamed, pissed in my pants, and then started to bawl." Everyone around the table give a chortle, including Tommy. He'd forgotten about Stephen's self-effacing style of humor, and how it had always tickled his funny bone.

"I heard a loud cracking noise as the figure knelt down. Honestly, I thought someone was shooting a gun, but it turned out to be the chains on my arms and legs bursting themselves open. No sooner had I gotten up, though..."

A girl sitting nearby interrupted Stephen. Tommy had seen her in the cafeteria before but didn't know her name or really anything at all about her; just that she was in one of the more advanced classes. "Wait a minute," she said to Stephen brusquely.   "I thought you said the chains were tungsten. Everyone knows tungsten kills magic, and that magic doesn't work on anything made of tungsten."

Stephen just shrugged. "I don't know. All I know is what I heard and what happened. One minute, I was chained up tightly, the next minute I was free, and he never even touched the chains."

Mae sniffed, and took on a lecturing tone that Tommy found endearing. "Mary, don't be so obtuse. Everyone knows tungsten is brittle, unless you mix it with steel. He didn't have to burst the chains. He could have used magic to throw something at them and crack them, or to make the air around them very cold so they could break. Oh! He could have also used magic on the locks, which probably weren't made from tungsten. Or, I've heard that he may have been able to, hrmmm..." She trailed off deep in thought, but her lips kept moving. Tommy realized that she was still talking, to herself, and that she didn't realize that she was no longer speaking out loud. Everyone was staring at Mae – Stephen with a kind of good-humored tolerance like an older brother to a silly child, the rest of the kids like they were looking at some strange and obnoxious insect.

To distract everyone, Tommy spoke up. "Uh... who is this 'he' you keep talking about?" Tommy's question appeared to snap Mae out of her reverie, but it was Stephen who answered. "Well, it was Micah, of course. Who else? He's really one of the only ones who makes a habit of going around rescuing kids, isn't he?"

Everyone at the table nodded. Mary pitched her voice low, in a whisper, but loud enough that all of them could hear. "I've heard that he does it because they took his kid. His son. Someone told me that they are holding his son in a prison somewhere, and that is what prevents him from just destroying all the prisons and freeing all the other mages."

Another boy that Tommy didn't recognize scoffed. "Don't be stupid. Micah's strong, no doubt. Stronger than anyone I've ever seen. But he's not strong enough to fight them all. Not with their tanks and soldiers and pet mages and everything. If he tried to attack one of the prisons, they'd take him out like that," and the boy snapped his fingers in the air. "That's why he tries to save kids before they get taken."

Everyone nodded thoughtfully at that. It did make a certain kind of sense, after all. Tommy, however, was thinking about a boy, trapped somewhere in a prison cell. Afraid, alone, and away from his family who loved him, guilty only of the crime of being the son of a man who freed captured children. Tommy found his respect and admiration for Micah growing, like a warm glow in his chest, even as he felt sad for the man, who must miss his family as much as Tommy did. Maybe even more. Tommy's sense that he had made the right decision increased, and suddenly he felt at home and happy to be at the school.

Suddenly, Tommy noticed that everyone was packing up their trays to leave. "Hey! You didn't finish the story!" he called to Stephen. Stephen merely turned his head and grinned as he walked away. "Another time, buddy," he called. "We're starting our first lesson in combat training early tomorrow morning, and I want to be ready and rested!" Mae let out a small squeal of delight and hurried after Stephen, leaving Tommy alone at the table.

"Combat training?" he mused to himself. "I wonder what they teach in that class?" He was still wondering and muttering to himself when he packed up his own tray and headed back to class.

CHAPTER ELEVEN

I t was several days later that Tommy actually managed to get in touch with the magical energy that he felt around him. He wasn't the first one in the class – that honor fell, of course, to Ryan, but Ryan had in turn given Tommy some tips the night before, and it was using Ryan's tips that helped Tommy succeed on his own.

Micah had begun the class that day in his usual fashion – with a lecture. Tommy didn't mind the lectures so much. They were often fairly interesting, and Micah had a kind of twisted sense of humor that appealed to Tommy. Plus, Tommy was forced to admit, he knew next to nothing about the topic and needed to learn more if he was to keep up with his classmates. Even though he had generally disdained his classmates and avoided contact with them in the past, one thing that Tommy had always been terrified of was being held back a grade in school. He couldn't imagine having to suffer that kind of humiliation on a daily basis and was determined that it wouldn't happen to him here.

Micah's lecture had been on 'Elemental Affinities'. "People", Micah had told them, "each have a unique and individual attunement to the classical elements – earth, air, fire, and water. Although magic does not naturally conform to any one element, each person has a different level of skill in forming magic in the individual elements. Most any effect you could desire can be caused by tuning magic to one of these elements – or, in some cases, by combining multiple elements. And just like everyone has a unique face and a different voice, so does everyone have a different level of ability – of elemental affinity, if you will."

Tommy thought on that, and decided it sounded reasonable. His father had always been hot, and his mother had teased her husband that he had fire in his veins. Tommy decided that his father was probably fire-attuned, and he hoped that he was, as well – he could see a lot of ways that fire could be useful, but couldn't see much application for the others. Evidently, he wasn't alone in his thoughts – James raised his hand and asked, "But what good is something like earth or air magic?"

Micah chuckled in response. "What good is air magic? Well, look, it's all around you. You move through it. You need it to breath. What would happen if a mage was to cause the air to abandon you," Micah asked, and suddenly the air in the room got extremely thin.   Tommy gasped and found it hard to breathe in. In the space of seconds, his head started to swim, and he felt dizzy. Then, suddenly there was a "whooshing noise, and Tommy found he could breathe again. He looked around, and found his classmates all gasping and panting from the experience. Micah, however, did not miss a beat and appeared not to notice their discomfort. "I personally believe that air magic is one of the most powerful elements, if not the single most powerful. But do not discount the others. You stand on the earth, and even the clothes you wear are made from fibers that come from the earth. Your body is over half water, and your brain is seventy-percent water. Many novices think only of the destructive power of fire, and while this is true, it is simply not the only application of fire. Fire is the application of energy, so consider things like electricity – the very stuff that is powering the lights in this room is generated using fire magic."

"Instead", Micah continued, "It might be helpful to think of the elements in a different way. Earth magic deals with solids, water magic deals with liquids, air with gasses, and fire with energy. Thinking about it that way, you can see more applications for each element. Only, we still refer to them by their classical names." Micah gave them a wry grin. "After all, who would want to say, 'I am a gas mage', or 'I'm a master of the gas?'" The whole class, Tommy included, laughed at that, and Ryan actually laughed so hard he snorted, which set everyone off giggling again.

After the levity subsided, Micah said they were going to move on to practice time. He spent some time going over everything again, even though they had heard it all several times before. Tommy sat back in his chair and tried to remember the tips that Ryan had given him, as well as everything Micah had taught them. At first, it had gone like every time before – Tommy got into a nice, relaxed state of mind where he could feel the energy floating around him. But every time he focused enough to reach out and touch it, he lost the relaxed state of mind and therefore lost touch with the energy.

Tommy decided that he'd try some of Ryan's suggestions. First, he tried to empty his mind. He had read a book on meditation once, and this was very similar – he simply tried to think about nothing at all, to calm the normally rampant thoughts that surged through his mind. Then, when he felt very calm and at peace, he could feel the energy all around him. This time, instead of trying to reach out and touch it, he tried to relax more – to simply allow himself to relax so much that his mind and his being flowed out and merged with the energy around him.

For several long minutes, nothing at all happened and it occurred to Tommy for a moment that Ryan might have been shining him on – it would fit with Ryan's general sense of humor, or lack thereof. Tommy pushed the annoying and distracting thoughts aside, since they would serve no purpose but to distract him. He calmed himself again, relaxed, let his consciousness expand beyond his body... And suddenly, his entire being was suffused with an immense energy. It reminded him of a time when he and some friends had stayed up all night drinking highly caffeinated and sugared energy drinks. He had that same tingly, excited, energy filled feeling all over his body, but at the same time he could feel that his body was still sitting passively. It was a unique feeling, not unpleasant, but certainly unaccustomed.

The energy continued to build and intensify, almost to the point of being uncomfortable. Suddenly, Tommy felt like he was going to explode, and the energy burst free from him in a torrent. It felt like he was trying to control a fire hose – the energy flowed out of him in a wild, uncontrollable stream that whipped around the room. Except, Tommy WAS the fire hose – he could feel the energy pouring into him, concentrating, flowing through him, and then shooting out in a stream. Tommy began to panic – he couldn't control the energy that was coursing through him, and neither could he stop it or slow it – quite to the contrary, Tommy felt like it was flowing faster and getting stronger the longer he held it.

Tommy opened his mouth to scream... when suddenly, he felt as if the fire hose was seized in a massive, iron grip. No longer flailing around, Tommy regained some sense of control, and his panic began to subside. When it did, Tommy recognized the force that was holding him steady – it was Micah, and he could sense the teacher's presence containing the energy and controlling it. It was then that Tommy realized just how strong the man was – if the flow of energy through him was a fire hose, then the man holding it was a gigantic mountain, vast, strong, and immovable.

With Micah steadying him, Tommy was able to slowly choke back on the flow. The stream of energy narrowed and thinned, slowed to a trickle, and then stopped altogether.

Tommy opened his eyes. He was sprawled on the floor, his desk and chair knocked askew and his papers scattered. Micah was kneeling over him, and the older man's eyes showed concern but there was a soft smile on his face. Micah extended a hand, and Tommy took it and let his teacher help him to his feet. A wave of dizziness hit Tommy, and he might have fallen had Micah not been there to steady him. Tommy looked around the room – his classmates were all looking at him with a mixture of surprise and pity. James stepped over and righted Tommy's chair, and he fell into it gratefully.

He was feeling very confused. This hadn't happened to Ryan when he successfully reached the magic, but Tommy found himself suddenly too tired to sort it out. All he could manage was a feeble, "Wha...?"

Micah set his desk back upright in front of him, but then turned and strode toward the head of the class, leaving Tommy's papers on the floor. Some of Tommy's surrounding classmates bent to gather them up and place them back on his desk, and he nodded to them thankfully. When he reached the front of the classroom, Micah turned to regard the class.

"It appears," he said with a serious voice that belied the smile on his face, "that our friend Tommy is a Channeler. You have my apologies, Tommy – I had my suspicions, but until this very moment, I wasn't sure."

Tommy was no less confused, and he looked around – the pity on the faces of all his classmates had been replaced with a look of respect.

CHAPTER TWELVE

In the days that followed, Tommy started to feel more alone. Mae and Stephen had moved up to a higher-level class, and their schedules were different than his. Tommy had become somewhat of a celebrity since word of his abilities had gotten around, and that had made Ryan increasingly acerbic. Even James had been somewhat distant; he still had not managed to touch the magic, while the rest of the class could almost do it at will. James' failure to keep up with the rest of the class had become somewhat telling, and he had withdrawn inward, spending much of his time trying to practice his abilities. Tommy had tried to tell him that he was trying too hard, that it would come easier if he could just relax and let it happen, but James seemed almost... spacey... when Tommy tried to talk to him, and Tommy was sure that his words weren't really getting through to the older boy. More than not, Tommy ate his meals alone, or sat with Mary, who had not passed her advancement test and had been left behind by Stephen and Mae.

Even with Mary for company, though, Tommy was often lonely. Mary often didn't want to talk, and frequently studied or worked on homework while she ate. Tommy sensed that she felt the sting of having been left behind and was spending her every waking moment trying to catch up. At first, he tried to talk her out of it – there was no pressure at the school and each student was allowed to move at his or her own pace. Then he remembered how he had felt every time Ryan had surpassed him at something and decided to keep his mouth shut. Tommy even tried to help her, tried to ask questions about the test she had failed and how he might help her study for it, but Mary rebuffed his efforts and told him that it she wasn't allowed to discuss the details of the testing with someone who had not undergone it.

All in all, Tommy thought that it was a pretty good life despite his growing loneliness and depression, and the days slipped by him in a blur.

Thus, it was several weeks later that Tommy found himself sitting alone at a table in the dining hall, feeling totally and completely sorry for himself. It was a "visiting day" for the students – the first ever visiting day for many of them – where the student's families were permitted to come to the school and spend the afternoon and evening with their loved ones. There were only a handful of other students in the dining hall – James was one of them, but he was sitting across the hall with his parents, and looked to be getting a stern lecture from his father – he was shaking his finger at James, who had his head down almost on the table. The scene made Tommy feel a little sick to his stomach. He would give just about anything to get a visit from his parents, and here James' parents were wasting the opportunity. After watching for a few minutes, Tommy packed up his tray and left the dining room.

He had no classes or assignments that night – everyone had gotten most of the day off for visiting day – so he let his feet wander. He briefly considered sneaking back to his room and stealing James' "Canadian Bacon" T-shirt – James wore the shirt all the time, despite the fact that Tommy had told him it reminded him of his encounter with the greasy man named Jordan, the man that Micah had killed. It seemed like it had to be years ago, not just a couple of months, but the sight of the shirt still made Tommy's throat clench, and he'd been trying to find a way to sneak it away. Ryan would probably be in the room with his parents, though, and would certainly tell James if Tommy tried to sneak into his things.

Tommy's wandering took him past several classrooms. Most of them were empty, but some had small gatherings of people sitting and talking, marveling over school work, or simply sitting and spending time together. This did nothing to improve Tommy's mood, and eventually he found himself in the channeling room. The giant blue crystal that dominated the room towered over him, and Tommy felt the same sense of peace and awe that he always did in coming here.

Tommy was way ahead on his channeling duties. Every mage that lived in the school was required to spend some time channeling magical energy into the giant crystal. This energy was used to power the school, maintain the illusions that hid the school from outsider eyes, and for a variety of other things that Tommy only half understood. Tommy's great ability to channel gave him a distinct advantage over the other students, here – while most of them had to spend several hours every week to meet their requirements, Tommy could fulfill his in just a half an hour or so. And he was getting stronger – much stronger – very quickly.

Despite not really needing to, Tommy decided that the calmness of channeling would help snap him out of his depression. He sat down on one of the padded benches, relaxed his mind, and opened himself to the power. Although it took him a few seconds to reach the right frame of mind, Tommy could reliably channel any time he wanted to, now. When he felt the flood of energy entered his body, Tommy directed it into the crystal.

Although the energy coursing through Tommy felt massive, like a raging river, the crystal soaked up every drop of it as if Tommy was pouring water into a vast, deep hole. Every time he did this, it always felt to Tommy like if he could just channel enough energy, if he could just force enough power into the thing, that he could fill it up. Of course, it never did, and Tommy knew that stronger people than him had tried. Still, he channeled as much energy as he could, straining to pull more and more. He could almost feel his ability gradually getting stronger, bit by bit, the more he tried and the longer he channeled.

After about twenty minutes, though, he could take no more. He lost touch with the power and his body slumped on the bench. Channeling was physically taxing, particularly for someone as new to it as Tommy, and he became tired rather quickly. Micah had told them that they would grow more accustomed to it – that their stamina from channeling would increase with their strength the more they practiced. He had likened it to muscles that were getting a workout, and gradually built strength and endurance the more they were used. Only, the muscle was in their minds, and it was one that they had never used before, so it took quite a lot of working out to build it up.

Tommy picked himself up off the bench and stretched. He was well and truly tired now, and he was sure that he could go straight to sleep, even if Ryan or James was still awake in the room. He was sure that one or both of them would be – it will still fairly early, and visiting day lasted for several hours, yet. He made his way slowly through the hallways back to his room, not dawdling, but in no particular hurry, either. It felt good to Tommy to slow down and take his time for once. Normally, things were rather hectic around the school, and it was a rare chance that Tommy got to take a walk without having the hustle.

So it was that when Tommy arrived in his room almost a

quarter of an hour later, lost in his own thoughts, he was completely surprised to find Micah himself sitting cross-legged on the empty bunk across from Tommy's. Tommy saw that he had a huge, goofy grin on his face, and in his surprise, it took Tommy a few moments to process the fact that sitting there, on his bed, talking with Micah, were Tommy's parents.

CHAPTER THIRTEEN

Tommy let out a cry of joy and ran to his parents, almost knocking them both over backwards onto the bed in his haste. Laughing, he wrapped one arm around each of them and hugged them tight as his laughter wound down and turned into sobs. He slowly sank until he was kneeling on the floor, one arm around the waist of each of his parents, and his mother softly stroked his hair as he knelt there, holding them and crying.

It was some time later when Tommy finally raised his head and looked around. Sometime during his fit of tears, Micah had stood and let himself out of the room. Tommy was alone with his parents. Slowly, he stood, still sniffing, and wiped the tears from his eyes. Sitting back on his bunk, Tommy noticed that both his mother and father had tears dripping down their cheeks, as well, and the three of them spend a moment putting themselves together.

Finally, Tommy's dad favored him with a grin and said, "So... how's it going, son?"

Tommy couldn't help but grin. It was almost like old times. "I'm doing really good, Dad. I'm working hard and learning a lot. I think you'd be proud of me."

Tommy's father reached out to him. "Oh, son, I've always been proud of you. Come here," and with that his father pulled him into a tight hug that set off another bout of tears in all of them.

Eventually, Tommy found the presence of mind to ask, "I don't understand. How are you here? Micah said you wouldn't understa... That is, I thought I'd never see you again."

It was Tommy's mother who answered. "Well, we didn't, at first. My god, Tommy, we were so worried about you. When you didn't come home, we were in a panic. We called the police, the local news stations, the school... everyone we could think of. Then, an old woman who lives near the school reported that she'd seen you walking down the railroad tracks. When it came out that there had been a mage battle and people killed right near where you had been walking.... Well, we feared the worst, and then a man from the federal government came around asking all kinds of questions about you. He told us the most horrible things about that man Micah, called him an international terrorist..."

Tommy interrupted her. "It's not true! Micah isn't a terrorist! He helps kids!"

Tommy's father patted him on the hand. "We know that. Now, we do, at least. How were we to know what to think, with the government and the news stations and everyone else telling us all these things about him?"

"Yes, everyone was telling us all kinds of stories. I'll be honest, Tommy, we'd given in to despair. We thought for sure we'd lost you." His mother began to sniffle and tear up again. "But then, just a few days later, a man showed up at our front door. He told us that he had information on you, and said that you were alive and safe. Your father threw him out."

"Dad?! You didn't?!" Tommy said incredulously, but his father just shrugged and held his hands out in a gesture of helplessness.

"What was I to do, Tommy? At best, the man could have been a fraud, trying to capitalize on all the media attention. At worse... well, at worst he could have been exactly what he was."

Tommy struggled to put himself in his father's shoes, and somehow couldn't. The picture of Micah the evil terrorist was so incongruous with the person he knew that he just couldn't make it fit.

"Anyway," his mother continued, "Your father and I talked about it for a few days. Eventually, we decided to talk to that man if he ever came back. We figured if he really was trying to scam us, he wouldn't return after your father had thrown him out. And he did come back, about a week later. So, we sat down and talked to him."

His father picked up the story. "I'll be honest, Tommy. We didn't like the things he had to say. Everything we'd been taught all along said that... people like him... were evil. It was hard to hear that our own son had been taken away somewhere to learn how to be like him, and that there was nothing we could do about it. But he was so damned... patient. He sat calmly while I shouted at him. He answered our questions calmly. He seemed to have a good answer ready at hand to every objection we could raise. He was just so... so... *right*."

"He came to visit us several times over the last few weeks, " Tommy's mother said, reaching up to stroke his hair. "He told us that you were doing well, gave us updates on your progress. He even told us you were enjoying your math class, which made me wonder if he'd gotten the wrong kid." She ruffled his hair affectionately. "By the time he told us that we could come visit you, we were both ready to leap at the chance."

"But why didn't you come earlier, when the rest of the parents came?"

Tommy's father answered. "Micah told us that men from the government were still watching us. We had to go about a normal day, and then sneak off together after bedtime. By the time we were able to meet Micah, it was the wee hours of the morning."

Tommy was confused at that. "It's not even bedtime yet. Have you been here all day?"

"No, just a couple hours, waiting for you. Micah told us that you'd come here after dinner, and he seemed perplexed when you didn't show. He even sent some people to look for you. As for the time... I think this place is somewhere in the East. Maybe even in Asia. Micah told us we were better off not knowing."

Tommy nodded thoughtfully. It hadn't even occurred to him that the school might not be in the United States. Since his foray outside, he'd imagined that the school was in the mountains somewhere, possibly the Rockies. He wondered briefly if there was a way to figure out where they were before he decided that his father was right; they were all better off not knowing.

His father grinned at him. "So, my little magician! Aren't you going to show us around? All we've really seen is this little bedroom. Which I see you've kept cleaner than your bedroom at home!"

Tommy rolled his eyes before bounded to his feet and grabbed their hands. "We're called mages, Dad. Not magicians." Tommy pulled his parents toward the door. He had a lot of things to show them, and time was short.

CHAPTER
FOURTEEN

The next morning, Tommy felt like he was floating. He was tired, sure. He'd stayed up extra late to spend time with his parents, and he hadn't gotten enough sleep. Even when Micah came and told his parents that it was time to leave and Tommy finally found his way back to his bed, he still found that he couldn't sleep. He was so ebullient at getting to see his parents that he thought he would bounce straight out off of his bunk. It had been the very wee hours of the morning before he finally found rest, and with his early classes the next day, the lack of sleep was starting to wear on him. Still, he reflected, it was worth every minute of being tired.

The previous night, he'd shown his parents all around the school. They seemed mystified at some of the things Tommy was learning – his dad still couldn't grasp why he'd ever need to learn how to use a sword, and his mom couldn't understand how Tommy would be able to channel magic but not do anything with it, yet; both his parents had eventually asked him for a demonstration. They were suitably impressed by Tommy's progress in Math, however. Tommy's dad had gone to college to be an electrical engineer but had never finished, and he'd always hoped that his son would someday fulfill his dream; Tommy's lack of interest and poor aptitude in the subject had always been a sore spot for his father. They were also very interested to meet Tommy's new friends, so he had introduced them to Ryan, James, Mary, and most of his other classmates. Stephen they had both recognized and remembered as being one of Tommy's friends from school. The one regret Tommy had had was that he couldn't introduce them to Mae. He hadn't been able to find her all evening, even though he and his parents made several laps of the novice area of the school looking for her. He hadn't told his parents that he had a bit of a crush on Mae – he didn't want them to jump to conclusions, tease him about it, or, even worse, give him a parent's lecture on dating, but he knew that his parents kind of suspected by the amount of time that he had spent looking for her.

So, Tommy had yawned his way through math that morning. The class had actually been fairly easy, and Tommy suspected that his teacher saw that he was not the only member of the class with bags under his eyes. Everyone knew about visiting day the previous day, of course – most students had spent a lot of time cleaning and decorating for the arrival of family members, an activity that Tommy had eschewed because he thought he would be doing no visiting. He wished he'd pitched in more, but there was always next time.

Now he was in physical fitness again. He was sparring with a sword with James, who also looked somewhat worse for the wear. Tommy had begun to enjoy the class now that he was matched with someone of equal ability. Although James was larger and stronger than Tommy, he wasn't nearly as quick, and the two boys gave each other as good as they got. He still remembered the drubbing he had taken at Ryan's hands, and was glad the boy had moved to a higher skilled class.

Today, though, neither boy was feeling particularly strong or fast, and Tommy grumbled a curse under his breath as he dropped his sword for the third time that day. James gave him a sheepish grin as he bent quickly to pick it up; Lord Kalish was particularly vocal about the evils of dropping a weapon in combat, and if the fallen weapon was noticed it was sure to bring a lengthy lecture on the topic. James had dropped his own weapon a few times, as well, and once gotten a lecture out of it, so it was plain that he sympathized with Tommy.

Suddenly, Lord Kalish loudly clapped his hands twice, the way he always did when he wanted the class's attention. Tommy groaned inwardly as he lowered his padded sword and stepped back from James, sure that he was about to get a lecture for the fallen weapon in front of the entire class. When he looked, however, Lord Kalish was facing away from him, and instead was giving his odd bow – bent at the waist, hands on his knees – to Micah, who was standing nonchalantly on one side of the room.

"My Lord, to what do we owe the honor of your visit?" Lord Kalish asked Micah.

"I came to check on the progress of our students, of course." Micah smiled and made a small gesture with his hand. Tommy didn't understand it, but Lord Kalish rose from his bow at the gesture.

"Ah, yes, of course. I believe that you will find them progressing satisfactorily, my Lord." Lord Kalish clapped his hands twice and shouted, "Resume."

All the students, Tommy and James included, raised their weapons in a salute to one another and then set to trying to brain each other with fervor. It was one thing to be sparring in class, it was quite another to be doing it in front of an audience. Tommy watched out of the corner of his eye as Micah walked briefly around the room, nodding at what he saw. He was actually watching Micah too closely – he brought his padded weapon up just in time to block a thrust from James that would have bashed him in the face. When he looked up again, Micah had turned and was leaving the gymnasium.

"My Lord," Lord Kalish called out hesitantly to Micah, who paused and half turned. "Perhaps you would care to give the class a demonstration? Show the young students what they should strive to reach?"

The entire class paused mid-sparring match as Micah cocked an eyebrow and walked back into the room. "It would hardly be a fair match, Lord Kalish. You practice every single day."

Lord Kalish bowed in acknowledgement and retorted, "As do you, of course, my lord."

Micah smiled and drew a sword from the belt at his waist. It was long and thin, with an ornate hilt and a keen edge on one side that curved inward at the end of the blade to form a fine point. The whole thing sparkled in the light, like it had been gilded its entire length in gold. "I assume you still use that giant club of a weapon?" he asked.

Lord Kalish bowed his head in a nod. "Naturally, as you well know, my lord." With that, Lord Kalish drew his own weapon. It was shorter than Micah's sword, but still larger than the sparring weapons that the students had been training with. The length was where any similarity between the weapons ended, however. Where Micah's sword was thin, Kalish's weapon had an extremely thick, double-sided blade with a wide crossbar of a hilt. The whole of it was a deep grey in color, the metal almost refusing to shine despite the obvious polish on the blade. Fine silver inlay made a pattern up and down the length of the weapon, and as Lord Kalish moved the weapon, Tommy thought he could almost make out letters and words worked into the pattern.

Tommy thought that the whole thing was rather odd. He'd never seen either Micah or Lord Kalish wear any kind of weapon. Lord Kalish might be able to hide a weapon in his voluminous robes, but there was no way Micah could have hidden one in his blue jeans and shirt. Tommy made a note to ask about it later, in magic class, when Lord Kalish barked an order. "Attend, class! But stand back and give the Lord archmage and I some room."

The two men walked to the center of the room and faced each other in two different fighting stances. Micah stood holding his sword in one hand, facing Lord Kalish sideways, with only the narrow part of his body exposed to the other man and his feet close together. Lord Kalish, on the other hand, faced his opponent directly, with his legs spread widely and his sword in front of him in both hands. Both men paused for a moment like that and closed their eyes. Tommy could feel something in the air, a tingling, rushing sort of feeling, and he realized that both men were channeling magic. They opened their eyes at the same time, and each man raised the hilt of his sword in front of his eyes in a salute to the other.

Tommy thought he had been making progress learning to fight with the sword. He thought that Ryan had been very skilled. But what he saw before him made Ryan look like a clumsy oaf swinging a wood axe.

The two men danced with their weapons. They moved smoothly, almost elegantly, in a series of cuts, strokes, and thrusts, each attack smoothly dodged or blocked by the other's blade. They moved like the weapons were light in their hands, like each sword was made of cardboard instead of solid metal.

At first, Tommy was barely able to following the cut-and-counter cut that took place, but after a few minutes he watched enough to pick up how each man had built on the basic techniques that they'd learned. Micah's attacks were quick, precise, and careful, while Lord Kalish favored broad, strong strokes with his larger blade. Micah lunged at Lord Kalish's shoulder, attempting to strike with the point of his blade. Lord Kalish swept Micah's smaller weapons aside, and followed through with a strong sweep at Micah's knees. Micah turned the blade aside with the back of his sword, stepped to the side, and cut at Lord Kalish's arm. Lord Kalish responded by spinning away and used the momentum of his spin to bring his sword around in a wide arc that was aimed at Micah's head, and which the man simply ducked under.

Back and forth across the gymnasium they fought. Some of the students had begun to cheer, but Tommy barely heard them. He was enraptured by the spectacle before him, and he kept having to force himself to remember to breath. Ten minutes went by, and still the two men fought, neither one showing the slightest sign of slowing or tiring, and as Tommy continued to watch, he noticed something else: Micah's movements were just a little TOO quick. Micah would begin moving his weapon to block a blow before Lord Kalish even began to swing. Evidently Lord Kalish noticed it, too, because a deep frown had replaced the look of intense concentration on his face.

Finally, Lord Kalish broke the rhythm of the dance with a fast series of wild attacks that ended with his blade smacking into Micah's hip at the exact same moment that the point of Micah's blade landed against his throat.

Both men froze for a moment in that position, as several students gasped in horror. Tommy found himself on his feet, ready to run to help Micah, but the two men stepped smoothly apart and bowed to one another. Tommy realized with a sigh of relief that both of his teachers were unhurt, and must have used magic to protect themselves. Tommy wished he could learn how to do that; it would be most useful if he ever had to spar with Ryan again.

"You have... improved... since our last match. If I may say so, my Lord" Lord Kalish intoned formally once the two men had lowered their weapons.

Micah nodded to acknowledge the compliment, and sheathed his sword at his side. Amazingly, once he let go of the sword, it vanished entirely. "You should spend some time at the fronts, Lord Kalish. No amount of practice can substitute for real world experience."

Lord Kalish bowed to Micah again. "Ah, well. I do not share your predilection there, my lord, as you know very well. Besides, Lord Kalish is not as young as he used to be, is it not so? Fighting is for the young. I am content to teach the young ones, that they might go where I can not."

Micah nodded as if he'd heard the speech before, bowed slightly to Lord Kalish, and turned to go. Tommy noticed that he had still not even broken a sweat. The entire exchanged seemed odd to Tommy. The men treated each other with respect, but it was a cool kind of respect, without friendship and full of formality. It occurred to Tommy to wonder what kind of history lay between the two men.

He didn't have much time to ponder, however, because Lord Kalish clapped his hands together twice and called, "Now you see! You have very far to go, yes? There is no learning in standing and staring! We have fifteen minutes left in class, begin again!"

CHAPTER FIFTEEN

Tommy lay on his back on his bed, staring nervously up at the ceiling. He was far too worked up to rest, even if it wasn't the middle of the day, but he was also too anxious to read or do anything else, really. Nearby, Ryan lay on his bed making a vain attempt to study his history textbook. Tommy noticed that Ryan had a distant, unfocused look in his eyes, and that he'd been "reading" the same page for over an hour, now.

"Hey, do you think we have to wait for James to get back," Tommy finally asked, breaking Ryan out of his reverie. "Maybe we can only go one at a time."

Ryan shook his head. "I don't know, man. You aren't supposed to tell anything about the tests, but think about how many kids there are in our class. James has been gone for hours. If they tested us one at a time, it would take days to get through us all, and they can't mean to keep us cooped up in here for days." Tommy couldn't argue with the logic.

They'd been woken very early in the morning by Chancellor Duvey. He had come in the room trailed by several other students that Tommy had not recognized; they must have been from a more advanced class. Each of the students carried a tray covered by a warm cloth. Underneath the cloth was a sumptuous breakfast; bacon and sausage; scrambled eggs with cheddar cheese mixed in; two fresh, soft biscuits with a side of peppery sausage cream gravy; a bowl of mixed fruit; and milk, tea, and a small cup of coffee to drink. Each tray was set on elevated legs, so it could easily rest on the bed over the boys' laps. Tommy had never been served breakfast in bed before, and as he set to eating, he started to realize why his mother had always gone on about it. It felt... opulent.

Chancellor Duvey had explained succinctly that today was a testing day, and that several students had been chosen to test for advancement into the next class. He told them they were not permitted to leave their rooms except to use the restroom facilities, and that even there they would be escorted by one of the more advanced students, who would be standing guard outside their doors. The chancellor also explained that it was forbidden to discuss, ask, or answer questions about the testing, and that doing so would be regarded as cheating and could result in expulsion from the school. He then swept out of the room with the other students in tow without another word, and closed the door behind him, leaving the boys to their food.

They had talked among themselves while they ate, wondering which of them would be called to test (because surely they wouldn't have been restricted to their room if NONE of them were going to test), what the test would be like, and how hard or easy it might be. Tommy surprised himself by cleaning his plate. He even drank a little bit of the coffee; Ryan and James drank it all the time, but he'd never really acquired a taste for it. He found, though, that when he sloshed a good portion of his milk into the cup that it was palatable, if not particularly great tasting.

No sooner had they finished eating than one of the older students had stuck his head in the room and called, "James Thorton!" James almost spilled the tea that he was sipping, he was so startled, but he stood and walked over to the door, giving the other two boys a sheepish grin. The older student beckoned for James to follow, and the two of them left, closing the door behind them. Tommy had shared a long look with Ryan before he gave a nervous laugh. "Well, at least we know we'll probably get called, right?" During their discussions, James had been worried that he might not be called to test; He had made decent progress in the last couple of weeks, but he was still struggling to keep up with the rest of the class. Ryan had only nodded absently, however, and had sat staring at the closed door. Tommy suspected that he was bitter over James being picked to go first. Ryan had never liked not being the first at anything.

After a while, Tommy had gotten antsy, and had gone and knocked on the door. A different older student opened it, and Tommy explained that he had to go to the restroom. The boy nodded and gestured for Tommy to follow without a word. Tommy tried to start a conversation, had even jokingly asked, "How did you get picked for this wonderful job?", but the older boy had firmly rebuffed his attempts, and had adamantly refused to speak even a single word the entire time Tommy used the facilities, washed up, and returned to him room.

When he got back, Ryan was gone, and Tommy felt a momentary stab of panic. Had he missed his own call to test? Had he been passed over for testing completely? He didn't want to get left behind his friends, like Mary had. He thought he would die of embarrassment if that happened. He had worked himself up into a pretty good panic when the door opened and Ryan stepped back in, fuming.

"They wouldn't talk to me. Not even a single word!" Ryan grumbled at the closed door.

Tommy nodded. "Me too. Maybe it's part of the rules, or something."

That seemed to calm Ryan down a little, and he quipped with a grin "I almost kicked him in the shin, just to see if I could get him to make a noise."

Tommy grinned back at the thought of the somber, older students howling and holding their shins, and they had sat on their bunks and joked back and forth about interesting and increasingly abusive ways to get their escorts to produce sounds.

Eventually, however, their talk had run down. Mirth gradually turned to boredom, and eventually both boys sat quietly, alternating between trying to study and sitting and staring. There wasn't much point to any channeling exercises; Tommy was far too nervous to concentrate, and in any case he wanted to be fresh in case that was part of the test, as he suspected it would be.

After several hours another group of students arrived with lunch trays; Roast beef and grilled chicken sandwiches, a hot and hearty vegetable soup, and a nice red apple for dessert. There was milk to drink, again, along with iced tea and a glass of ice-cold water. Again, the other students spoke not a word; they simply laid down the lunch trays, gathered up the remains of the breakfast trays, and left.

Shortly after they finished lunch, the same student who had come for James called for Ryan. Ryan paused and shared a nervous look with Tommy, and then he was gone out the door. "Good Luck!" Tommy called after him feebly, but the door was already almost shut, and Tommy had no idea if the other boy had even heard him.

With Ryan gone, the waiting became almost unbearable. Tommy paced back and forth in the room, unable to sit still. He had never dealt well with waiting and had had a tendency to worry himself sick when he was nervous. That was why Tommy had almost never broken the rules at his old school – when he did, he always worried himself so sick over possibly being caught that it became easier just to obey the rules. He had never understood how the "bad kids" could live with themselves.

Tommy's pacing gradually increased in speed and urgency. After almost an hour, his stomach was tied firmly in a knot and he was considering asking to go to the bathroom so he could be sick. In his mind, he saw Ryan and James and all his other classmates, sitting at a graduation celebration and laughing about how stupid Tommy had been left behind. His mind spun the dread fantasy up again and again, worse each time, and he was right to the part where his room got moved into another area so he could be with a "younger class" when suddenly the door opened again, shocking him out of his daydream.

The same boy stood there in the doorway. He locked eyes with Tommy and said, "Thomas Nelson? Come on; it's time."

CHAPTER SIXTEEN

The boy lead Tommy to a part of the school that he'd never been to before. That wasn't surprising; the school was vast, and students at Tommy's level were actively discouraged from roaming the school at random; they'd been told that it was for their own protection, that, lacking experience, they may very well wander into something harmful. Tommy had never even been to the area where the more advanced students, like Stephen, Mary, and Mae lived. For that matter, he didn't even really know how to get there.

They walked for quite a while – Tommy guessed that it was over fifteen minutes – and took so many turns and sets of stairs that Tommy was totally lost. He began to wonder if this was part of the test and was grateful for the physical fitness training he'd been attending over the last couple of months. The boy set a pretty brisk pace, and "old Tommy' would have been winded.

Eventually, the boy opened a door and motioned for Tommy to step inside. It was a plain stone room, much like any other room in the school; it was lit by glowing bulbs from above and had the same smooth walls without crack or mortar. On the far end of the room was a narrow archway that lead to an unlit hallway that stretched into darkness. There was a small wooden table in the center of the room. On it was a metal lantern, like the gas lantern that Tommy's dad had in the garage for the camping that they never actually found time to do.

The boy walked to the front of the table and turned back to face Tommy. "Listen carefully to my instructions," he began. "You are not permitted to ask any questions, and in any case, I am not permitted to answer them. The lantern on this table is powered by magic. The first part of your test is to channel into it until it begins to shine. Then you will take it and proceed down the hallway behind me," the boy intoned, gesturing to the darkened hallway opposite the door through which they had entered the room. "You may take as long as you need to complete the test. If at any time you decide that you cannot continue or you need to give up on the test, simply say the words 'I give up' out loud, and the test will be over. However, if you give up on the test, you will fail and will have to return to your previous class. Once I leave this room, there is no turning back. Do you understand these instructions?"

Tommy thought about it and decided that he did. His palms were damp with nervousness, though, and he felt a trickle of sweat running down the side of his chest inside his shirt, so instead he asked, "Is this dangerous?"

The boy took on the annoyed expression of someone who had been through this several times and simply repeated, "Do you understand these instructions?"

Tommy realized he'd get no further explanation from the other boy, so he nodded his head and replied "Yes, I understand."

"Good," the boy said curtly. Then, "Are you ready to proceed?"

"Uh. I guess so. I mean, yes."

The boy nodded his head once, said, "Good luck, then" with the practiced voice of a ceremonial invocation, walked to the door, and left the room, closing the door behind him.

Tommy watched him go and then walked to peek down the hallway. It got very dark rather quickly; Tommy could barely see more than fifteen or twenty feet, and there was nothing there to see but hallway and darkness. He walked up to the lantern and picked it up. It clanked faintly with a loose-metal type of sound, and Tommy could see that it was almost exactly like the lantern that had hung in his father's garage.

"Well, here goes" he said out loud, then immediately regretted his articulation. If he could quit the test by speaking out loud, then surely someone was listening to him. The thought made him look around the ceiling of the room, but it was blank and smooth; there were no cameras or microphones to be seen. He supposed that there might be a microphone in the lights somewhere, but then decided that the whole exercise was moot. In any case, he'd have to be careful what he said out loud. He certainly didn't want someone mistaking his words for him giving up on the test.

Tommy sat down on the stone floor and closed his eyes. He relaxed his mind and body in the way that he'd been taught and tried to channel. It was somewhat more difficult than he was used to due to the fact that he felt nervous and pressured, but after a few minutes he felt the power flow and he directed it into the lantern. It was like channeling into the crystal in the channeling room – he could feel the power flow into the device and begin to fill it – but unlike the crystal Tommy could clearly feel the limit of what the lantern could hold. It only took a few moments, and Tommy realized that the lantern was now full – the energy he was channeling poured around the lantern and off into room as if it had never flowed into the device.

When Tommy opened his eyes again, he saw that the lantern was shining brightly with a clean, white light. Pleased with his progress, he picked up the lantern carefully. At first, he expected it to be hot, but then he realized that was silly; there was no fire to generate heat, and all the light was provided magically. Tommy shook his head at himself and smiled before setting off down the hallway.

The hall was more of the same unrelieved grey stone and curved slightly to the left. Tommy quickly lost site of the entrance archway around the curve, and soon he found himself walking down an unadorned stone hallway with only the lantern for light. He didn't walk for very long, but it seemed like an impossibly long time to be walking down a hallway inside – at least 10 minutes, possibly longer. Eventually, he came upon a large metal grate that completely blocked the hallway.

He stopped in front of the grate and stood for a minute studying it. It was made of a dull grey metal, and after studying it for a moment, Tommy was sure he knew what it was. Just to be sure, he relaxed himself, embraced the power, and channeled it at the grate. The energy warped and bent around the metal, refusing to touch it, and Tommy's suspicions were confirmed – the grate blocking his passage was made from tungsten.

Setting his lantern down on the floor, Tommy grabbed the grate with his hands and pushed, but the hard metal didn't budge even a hair's breadth. He tried pulling, lifting, sliding, twisting, turning – all to no avail; the grate stood immobile in his path. Stepping back, Tommy scratched his head. After a moment's thought, he decided that he must have missed something back down the hall, so he picked up his lantern and began retracing his steps.

He didn't get very far down the hallway before it abruptly

ended in a blank stone wall. Tommy was surprised and confused. He was sure he had walked much, much farther down the hallway the first time, and he decided that the hallway must have closed up after he passed. Just to be sure, he put his hand against the wall and pushed; it was as solid as any of the other walls. Frustrated, he decided to return to the grate.

When he got back, the grate was still there, and he noticed that his lantern had begun to dim significantly. He fought down a brief panic at the thought of being alone in the pitch blackness. It took him several minutes of deep breaths and trying to relax before he felt ready to channel again, and the lantern had almost gone out by the time he refilled it with magical energy.

Once the lamp was shining brightly again, Tommy turned to regard the metal grate and saw something he hadn't noticed before. Down the hallway, just at the limit of his light, was a small metal arrow protruding from the wall. It was bright, shiny, silvery, and pointed straight up at the ceiling. Suddenly, Tommy understood. He went through the mental exercises that were becoming second nature to him, focused his will, and channeled energy directly at the arrow.

Almost immediately, the metal grate began to rise into the ceiling. It moved slowly but steadily upwards, and after a few minutes, Tommy was able to step forward through the grate. As soon as Tommy moved he let his concentration lapse and lost contact with the magical power, and the grate began to sink back down to the floor. Tommy realized that it was only the energy that was keeping it up, and he stepped quickly away as the grate sank down and crashed into the floor with an immense bang that reverberated up and down the hallway.

He smiled, suddenly pleased with himself, and set off down the hallway. He only paused briefly to examine the metal arrow that he'd seen through the grate. It was as cool and smooth as he thought it would be, but it had served its purpose in his test, and he had no further business with it. He hadn't gotten very far – just far enough to begin to wonder if that was the end of the test, if he'd finished it so quickly, when he came to another grey metal grate blocking the hallway.

This time, he knew exactly what to look for – peering through the holes in the grate; he saw not one, but two things protruding from the wall down the hall. On the right-hand side of the wall was another silvery arrow, pointing to the left, this time. On the left-hand side was a strange square made of the same grey metal as the grate – tungsten, again, Tommy surmised – but with an upwards pointing arrow etched on it in silver. Tommy channeled at it experimentally, but predictably the energy just slid off the square and refused to touch it. Tommy had fully expected the result, so he turned the focus of his energy over to the silvery arrow.

He had fully expected the grate to slide to the side and was surprised when it didn't. What did happen was that the strange metal square down the hall slide to the left and into a small hole in the wall that Tommy hadn't been able to see previously and exposed another silvery arrow that had been behind it, this one pointing up. Tommy guessed the nature of the test – one arrow to move the metal panel, the other to move the tungsten bars blocking his path. He shifted the focus of his channeling to the new arrow and was completely surprised when the tungsten square immediately snapped back into place, blocking him.

The shock caused him to completely lose focus, and the magic power drained away from him, so Tommy doggedly began the mental exercises required to seize it again. This time, it didn't take him long to figure out what to do; He focused his energy into two different channels. They'd practiced this in class before, several times – some of the students were so good at it that they could channel at ten different targets at once, but Tommy found it difficult to split the massive flow of energy he handled into more than three or four streams. Micah had told him he'd get better at it with practice, but he still felt like he should be able to do more.

The energy touched the left-pointing arrow, and the metal panel slide to the side again. That left the way clear for Tommy's second channel to contact the up arrow that had been behind it, and sure enough, the gate began to rise. It took just a couple minutes of maintaining the two flows of energy before the gate was high enough that Tommy could step underneath it. Like before, as soon as he moved and released the magic, the gate began to slide back toward the floor, sinking faster and faster until it slammed into the floor with a jarring boom.

Tommy quickly turned away from the closed gate and continued down the passage. His step was light; He'd faced two challenges and, after a few moments of thought, defeated them both quite handily. He set off down the hallway at a determined pace and stepped briskly past the two silver arrows, ready to face what might come next.

He was quite surprised, however, when after a short walk he found not another grate blocking his path but a blank stone wall. The hallway simply ended. Frowning, Tommy put his hand against the wall and pushed, but to no avail; the stone was as solid as any of the walls he'd walked past.

A sudden burst of inspiration took Tommy. Maybe he'd walked right past some more of the silvery arrows and not even noticed them. He turned to retrace his steps and was immediately confronted by another large stone wall, this one with giant metal spikes protruding from the wall. As Tommy approached to inspect the wall and its spikes, he saw that they looked extremely sharp.

He also quickly realized that the spikes were moving slowly but inexorably toward him.

CHAPTER
SEVENTEEN

Tommy felt sweat break out across his forehead and the sides of his face, and felt the tension in his arms and shoulders that signaled a panic attack. Stepping back from the wall, he forced himself to take several deep breaths, and then began the mental calming exercises that he'd learned in channeling class. It took him several minutes to gather the power, since he kept having to stop and open his eyes to check on the progress of the wall, but he finally managed it. The wall was still a good fifteen feet away, and hadn't made much progress, but it was creeping steadily nearer.

Tommy focused his will and channeled at the wall and the spikes, but nothing happened. He felt the power flow, but there seemed to be nothing for it to contact, and it just vanished into the air. He struggled for a moment, then successfully fought down a surge of panic that threatened the calm state of mind that allowed him to channel. Calm again, he noticed that the wall was definitely moving toward him, but slowly enough that he had some time to think.

He turned his back on the spikes for a moment (although

he was constantly looking over his shoulder to be sure they weren't getting closer) and studied the end of the passageway. A faint shadow caught his eye, and he got closer to inspect it. There, carved very lightly into the stone directly in the center of the wall, almost so lightly that he couldn't see it, was a spiral pattern. Tommy traced it lightly with his finger for a moment before inspiration struck and he stepped back and channeled directly at the pattern.

Immediately, the wall faded from view and became an open hallway again. Tommy stepped forward quickly, and found that the hallway ended after just a few feet and ended in a giant stone room. The room was fairly massive – at least as big as his school gymnasium back home – and had large, ornate stone columns lining either side of the room and supporting a flat stone ceiling carved with pictures of clouds. In the very center of the ceiling was a wide open hole through which a brisk breeze and even a few flurries of snow fell; Tommy assumed the room was paradoxically high up on the mountain, even though he had descended deep into the school in order to take his test. Beneath the hole in the roof was a low stone rim on the floor that surrounded what looked like a shimmering pool, and sitting a distance away from the pool was a small raised dais with a huge stone throne at the top. Sitting in the throne in a casual, bored posture, one leg thrown idly over one arm of the throne and his chin resting on his fist on the other, was Micah.

Tommy's face broke out into a smile, and he started across the room toward him, forgetting to even look behind him to notice that the hallway he had come through had vanished, and there was now only unbroken, smooth stone. As he passed the pool with its raised stone lip, Tommy cast a quick glance down. He gave a double-take and stopped and stared. It was no pool at all, but a vast, open hole that lead to absolutely nothing – Just wide open sky, limitless, as far as Tommy could see, with no sign of the ground. Tommy's head swam with vertigo, and he took an involuntary step back from the pool. He was still staring when he heard Micah chuckling.

"It's not really endless, Tommy. That is just an illusion that relaxes me."

Tommy nodded slowly, never taking his eyes off the pool, and edged around it toward Micah. Only once he was past the area and several feet away did he turn his head to the man on the throne. "So that's all, then?" he asked. "I passed?"

Micah gave a "so-so" shake of his hand and head. "More or less," he replied. "You're done with the difficult part of the test, anyway. Now all you have to do is get past me."

Tommy favored the man with a worried half-smile, and said "Ummmmm, okay?"

Micah sat up in the throne. "Every student must undergo an interview before they are ready to advance. Sometimes I conduct the interviews; sometimes one of the members of my coterie does them. But you cannot pass the test until we've completed our discussion."

Tommy nodded. "Ok, I'm ready."

"Very well, then. First, I need you to channel at me. Directly at me, like you did to the objects in the test."

Tommy nodded his head again and took a deep breath, beginning to relax. He half expected Micah to jump up, to startle him, to do something to make the task more difficult, but he just sat and watched, the peculiar half-smile that he wore so often adorning his face. Tommy began to channel, and he directed the energy at Micah. He immediately felt the energy seized as if in a giant fist, like he had the first time he had channeled in the classroom so long ago. Micah held the stream of energy fast, and when Tommy opened his eyes, he saw that the man had neither moved nor changed the expression on his face. Tommy met his eyes, and after a few moments Micah nodded and said, "Enough." Tommy immediately stopped channeling and let the power drain away from him.

"Well, it seems that you have a minor Earth affinity, Tommy."

Tommy was surprised and a little dejected. "Are you sure?" he asked him.

"Absolutely sure. Why does that bother you?"

Tommy shrugged and looked at the ground. "I don't know," he muttered sullenly. "I kind of hoped that I'd be good at air magic. You know, like you are."

Micah chuckled at that. "You don't have to be like me, Tommy. In fact, you'll be much happier in the long run if you decide to be like you."

Tommy could only shrug again. "I don't know. I guess I also kind of thought... I dunno. That maybe someday I'd be the one to figure out how to fly with magic. I've always wanted to fly."

Micah's face took on an unexpectedly stern appearance. "No, Tommy. I don't want you even trying it, you understand? Many, many people have been badly hurt attempting to do what simply cannot be done. You cannot use magic to fly any more than you can use your arms to lift your legs off the ground. Do you understand me?"

Tommy was momentarily taken aback at the rough tone in the man's voice, but he nodded his understanding. His mind raced with half a dozen excuses why he might be permitted to attempt learning to fly, but the look on Micah's face made him discard them all. He struggled to think of a reply, and came up with a question. "If I'm an earth mage and you are an air mage, does that make us… umm… like, enemies?"

Micah truly did laugh at that, throwing his head back in a hearty chortle, and Tommy felt his face flush with embarrassment. "No, Tommy," the older man said. "We aren't enemies. In fact, I hope you'll always regard me as a friend, even when you've learned all that the school has to teach you. You've listened to my lectures in class. You know that all mages are able to use magic of all different types, regardless of their particular affinity… and in any case, the affinity in your case is slight. You'll find earth-focused spells easier to learn and master, and you'll find that they use less energy and tire you less than other magic, but that is all."

Micah sat back as Tommy absorbed that, then furrowed his brow and stared into the distance for a moment. "We have a few more minutes to talk, Tommy. So tell me, how are you liking the school?"

"I think it's great," Tommy blurted. "It's much better than my old school."

Micah nodded. "Just remember to stay up on your other classes, as well. I know we ask a lot of you, but you need to get an education as well as learn how to use magic. If we notice that you are falling behind in your academic classes, we'll pull you out of magic class until you catch up. I have spent a great deal of time assuring your parents that you are getting a quality education."

Tommy was enthusiastic. "I like my classes. Even math.

Well, most of the time, anyway. I was sad about missing my parents for a while, but now that I can get to see them again, I think everything is great!"

"I'm glad, Tommy," Micah smiled. "But make sure you keep working hard. It only gets more difficult from here."

"Difficult how?" Tommy frowned. He was already working on school work for most of the day every day, with few breaks. He didn't understand how it could get any more difficult.

"Up until now, we've coddled you, Tommy. Your room, your clothes, your food, everything was provided for you. Sure, we asked you to spend some time channeling for us, but that was mostly to give you practice. But now, you have proven that you can channel well enough on your own, and you will have to earn everything you get. We're going to be asking a lot more of you. Some of your classmates may be hard pressed to keep up. James, for example."

"Um... Why?"

Micah paused and blinked. "Why, what, Tommy?"

"I mean, why make it hard for James? Why not just let him channel what he can?"

"Running the school isn't free, Tommy. It takes energy to make all these things happen. Energy to grow our food, energy to make our clothes, energy to power the lights. Everything has a cost, and everyone must bear their share of the cost."

"I know! I mean, I wasn't suggesting that. But... I mean, I can channel a lot. Maybe I could make up for what James can't do."

"You could, Tommy. And what about your friend Mae? She's been struggling some, too. Would you spend your time channeling to help her?"

"Yes! Of course! I'd be happy to!"

"And tell me, while you are spending so much time channeling every day… When are you going to find time to practice your own skills? Are you going to get left behind, allow James to graduate ahead of you, because you are spending your time paying his dues?"

"Of course not! I don't know… maybe we could all share it, you know? The whole class?"

"There are several students in your class who are struggling, Tommy. Is the class going to support them all?

"Well… I guess we could, yeah."

"And when your fellow students, Ryan and the others, start to fall behind in their studies because they have to spend extra time channeling? Is it fair to them to burden them, to limit them, just because James is unable to live up to his potential?"

That caused Tommy to frown in thought. "Well, I guess not. But it just feels to me like we should be able to do something for James. Anything."

"We ARE doing something for James." Micah replied firmly. "We are giving him the chance, the same as everyone else. James has a lot of potential, but right now, he's going to have to work extra hard to live up to that potential. It is easier for some people than for other people. Someday, you may be struggling with things that James finds easy. That's just the way the world works, Tommy. But we don't do James any favors by making everything easy for him. All that does is cause him to become dependent on us. James NEEDS the opportunity to overcome his own challenges. To learn for himself that he CAN do it, if he'll only work hard enough. James needs to decide that his future is worth the time he spends now, to focus on the things that matter, and then he will succeed. Or, perhaps he won't. Maybe he'll fail completely. Better he learns today that he's not cut out for this life than to lead him on for months, or even years. If he fails, let him fail and move on to something better suited to his abilities. You help him more in the long run by letting him struggle a little now."

Tommy could only nod thoughtfully. Micah made an awful lot of sense, and he was right – it wasn't fair to the others to limit their success just so James wouldn't have to work hard.

Micah's voice broke Tommy out of his reverie. "We have just a few more minutes, so do you have any questions for me?"

The question gave Tommy pause. He did have questions for Micah. A great many questions, in fact, but he couldn't decide if any of them would be polite to ask. He briefly considered asking about the rumor the other students had been discussing about Micah's son, but discarded that; He didn't want to make the man sad or angry. Finally, he settled on asking, "Stephen and Mae were talking about doing combat training. What's that?"

"One class at a time, Tommy!" Micah chuckled. "Once you learn how to use magic – actually use it, that is, not just channel it – then we'll teach you how to use it to defend yourself. Don't worry – you don't have to spend a lot of time learning to fight, if you don't want to. Many of our graduates and students are pacifists. But we DO require you to at least learn how to defend yourself if the situation requires. We are hunted by far too many people to let our students run around defenseless. And if you decide you want to learn more... well, once you graduate beyond Novice, we allow you to customize your course of study, and there are always the Games if you have an interest."

It was the first time Tommy had heard that word; Games. He could definitely hear the capital letter when the older man said it. So he asked, "What are the Games?"

"Ah. I always forget, you haven't been one of us for long. The school sponsors mage games, where students can test their strengths and skills against one another in a safe environment. We sponsor duels as well as small and large team events. It's a lot of fun, and even if you don't participate, everyone gets a thrill out of watching the games. Some of the students even place small bets on the outcomes. Sadly, though, you cannot participate, even as a spectator, until you've learned more."

"Why not? Why can't we watch?"

Micah sighed. "You'll understand soon enough, Tommy. Suffice to say that you simply cannot. It is not a matter of permission, or danger, or anything else. Right now, you simply lack the abilities to be able to spectate. Soon enough, I promise. Okay?"

Tommy didn't really understand, but he also didn't see the point in questioning further, so he simply said, "Alright."

Micah raised his head and looked off in the distance again for a moment. "We're just about out of time, Tommy. Last question."

This time, Tommy knew exactly what he wanted to ask. "Did I pass?"

"Now, just remember that you may not talk about the test

with anyone who hasn't gone through it, Tommy. I can't have you tipping off the next class. But yes, congratulations Tommy, you passed your first test."

CHAPTER EIGHTEEN

When Tommy got back to his room, he discovered two very important things.

The first was that both Ryan and James were back from their tests, and that both had passed successfully. There was a good deal of cheering and back-slapping among the three boys, although James looked extremely wan and tired. They weren't able to discuss anything specific about the test, however, because of the second discovery.

While Tommy was gone, a new boy had moved into the fourth bunk of the room. He was young, more than a year or two younger than Tommy, and very short – quite possibly one of the shortest people Tommy had ever met. The boy had a slightly unkempt mop of straight hair on his head, colored so brightly red that Tommy would have called it orange, and the pale skin of his boyish face was covered with brownish-orange freckles. He was thin and lithe, smaller of frame than even Ryan, who was shorter than most of his classmates. He met Tommy's eyes somewhat shyly, but his face split in a big grin that revealed the gap between his two front teeth.

"Hey! I'm Sam!" the boy said.

Tommy disengaged from Ryan and James and stuck his hand out. "I'm Tommy, good to meet you."

"Hey Tommy," the boy said, shaking Tommy's hand, "I'm Sam!" Then, realizing he'd repeated himself, the boy flushed a bright crimson that effused his entire face. Tommy couldn't help but chuckle.

"Sam is part of the new class of students," Ryan chimed in from behind Tommy. "Now that we've moved up, I mean. I haven't heard that anyone in the class failed."

Tommy went to his bunk and sat down on it. The room suddenly felt crowded with the addition of the fourth boy. Tommy had grown used to having the bunk across from him be empty, but he tried not to hold it against the younger boy, and for the most part, he managed; he only felt bitter about it a little bit. The boys spent the next couple hours catching up on their respective backgrounds. Sam was from an old Italian American family, and although he didn't have much of an accent, he occasionally used words that Tommy was unfamiliar with. He came to the school in a way similar to Tommy and his friend Stephen – he had started to exhibit magical ability in the past few weeks, and his family immediately shipped him off to the school, lest he get caught and imprisoned or worse.

Before too long, their talk was interrupted by a loud snore from James, who had collapsed on his bed and gone to sleep. After giggling for a few minutes, the boys all agreed that they were tired, so they turned off the lights and went to bed.

The next day began in much the same way that the previous days had, with math class. Tommy had expected that passing the test would mean a different schedule, but the day went by pretty much the same as other days. He hadn't seen Sam all day, and figured the boy had a different schedule being in a different class, but when he got to the dining hall for lunch, the boy was already seated next to James, so Tommy joined them and they all chatted about their days. It turned out that Sam had a schedule that was almost completely opposite of Tommy's, beginning his day with magic class and ending with math.

In fact, it wasn't until Tommy got to his magic class that the day got any different.

Micah stood at the head of the class, as usual, but seated next to every student's desk in a roll-away chair was another, older student. Tommy glanced at his friends in confusion, but Ryan simply shrugged and went to take his seat, so Tommy and the rest of the class followed. As soon as everyone was seated, Micah clapped his hands together in the way that Tommy had come to realize was his signal that class was beginning.

"Okay. Everyone here has passed their first test. Everyone here can channel at least marginally. You can feel the magic around you. You can tap into it and focus it to your will. Perhaps some of you can even sense or feel when someone around you is using magical energy. But what you cannot do is perceive the magic. You cannot view it, you cannot see a spell being wrought. And because you are unable to see what I am doing when I cast a spell, I am unable to teach you how to do it. Does that make sense to everyone?"

Tommy nodded slightly, although he felt like he only barely understood.

"Good," Micah went on, taking the classes feeble nods as assent. "To help me today, we have students from one of the senior classes. They are going to cast a spell on you. On your eyes, specifically. This spell will allow you to perceive the magic as I work with it. Once you can see what I'm doing, I will teach you how to cast the very same spell on yourself. This is the first lesson everyone must learn; In order to proceed, you must be able to see what another mage is doing. Are there any questions?"

Tommy briefly considered raising his hand and asking if it was dangerous, but then decided against it; he had confidence that Micah would not expose anyone in the class to danger.

"Alright then, let's begin."

Tommy turned to regard the boy sitting next time. He was older. Much older, in fact; Tommy could only call him a boy by the broadest of definitions. For a long moment, nothing happened, and Tommy began to wonder if he'd feel anything different. Then, all of a sudden, a mist passed briefly over Tommy's eyes, and a new world opened up to him. Suddenly, he could see what he had only previously felt. He could see the magical energy in the air around him; it appeared as a dim, violet haze in the air, turbulent and churning, and although it was everywhere around him, somehow it did not block or limit his vision of the room. He could also see the energy as it flowed into the boy next to him, could see how the boy accepted the energy and focused it, and perceive how the boy used the focused energy, forced his will upon it and formed it into the spell that was affecting his eyes. Suddenly, Tommy *understood.* He even felt like he could duplicate the feat, and was about to reach for the magic to try when Micah spoke up.

"Calm, now, everyone. No rushing ahead. Let me remind you of the dangers. This is a very basic spell, and you'll learn how to cast it on yourself soon enough, but try too soon and you could damage your eyes. You could even make yourself go blind. So, relax, now, and watch me as I step through the casting."

Micah stepped them through the casting slowly, one step at a time, over and over again, until Tommy thought he could have repeated it in his sleep. It was much easier to understand now that he could see it, and Tommy thought that he might be able to work out how to do some other things, as well. He certainly thought he saw how he could alter the steps in order to make someone go blind, although he swore to himself that he would never do something like that. Still, now he understood a great many things; He didn't think he could possibly have described the casting to someone, without actually showing it like Micah was doing.

After an hour or so of watching the demonstrations, Micah dismissed the older students, and they got up and left. The extraordinary vision that Tommy experienced vanished with the other students, and Micah grinned at them all. "Ok, class," he began, "Now it's time to try it on yourself. At first, you'll only be able to support the spell when you need to learn how to cast a certain spell, but eventually, you'll get good enough at it that you'll have it on all the time. Most of the senior mages at the school keep their vision enhanced all day, so that they are never surprised by what is going on. Certainly no one leaves the school without the ability to maintain the spell for the duration of their sabbatical; the moment it takes you to enchant your vision could be all an opponent needs to beat you."

The entire class sat and practiced casting the spell. It was surprisingly more difficult than Tommy expected. He could recall the steps that Micah had walked through, but watching them done and actually doing them proved to be two different things. At one point, Tommy and several of the other students were getting frustrated, but Micah soothed them. "Don't get upset if it is more difficult than you expect. You are using your mind in a way that it has never been used before. It's almost like trying to learn a new, totally different language. You have to train yourself to think in a different way, and that takes time and practice."

So the class practiced, and practiced more. Eventually, everyone in the class was able to duplicate the spell and enhanced their vision without mishap. Tommy and Ryan favored each other with a big, goofy grin when they both finally managed it. But Micah was relentless; When they successfully cast the spell, he quickly made them dismiss it and start over again. Tommy thought it might be difficult to dismiss the spell, but it turned out to be simply a matter of no longer channeling energy into it - as soon as he stopped channeling, the spell and its effects evaporated.

By the time Micah dismissed the class, Tommy felt confident that he could cast the spell with his eyes closed... which was, of course, essentially what he was doing, working with the magical energy before he was able to see it. Tommy left the room feeling very sure of himself, and very, very exhausted.

CHAPTER NINETEEN

For a while, the days started to just slide by Tommy. He still rarely got to see Mae and Stephen and missed them terribly, but he was enjoying spending time with James, Ryan, Mary, and his new friend, Sam.

His classes continued to go well – he was learning how to craft new spells every day, and although they'd been specifically instructed not to branch out on their own, Tommy thought he could see different ways of doing the same things, or even ways to innovate and create new effects based on the old ones. He was doing pretty good in his academic classes, although not as well as he was in his mage studies – he enjoyed the academic well enough, but found the material not as fascinating as his magical classes.

Still, everything seemed to be going pretty well. Christmas was rapidly approaching, and Tommy was looking forward to getting to see his family during the holiday break. All in all, life was pretty good for Tommy, and there was almost a skip in his step as he headed back to his room after dinner. He'd been having an intense discussion with Mary over dinner, arguing over the motivations of the characters in a book they were discussing in English class, and neither of them had noticed when James, Ryan, and Sam had all left. After the debate, Mary had to go spend some time channeling, so Tommy was walking back to his room alone.

He was in the middle of a reverie, thinking over the argument with Mary and trying to decide how he could have made his point better when he was stopped in his track by an odd thing in the middle of the hallway. It was a small creature - if the word could be used to describe the thing before Tommy. It was small, about a foot and a half tall, and roughly anthropomorphic in shape. It appeared to be made entirely of ash, with hot coals for eyes and tiny claws at the end of its hands. The smell of the thing was horrible – it clogged Tommy's nose, and reminded him vaguely of a store at the mall that sold rubber masks and other Halloween-type outfits and decorations year round. The smell was like moldy rotting plastic left too long in a damp room with no ventilation, and it made Tommy want to retch. Tommy took an involuntary step backwards as the thing opened its mouth and hissed at him, spraying a tiny jet of flame into the air as it did so.

Tommy was about to turn and run from the thing when it leapt high into the air, straight at his face. Tommy shrieked in terror and his feet tangled together as he tried to turn to run and step backwards at the same time, and he ended up falling backwards onto his back, sending the textbooks and notepads that he had been carrying flying into air and skimming across the floor. The wind flew out of Tommy's lungs, but his falling might have been fortunate – the ash creature ended up crashing into the floor instead of Tommy's throat.

It didn't pause for long, though. The thing was quickly back on its ashy little feet and turned to hiss at Tommy again as he struggled to both breathe and rise at the same time. The creature lunged at Tommy, and he put his hand up to ward the thing off.

Its little claws scored a series of deep scratches across his arm that burned like nothing Tommy had ever felt, and he let out an involuntary shriek as the smell of burning hair and skin mingled with the rotting plastic scent of the creature.

Clutching his arm, Tommy scurried backwards until he knocked his head painfully against the stone wall of the corridor. The thing continued to stalk him, however, and made as if to lunge at him every time he tried to stand up. After a few such attempts, the thing actually did leap, straight at Tommy's face, with its sharp little claws extended toward his eyes. Tommy screamed and tried to channel, but he was far too afraid, and the magic would just not come.

Tommy was sure he was about to be blinded by the horrid little creature when a thick, dull-grey sword flashed from behind his head. He felt the wind of the blade's passing in his ear right before it struck the creature, and Tommy noticed silvery runes set in the blade flare to life as it hit, cleaving the creature in twain and sending the two pieces sailing several feet down the hall. The halves of the creature struck the floor and burst apart, sending ash and tiny hot coals that quickly cooled scattering across the clean stone floor.

Tommy looked up and was surprised to see Lord Kalish there, dressed in his normal long, flowing robes, his massive broadsword gripped in one strong fist. The man extended his other hand down to help Tommy up, and he accepted it and gratefully rose to his feet.

"What... what was that?" Tommy asked his teacher.

"An abomination, yes?" Lord Kalish replied. "Something you were told not to do."

"Me? I didn't do it!" Tommy protested, and Lord Kalish replied with a grunt that could have been taken for either doubt or acceptance, but he continued to stare at the scattered ashes for a few moments before Tommy realized he was sniffing the air.

"Ugh, what is that smell? It's horrible!" Tommy asked and was incredibly surprised as Lord Kalish turned toward him and leveled his sword at Tommy's throat.

"And how is Mister Nelson able to sense that smell, hrmm?" Lord Kalish asked in a curious voice that was full of placid anger.

Tommy babbled, terrified for the second time in mere minutes, and managed to stammer out, "I... I... don't know? It smelled like old plastic."

Lord Kalish pushed his sword further toward Tommy's throat, and it was only when he backed into the wall again that Tommy realized the man had been forcing him backwards. "It is only those who have touched the darkest magics that can smell that scent, yes? So tell Lord Kalish, Mister Nelson, when have you been touching dark magics? You created this abomination, yes?" Lord Kalish leaned in a bit further with the sword.

Tommy didn't know what to do. "I didn't! I never, I swear!" he managed to stammer. "An evil mage used black magic on me! I mean, before I came to the school! That's how Micah found me! You can ask him if you don't believe me!"

Lord Kalish stared at him for a long moment before lowering his blade and sinking to a single knee next to Tommy. Tommy realized he'd been holding his breath and let it out with a sigh of relief. Lord Kalish simply reached out and grabbed hold of Tommy's arm, turning it over to expose the wound where the creature had scratched him. There were three long gouges on Tommy's arm, not overly deep but extremely narrow, like a bad paper cut, and scabbed over with burned skin. Lord Kalish held his hand over the scratches, and the hurt faded and became an intense itching sensation that had Tommy squirming in the older man's grasp. "Be still!" Lord Kalish barked, and Tommy did his best to grit his teeth and deal with the itching. After just a few moments, the itching faded, and Lord Kalish swept his hand along Tommy's arm. The burned skin fell away leaving behind skin that looked pink and newly healed.

"You will have a small scar, yes?" Lord Kalish said, still gripping Tommy's wrist in one of his rough, weathered, leathery hands. "But you will listen to Lord Kalish, now." The man had a very firm tone in his voice, and jerked Tommy's arm slightly so that Tommy was looking him straight in the eyes. "Your 'friend' Lord Micah, he is a good man, yes? This is why Lord Kalish follows him, even though Lord Kalish and Lord Micah do not see eye to eye on many things. But you must not put all your faith in him. Lord Micah is still a man, no matter that the other members of the school like to pretend otherwise. Mister Nelson should follow Lord Micah, and learn from him, but you must not be blind in your following. Lord Micah plays a very deep and hidden game, yes? Everything Lord Micah does, he does for a reason, and neither Lord Kalish nor Thomas Nelson will know that reason until the game is done. Do you understand, Mister Nelson?"

Tommy didn't really understand. "You make him sound so... cold. Calculating, I guess," Tommy protested.

Lord Kalish nodded; it was not the reaction Tommy expected to get. "Calculating, yes. This is a good word to describe Lord Micah. You must remember this word when you deal with your 'friend'. A man like Lord Micah does not have friends. A man in Lord Micah's position must not let himself see people, but instead see tools to be used, yes? Remember that Lord Micah does the things that he does for his own reasons, and those reasons are likely to be what is best for Lord Micah or for the school, but perhaps NOT what is best for Mister Nelson, yes?"

Tommy was thoughtful, but he nodded. He understood what Lord Kalish was saying, even though he didn't agree with it. Micah calculating? It couldn't be so. Micah was warm and caring and always bore that knowing, half-smile on his face that made him look like he was about to tell a joke. Lord Kalish took his nod as acceptance, however, and stood up, sniffing the air once more.

"Gather your things and come along, Mister Nelson." Lord Kalish paused briefly to allow Tommy to gather his books and papers before he swept down the hallway, still sniffing the air, and Tommy hurried after. They walked directly to the door to Tommy's room, where Lord Kalish paused briefly, sniffing the air, before turning and going inside.

The room was as it should be, except for James, sleeping on his bunk, still in his clothes and shoes. Lord Kalish sniffed the air again, and narrowed his eyes and stared at James for a long moment. Tommy sniffed, too. He thought he could detect a faint hint of the scent, but the smell was so pungent that he couldn't be sure if the air in the room bore the rotting plastic scent, or if it was still clogged in his nose from before. Either way, it made Tommy rub his nose.

Lord Kalish stood in the doorway for a while, still peering intently at James, before he turned and whispered, "Remember what Lord Kalish has told you, yes?", and then without another word he swept back down the hallway, leaving Tommy alone in the room with the still-sleeping James.

Tommy slumped down on his bed still dressed, sure that

he'd not be able to rest, but the adrenaline from the event drained out of him, and he quickly slipped down into sleep, where he had a night full of dark dreams about Micah chasing him through the school's halls wearing a rotting rubber mask.

CHAPTER TWENTY

It was exactly one week after the event with the creature that Tommy found himself outside the school, in the protected "courtyard". He had been assigned several chores that were supposed help the school while giving him an opportunity to practice his magical ability. In this case, he was using magic to cause the ground to erupt in a long series of miniature explosions that were creating long furrows in the ground that a farmer would use for planting. He'd had to work the spell out for himself; it was part of his education that he do so, and Tommy suspected that the farmers would have found it quicker and easier to plow the fields themselves, but it was work that had been assigned to him, and he was determined to see it through.

The work wasn't particularly difficult, but it was tiring – creating a series of small but controlled explosions to furrow the ground was a lot of repetitive work – channel, focus, release, over and over again. Tommy suspected that was why he'd been assigned this task – to give him practice doing an extremely repetitive task while trying to avoid making him feel like he was doing busy work.

The air was warm, and Tommy was working up a bit of a sweat with the effort. He used his hand to wipe the sweat from his brow, and as he did so, he noticed something from the corner of his eye. Micah and several other people had just come out of the front doors of the massive building Tommy had learned was the Hall of the Paladins. Tommy tried to watch the men without seeming like he was staring. He could see that the men were talking, but he was way too far away to hear what was being said. Finally, the men all shook hands with Micah one a time and dispersed in different directions. When the last man was gone, Micah looked straight at Tommy and met his eye. Tommy felt like Micah knew he'd been watching them and was embarrassed to have been caught snooping; he felt the blood rush into his face as quickly turned his attention back to the field and began making more furrows.

Glancing back, he saw that Micah was striding toward him across the courtyard. He paused to exchange some words with a farmer who was busy planting another field that Tommy had already furrowed. Then two men spoke for a minute, shook hands, and then Micah resumed his trek over to Tommy.

"You are doing that the hard way, you know." Micah said to Tommy when he was close.

Tommy regarded his work in the field. His small explosions threw dirt and rocks everywhere, and it was very messy. He'd been sure that there must be an easier, and cleaner, way to do the work, but he hadn't been able to figure out just what it was, yet. He expressed as much to Micah, who nodded.

"Do it again," Micah asked, and Tommy obliged.

"Yes, see," Micah instructed, wiping away a small bit of dirt that had hit him in the face. "You are using too much fire and air in the spell, and not enough water. That's why you are getting 'explosion' instead of 'hole'. Here, let me show you. Enchant your sight."

Tommy obliged, and colors and sensations exploded into his vision. Micah's eyes glowed a faint bluish color, and Tommy knew that the older man also had his vision enchanted. There was something new that Tommy hadn't seen before, however. To Tommy's enhanced vision, Micah appeared to be surrounded by a shimmering, golden field – almost like a prism or some sort of faceted gem, except less solid and more ephemeral. He was about to ask about it when Micah distracted him.

"Now, watch how I do it." Tommy watched as Micah plowed the field in one smooth, long furrow. There were no explosions, no dirt getting flung everywhere, and overall it seemed to take a lot less effort. Tommy nodded his understanding, then tried it himself as soon as Micah stopped. It took a few tries – the first time, he made the spell too strong, and dug a very deep furrow that Micah helped him fill in. But after a few attempts, he had it down pat and the work went much more smoothly.

"Thank you so much," Tommy said, full of genuine gratitude. "I had to try to figure it out myself, and I guess I didn't..."

Micah interrupted Tommy mid-sentence. "I heard about your little run-in in the hallway outside your room, Tommy."

Tommy was surprised by the change in topic. "I... I didn't do it. I think Lord Kalish thinks I did, though."

Micah shook his head. "No, Kalish suspects James. I'm not entirely sure that I don't, as well. It would make sense, after all. Often, when people are struggling to keep up with their peers, they become tempted to turn to the darker arts in an attempt to take the easier path. Particularly folks like James, who have never had to work for anything in their whole lives."

Tommy was somewhat shocked. "No," he said. "Not James! He wouldn't try that! Why would anyone do that, after you warned us not to?"

Micah sighed and looked off into the distance for a moment before replying. "Evil is not fanged and horned, like in the stories, Tommy. Evil is insidious. Evil wears a congenial smile and a brightly colored shirt. It doesn't attack you to your face, but instead whispers in your ear, leading you slowly but steadily off the path of righteousness in a series of small but perfectly reasonable steps, each one taken with the purest of intentions at heart, but leading inexorably to increasingly darker deeds until the light is just a memory, and the only paths open lead to more darkness." He turned back to regard Tommy. "Do you understand what I'm saying? Almost no one sets out to corrupt themselves. They think, 'Just a little bit, to help me catch up. I can handle just a little bit.' But then the little bit turns into more. Now it's, 'Just a little bit more, just enough to get ahead. I can handle a little more.', and before you know it, the person is lost."

Tommy nodded thoughtfully. He could see how things like that could become seductive, but he just couldn't wrap his head around why someone would try something that dangerous in the first place. If people KNEW that a little bit would lead to more, why did they even try the little bit? And James! James was his friend! He was certain no one he knew and called friend would ever try something so deadly.

"Which reminds me, I've brought you a little gift," Micah's words intruded on Tommy's thoughts.

"A gift?"

Micah nodded and drew a small item from his pocket. It was long and thin, almost the length of Tommy's hand, and narrowed toward one end like a greatly oversized needle but without a sharp point. And it looked to be made of gold, or some gold-like metal – it shone faintly in the fading light – and Tommy's enchanted vision detected a shining light moving over the surface, almost like sunlight shining through water. Micah turned it over in his hands a few times before presenting it to Tommy thick-end first.

"It's beautiful, but what is it?"

Micah shrugged. "There are some who would call it a wand, just because of its shape and perhaps its function, but the proper term for it is a 'spell binder'. Honestly, it could have been made in any shape, this one was just convenient for the purpose. It contains all the makings of a spell. In this case, a very specially crafted spell that will do incredible damage to a creature made from dark magic, but that will not harm anything else. The spell is there; all you have to do is provide the energy and point the spell binder."

Clutching the spell binder to his chest, Tommy smiled gratefully. "Thank you! Thank you so much," Tommy said, touched "I've been scared to walk alone ever since... well, you know."

Micah smiled, and laid a hand on Tommy's shoulder. "You are welcome. Just be very careful with it, okay? Spell binders are difficult to make, and this one was particularly hard. Oh, and one more thing – don't show it off to anyone, alright? Keep it a secret between you and I, please. Otherwise, someone might take it away from you."

Tommy nodded and looked around, suddenly conscious of who might be watching. He stuffed the spell binder down into his pocket, and turned to thank Micah again, but the older man had already turned and started walking away.

"Huh." Tommy said to himself. He continued to watch Micah until the older man reached the doors to the school. Opening the door, Micah turned, and Tommy thought the that older man pointed at him briefly before turning back and entering the school.

Tommy shook his head in confusion and resumed plowing the field. It was getting dark, and he wanted to finish the job before he went in to wash up for dinner. And he certainly needed to wash – he was covered in little bits of dirt and rocks from all the little explosions he conjured. This time, though, Tommy plowed the fields the right way, the way Micah had shown him.

CHAPTER
TWENTY-ONE

Tommy's skill continued to improve, and so did the tasks expected of him. One day, their history teacher had made them research a topic in the school's massive library, and then prepare a speech on the topic. Micah had made them all deliver the speech in front of the magic class, while spinning three multi-colored balls in the air. The spells that the class learned got increasingly complex, and Tommy felt his abilities growing in time with the new challenges.

One spell Micah taught them was so complex, and required so much magical energy to fuel it, that Tommy was the only student in his class that was able to make it work. Using the spell, Tommy was able to take an ordinary stone, melt it, and spin the molten rock into complex shapes before cooling it down. Tommy really liked that particular spell, and after working with it for a while, he was able to figure out how to strengthen the stone at the same time, enabling him to make shapes that were improbably thin. Tommy used it to make bracelets for Mae and Mary, and made a matching pair of rings for his mother and father out of a beautiful striated crystal stone he'd found while plowing fields out in the courtyard - he intended the rings as a Christmas gift for his parents. Micah had praised them when he saw them, and stated that perhaps someday Tommy could help earn money for the school by producing and selling the jewelry, if he decided to stay on after he graduated; Tommy beamed at the compliment and said he was absolutely interested. Micah had even asked Tommy to craft a couple of the rings for him, a request that Tommy was happy to fulfill. It was a new feeling for Tommy. He'd never thought of himself as being able to make something, to create something that someone else might want for money, and for the first time in his life, he felt like he could see a future ahead of him.

Eventually, the Christmas season came, and almost all the students had family come to visit. The school closed all classes for the entire week and opened up a rarely-used wing of the school to host all the family members that had come to visit, so that they might have a place to stay. Tommy's parents were among the visitors and had been given a pleasant if somewhat smallish room that was, admittedly, quite a long walk from Tommy's room. Still, with the school's population swelled to over triple size, everyone made do with what they could.

For Tommy, the time with his parents was a joy. He'd never been overly close with his family when he lived with them, but having been apart from them and assuming that he'd lost them forever had given both Tommy and his parents a new found respect for each other. Further, Tommy noticed that they'd begun to treat him as less of a child. They chatted about any number of topics, and Tommy's father had asked for Tommy's opinion of things, something he had never done previously, and Tommy's mother commented that he was growing up so fast so many times that Tommy almost got sick of hearing it. After some reflection, Tommy realized that his parents were right. He *was* starting to grow up a bit. The school taught students to be responsible for themselves and gave them the freedom to manage their own time and responsibilities. By letting Tommy know what was required for his continued progress and leaving it to him to figure out how and when to accomplish those goals, the school had effectively given Tommy ownership of his destiny, and he had responded by stepping up to the demands placed upon him.

For Christmas, Tommy presented his parents with the rings he'd made. They both marveled at the beauty of the rings, and were extremely impressed when Tommy told them that he'd made them himself, from a spell that he had figured out. His parents tried the rings on immediately and were slightly embarrassed when neither one fit – his mother's ring was too large, and his father's ring was way too small – but they were further impressed when Tommy used magic to immediately correct the sizes. Tommy also gave Mary and Mae their bracelets. Mary seemed genuinely touched, and clutched her bracelet to her chest for a moment before putting it on. Mae, on the other hand, seemed puzzled by the gift, and spent the next hour forcing Tommy to show her the spells he'd used to make it. Mae couldn't quite make the spell work, but that didn't stop her determination to become able, and although Tommy relished the time with her, he began to wish that they would talk about something else.

At one point during the week, while his parents were taking a nap and Tommy was at dinner trying to shovel bites of food into his mouth in between demonstrating his spell to Mae over and over again, his friend Stephen came into the dining hall and presented Mae with his own Christmas present – a large, beautifully worked book of fairy tales that was full of hand-drawn illustrations. Mae had bounced in her seat and clapped her hands with joy before jumping up, throwing her arms around Stephen, and giving him a kiss full on the mouth. Tommy's heart fell into his shoes at the sight of that, and he would have fled the room had Mae not immediately bounded out to show the book to her own family. Stephen and Tommy both watched her leave the room, the former boy smiling and the latter frowning, before Stephen turned back and took the seat at the table that Mae had been occupying.

Stephen turned to say something to Tommy, but, seeing the look on his face, stopped for a moment in surprise and said, "Tommy, what's wrong?"

Tommy could only scowl. "I think you know."

Stephen looked around. The dining hall was lightly occupied at this time of day, and there was no one else nearby. Stephen shook his head. "I don't know, Tommy. Honest truth, I don't."

"You know. You and Mae."

Understanding slowly dawned across Stephen's face, and with it came mirth bubbling up and bursting forth as overwhelming laughter.

"It's not funny, man." Tommy scowled, feeling mocked, but Stephen could only laugh harder and shake his head back and forth. Tommy started to stand up to leave, scowling even darker, but Stephen laid a hand on Tommy's arm and half-pushed him back down into his seat.

"No, Tommy. No. I'm sorry for laughing, but you've got it all wrong," Stephen managed to choke out between laughs, wiping tears from the corner of his eyes. "You have to understand, Mae is like a sister to me. It's not like that with us. I don't like her in that way."

Tommy was only slightly mollified. "She seems to like you in that way."

That sent Stephen into another round of chuckles, but he was shaking his head again, as well. "No, Tommy, I promise you, I *swear* to you, it's nothing like that." Stephen turned toward him, swinging one leg over so that he was sitting on the bench with one leg on either side, facing Tommy directly. "You see, Tommy, I don't like girls in that way. My preferences lie in another direction." Stephen paused for a moment and took a deep breath before continuing in a rush. "I'm gay, Tommy."

Tommy was so surprised that he almost couldn't process what he was hearing. "Gay...?" was all he could say.

Stephen nodded emphatically. "Yes. I like guys, Tommy. In fact, I have to tell you, I'm a little bit disappointed to find out that you are so interested in Mae. I had kind of hoped that you and I might be able to have a date sometime," he finished with a chuckle.

For Tommy, the hits just kept coming, and his head spun. "What? But... I mean, how could you be gay? You went out with that girl in school. You two were always together. What was her name? I can't remember."

"Phan Ho. That was her name. We hung out together all the time, and we told everyone that we were girlfriend and boyfriend, but it was... ahhh... a relationship of convenience, you might say? You see, Phan only liked women. Since she was Vietnamese as well, and both our families were very traditional and would have been completely not accepting of either of us, we came up with the deception. The families approved, and we were both free to be secretly gay while avoiding the censure of our families and the teasing of our classmates."

"But... why keep it a secret, I mean?"

"You remember how high school was, Tommy. The teasing? The bullying? I got enough teasing for being Asian, the other kids always calling me slant-eye and the like. Could you imagine if I'd come out publicly as gay? I'd have been the slant-eyed pole smoker." Stephen shook his head. "I wasn't up for that amount of teasing, and I certainly didn't want my parents finding out. With Phan, no girls ever asked me out, no one really bothered me, and kept my secrets hidden and contented myself to look for love online. But here, Tommy! In the school, no one judges me. I mean, some kids do, a little, but most of them don't even care. It's not that they 'support' me, or grudgingly accept me. They quite genuinely don't care one little bit. It's a non-issue for them. They treat me no different from anyone else. It's everything I could ask for, Tommy. For the first time in my life, I don't feel abnormal, like I'm some kind of freak. I can be myself, and I feel... complete."

Tommy was still struggling to wrap his head around the concept. "But... why me? I mean, I'm not... you know. Gay. I'm not gay, Stephen."

Stephen grinned. "Don't knock it 'til you've tried it," then, at the look on Tommy's face, "Oh, relax, I'm just teasing you. I'm not going to hit on you or try to kiss you, Tommy. You can't blame a guy for hoping, though, right?"

Tommy found himself grinning in spite of himself. Stephen seemed just so... happy. Full. Real, like a whole person. It was hard for Tommy to find any fault with something that could make his friend seem so complete. He stuck his hand out toward Stephen, and the two boys shook hands. "I'm really glad to see you happy, Stephen."

"Thanks, Tommy. You're a good friend." Stephen frowned for a moment. "As for Mae... You've got your hands full, there. I'll warn you, Tommy. I don't think Mae knows you like her. Heck, I don't think Mae would notice if anyone liked her. She's... interesting." He paused for a moment in thought. "Tommy, Mae is so interested in magic, in learning as much as she can, that I don't think she even spares a thought for dating."

Tommy nodded. "Yeah, I'm starting to find that out. She's been pestering me to teach her a spell, and she can't quite make it work no matter how many times I show it to her."

Stephen whistled through his teeth. "That's a doozy. I can't think she's very happy with that. Still, if you want to work your way into her heart, I can think of no better way than teaching her new spells. The more complex, the better."

Tommy considered that and decided that he should rethink his annoyance at trying to teach Mae the spell. If magic was her interest, then Tommy would just have to see what else he could do to capture that interest. He briefly considered showing her the spell binder, and then decided against it. He couldn't really explain what it was or how it worked, so it would only create more questions than he had answers, and Micah had told him to hold it in the utmost secrecy. Instead, he asked Stephen, "So, is there anyone else that interests you?"

Stephen smiled and chuckled mischievously. "I dunno. What do you think about your friend James?"

This time, it was Tommy's turn to laugh until he couldn't breathe.

CHAPTER
TWENTY-TWO

Tommy had both hoped and planned for the week after Christmas to be a slow week. Most of the school's instructors were still away from the school for the holidays, or had cancelled classes for a period of rest, or both. Tommy's parents had given him, as a Christmas gift, a stack of novels that he was desperate to break into and start reading. The stories were set in a fantasy land, and appeared to be about a pair of women who obtained magical powers and set out to right the wrongs in the world – precisely the kind of book Tommy loved, even though fantasy novels had fallen out of favor with the masses around the time that magic had become a reality. Moreover, each of the books had been signed personally by the author – quite a feat, since they had been published over twenty years ago.

Micah, however, had other plans for the class, and summoned all the students to their classroom just after breakfast that Monday morning. On each student's desk was a series of large, laminated sheets of paper, loosely bound together by a piece of twine looped through a hole in one corner. Each page was covered by a series of long, curving lines, small, different colored triangles that pointed in different directions, and other shapes, letters, and markings that made even less sense to Tommy. He flipped through the pages briefly. Each one contained more drawings, and they got increasingly complex, with more symbols and more *kinds* of symbols on each successive page. Tommy stared at them in confusion, unable to make heads or tails of any of it. He was still trying to puzzle it out when Micah, as he always did, clapped his hands together to signal that the class was now in session. Tommy turned his attention to the man.

"Can anyone here read music or play an instrument?" Micah asked. A couple students in the room raised their hands, and Micah nodded. "Not very many. Just as well. What you see before you, on your desks, is the mage's equivalent of sheet music. It may look like nothing to you now, but once you learn how to read it properly, you will be able to cast the spells written on the paper."

Tommy was shocked. It had never occurred to him that it might be possible to write down magic. Evidently, he wasn't alone; he could see the other students in the class looking at the laminated papers, and then back in forth to one another, in surprise.

Micah was continuing, though. "We waited until now to teach you this because you couldn't have understood it before. Think about it. if someone tried to teach you how to cast a spell before you had actually done it, you wouldn't have had any idea what they were talking about. Almost like teaching a fish to fly, as it were. And you will find that there's a wide difference between being able to read the texts and being able to cast the spell, just like there's a difference between being able to read and understand music, and being able to play a particular instrument. To carry that analogy just a little bit further, just like music, it's going to take a lot of study, work, and practice. We're going to take advantage of this week to buckle down and do some serious studying."

There were a couple groans around the class; Tommy wasn't the only student who had been looking forward to a little more time to rest and relax. Micah only grinned, though. "Think of it as stealing a march on the other classes. We're going to cover in a week what the other classes cover in a month. All while they are off goofing around."

The instructor's grin was infectious, and Tommy saw several of his classmates grinning along conspiratorially.

"Alright, let's get to it. Pick up the first sheet. You'll notice the colored triangular marks. The color symbolizes the type of magic to be used. Red for fire, blue for air, green for water, and brown for earth. Now, the direction that the triangle is pointing shows you...." Tommy wished he'd brought a piece of paper to take notes. Everything on the paper had meaning, even the thickness and direction of the lines. However, as Micah talked, Tommy began to see how the instructions on the document could be translated into a spell. After a couple hours of instruction, Tommy could even begin to see what the spell on the paper was supposed to do; in this case, it appeared to be a spell to create a small flame, like that of a candle. It turned out, however, that Tommy didn't need notes. Micah walked them through it again and again, often showing them with magic what the symbols on the page stood for.

The class spent the week studying increasingly complex charts. With every new chart, Micah added new symbols, and then showed the class how to translate the symbol into magical practice. The spells grew in complexity, and soon the class was learning spells that took several sheets of paper.

Halfway through the week, it occurred to Tommy that he

should write down his stone-working spell, so that Mae could stop pestering him to demonstrate it. However, when he tried, he realized he didn't quite know all the symbols required to translate it to a drawing, so one day after class, he approached Micah with the problem.

What he didn't expect was for Micah to chuckle at his conundrum. However, after seeing the scowling look on Tommy's face, Micah was quick to explain his amusement.

"You can't write the spell down because the symbols required to do it don't exist."

Tommy frowned deeper. "What do you mean? I don't understand."

"Tommy, the symbols I'm teaching the class are only the most basic. The most commonly agreed upon methods, if you will. The more advanced spells require symbols that don't exist. They require you to manipulate magic in ways that other people don't normally do. So each mage comes up with his own set of symbols to define those odd twists and such that the spells required." Micah sighed. "And, unfortunately, the only way to decipher the script is to either ask the mage who wrote it to demonstrate, or to try to figure out what they meant through trial and error. That's why your friend Mae can't seem to make your little stone bending trick work."

Tommy blushed a little at the mention of Mae's name. "You knew about that?"

Micah returned wry grin. "Anyone who has eyes knew about that, Tommy. You've been spending almost as much time trying to teach her as you have studying your material. But Tommy, the fault does not lie with you. If anything, the fault lies with Mae. She's only focused on the methods that she knows and has studied, and she's hasn't considered the simple truth – that you have discovered a new way of working magic that no other mage has discovered before."

Tommy blinked. "I've discovered something new?" He'd thought his spell was innovative, to him. An interesting trifle, perhaps a way of doing something differently that other people had done before, but it never occurred to him that he'd discovered something unique.

Micah nodded. "You have an interesting way of looking at magic, Tommy. Probably because, unlike most of the students here, you've only just begun to study it. You have no preconceived notions, no bad habits to unlearn before you can learn. It gives you a new insight into the workings of spells. A fresh pair of eyes, if you will. I only hope that you can maintain that fresh viewpoint as you become more skilled and learn the things that you need to know in order to really become one of us."

Tommy nodded, thoughtful. "I'll try my best," he said, although he honestly had no idea how to go about that.

Micah seemed to accept his answer, however, and changed the subject. "While we are talking about Mae... Tommy, do you realize Mae probably doesn't even notice you are interested in her, right? She's been so wrapped up in being scholarly for so long that it doesn't even occur to her that someone might find her attractive, and if she did notice, she'd probably just want to study the phenomenon."

Tommy grimaced throughout his instructor's speech. Finally, he burst out, "Is there anyone in this school who doesn't know that I like Mae?"

Micah threw back his head and laughed. "Unfortunately for you, Tommy, Mae is probably the only one."

CHAPTER TWENTY-THREE

After his meeting with Micah, Tommy went to the dining hall to get some food, still mulling over the man's words. He knew that he was a channeler, and that that meant that he was able to focus and refine more magical energy that most mages could dream of. He hadn't failed to notice the looks that his other classmates had given him following that discovery. Some of the looks were envious, some of them were looks of respect, but invariably, all of them made him feel like something foreign. Like an outsider who was isolated from the rest of the students at the school. Tommy decided, as he pulled open one of the double doors leading to the dining hall, that he would keep Micah's words secret. He didn't need any more jealous looks, and he was sure to get them if he went around bragging about discovering new spells. Mae would just have to keep trying to puzzle it out on her own. It would keep her interested in him, at the very least.

When Tommy got his food and arrived at the table the group normally sat at, he noticed that James and Ryan were not there. In fact, it was only Mae and Mary who were there, and Tommy quickly realized he'd be giving no lessons today. Mae and Mary were right in the middle of a heated debate.

"Clearly," Mae was saying, "Magic is not a new discovery. There have been stories of magic and wizards for thousands of years. Therefore, we must assume that, for some reason, the magic went away for a while, and for some other reason, it came back."

Mary, however, shook her head. "There have been stories of dragons for thousands of years, too. Yet there's never been any indication that they existed. No fossils, no records, no nothing. Besides, how would an animal breathe fire like that, anyway?"

Mae was insistent. "How would something breath fire? Well, MAGIC, of course! And what about dinosaurs? Primitive people could have found those skeletons, and conjecture that dragons might exist."

"It's a long leap from seeing some fossilized bones to creating a creature that breathes fire, Mae."

"So what? It's a long way from hearing thunder to believing that angels are *bowling*, of all things, yet my mother told me that for years, and I believed it. Besides, you are diverging from my original argument – that magic must have existed at one time, and that it went away for a while. What if it goes away again?"

"What if the world ends tomorrow? What if you have a heart attack in bed tonight? It's possible, you know – the way you eat, all that fat and no vegetables. I'd say it's a lot more likely than magic ever going away again, but even so, what does it matter? If magic goes away, we all go back to normal people. We don't have to hide any longer, we don't have to get sent to prison or treated like something less than human. In a way, it would be a blessing."

"Speak for yourself," Mae countered. "I wouldn't want to live without magic. And I think if you think about it, you wouldn't either. Going back to being a normal person would be so... Dull."

Mary sighed. "What I was trying to say, was, it's a pointless thing to worry about. If magic is going to go away again, then it will, and nothing we can do is going to stop it. We might as well not worry about it, there's no sense borrowing trouble from something that may or may not ever happen."

But Mae was shaking her head again. "That's short sighted. If we can understand why the magic came back, then we can understand why it went away, and maybe someday we can figure out how to keep it from going away again. Or even," Mae continued, her eyes shining in the light of the dining hall, "strengthen it."

"You don't even know for sure that the magic ever went away to begin with. What if... what if we *created* the magic, ourselves? What if it's the strength of all our human imaginations, finally reaching a critical mass, and creating something that wasn't there before? Or, heck, I don't know. Something like that. There's a lot of people on the planet. More than there ever has been."

"That's completely ludicrous!"

"It's no more ludicrous than any of your theories!"

Tommy finally chimed in. "Well, I don't know. Micah told me once that light magic was created by people's hopes and dreams, and that dark magic was created by their fears and nightmares."

Both women turned to regard Tommy, looking at him like a fly they'd suddenly found floating in their soup.

"That's completely ridiculous!" Mae said, and at the same time, Mary started with, "Well, that's not quite right..." The two women cut off and paused to regard each other for a moment, then Mae began speaking in the lecturing tone that Tommy had learned to know so well.

"Although it may seem like that to a casual observer, I believe that both light and dark magic are actually *refined* by human emotion. You do know that just about any person can learn to be a mage, right?" Mae asked, then continued when Tommy nodded. "Strong human emotions affects the magic around them, just like we do when we channel it, only we are doing it on purpose. Just like when we align the magic to an element, like Fire or Water, people can align the magic around them with their emotions. You wouldn't notice it at all for one person, or even ten, but a large group of people suffering, or being excited, or feeling any other strong emotion can affect the magic around them."

"... and thus, could have created the magic in the first place!" Mary finished, but Mae just rolled her eyes.

"So, could anyone use light and dark magic, then? If there is enough of it around, I mean?" Tommy asked. He didn't like to reveal his ignorance in front of Mae, but she knew that he didn't come from a magical background, and she often explained things in a way that, while long winded, was still something Tommy could understand.

"Only with very special and time-intensive training" spoke a new voice from behind Tommy, and when he turned around, he saw that Micah was standing there, holding a tray full of food that looked nearly identical to the one that Tommy had in front of him.

Suddenly, Tommy became aware of what was going on

around him. The entire dining hall was dead silent, which was a rare thing – normally, there was at least a small buzz of conversation. But none of the students were eating. They were, one and all, sitting and staring at Micah… and at Tommy.

"May I join you, if I'm not interrupting?" Micah asked, gesturing with his tray at an open seat next to Tommy.

Tommy didn't get to respond, however. He was still too surprised. Instead, it was Mae who said, "Yes, sir, of course, sir, please, it would be an honor, sir!"

Tommy heard a soft chuckle from Micah as the man sat down next to him, and peered at Mae. The sycophantic groveling didn't fit with her personality – she had always been self-assured and almost cocky about her knowledge, and it Tommy found it almost painful to listen to her be so obsequious.

"As I was saying," Micah continued as he wrapped a piece of meat up in a slice of bread, and dipped it in the gravy on his bowl, "It takes years of practice to learn how to use light magic. The creation process - being exposed to strong human emotions - makes the energy particularly… slippery… and difficult to channel. And even then, it is of limited usefulness. Dark magic, for example, can only be used to cause pain or hurt. Any attempt to use it otherwise would fail, or perhaps even backfire." Micah popped the meat and bread roll, now dripping gravy, into his mouth as he finished, and began to chew thoughtfully.

"Thank you for the lesson, sir." Mae bowed her head at Micah, and made Tommy feel embarrassed on her behalf.

To cover the rising blush in his cheeks, Tommy said, "We were just talking about if magic went away for a while and came back, or if it was something that was created by having so many people."

Micah's eyes got a faraway look in them. "Created by people?" he murmured. "No... No, I don't think so." Once again, Tommy got the feeling that there was more there that his teacher wasn't saying, and that, if he just waited long enough, the older man would continue.

He didn't get the chance to wait long enough, however, as Mae chose that moment to have her cockiness reassert itself. "HA! I told you!" she said, jabbing a finger Mary, who flushed red, picked up her tray, mumbled a soft, "Excuse me" to Micah, and turned and fled the room.

Micah stared off at her retreating back for a moment. "What was that all about?" he mused softly. Then, shaking his head, he turned toward Tommy. "This wasn't supposed to be a lecture opportunity. I came to make sure the food you were getting here was still good. And to ask you a favor, Tommy."

Tommy was bewildered. What could Micah want from him? "A favor?"

Micah nodded and went on as if he'd expected the question. "Yes, a favor. Remember that stone crafting spell you came up with? The one you used to make that jewelry?"

Tommy nodded in return - How could he forget? Mae had pestered him about it non-stop for over a month.

"Well, I took the liberty of showing the rings you'd made for me to a... friend of mine." Tommy puzzled momentarily over the pause before the word "friend". It was like Micah couldn't really decide what to call the person. "He runs another school, and they were able to take the rings you made and add an enchantment to them."

Tommy frowned. "Enchantment?"

Micah nodded, reaching to his side and pulling a ring out of his pocket. It looked like the one Tommy had made for Micah, except the one Tommy made was shiny, glossy, grey, and smooth. This ring looked... almost corroded. It had turned a brownish color and had shallow pits and pock marks across its surface.

"It doesn't really look like mine..."

"The people at my friend's school have been able to take the ring you made and enable it to use magic without someone channeling. This ring, for example, removes poisons and toxins from a person's bloodstream as they wear it. It's a fantastic discovery!"

Tommy nodded, and heard a soft, awed noise from Mae. She was staring at Micah, her jaw dropped. "That's...incredible!" she breathed, too stunned to remember to grovel at Micah.

Micah, though, didn't appear to notice. "Further, they are willing to share the method of crafting with us, so we could make our own. Even improve upon their design, perhaps. But, Tommy, there's one catch – in exchange, they want you to go there, personally, and demonstrate your crafting spell for their school."

Tommy frowned, considering. He didn't want to let Micah down, but he didn't really know how he was going to show his spell to an entire school. Surely, they could figure it out on their own?

Mae interrupted, echoing Tommy's thoughts by interjecting, "But, sir... he's not a very good teacher. He couldn't even teach me. Sir."

Micah turned to regard Mae, staring at her pointedly for the first time. "Mae Ramirez... Have you considered that the error might lie with you? I was able to learn the spell from Tommy just fine. You believe that you know everything there is to know about magic. The fact that you are a student at my school proves that you do not. Perhaps you should open your mind and be more accepting of others' gifts and less blinded by your own."

Tommy was shocked by the vehemence in Micah's tone, and Mae lowered her head and stared at her plate, abashed. An awkward silence stretched for several moments, as Micah continued to stare headedly at Mae.

Finally, Tommy could take the silence no longer, and he spoke up in Mae's defense. "Uh... she's right, though, Micah. Why me? I'm not a good teacher."

Micah turned his head to regard Tommy. "You were able to teach me, weren't you?"

Tommy could only shrug. "Yeah, but... you are... well... YOU. If you know what I mean. Besides, you know the spell, why couldn't you just go share it with them?"

Micah was shaking his head before Tommy finished speaking. "Another school wouldn't let me in, Tommy. Mages are very secretive people, and the master of the school would never permit someone of my ability into the school. It's just too risky. And besides, Tommy... the spell isn't mine to share, it's yours. If anyone shares it, it should be you."

"But... you can share the spell with whomever you like."

"Don't be so quick to toss away your discoveries, Tommy. If everyone knows how to do them, they become less special. And mark my words, I think this could be very special."

Tommy had to think about that for a moment before he made his decision. "Okay, if you think it will help the school, I'll do it."

Micah grinned broadly, and clapped his hands together like he often did. "Excellent! I'll set up the visit and let you know, then." With that, Micah rose to his feet, picked up his tray, and walked briskly out of the room. Tommy watched the older man's back recede for a few minutes, contemplating what he'd just agreed to. He turned to ask Mae a question, only to discover that, sometime during his conversation with Micah, Mae had also fled the room, and Tommy was now sitting at the table completely alone.

CHAPTER
TWENTY-FOUR

Tommy stumped sullenly back to the room that he shared with Ryan, James, and Sam. What had started out as a interesting discussion between Mae and Mary had turned into both girls being embarrassed and running away, leaving Tommy to finish his dinner alone. Worse, he'd been caught up in the discussion, and the talk with Micah afterwards, and his food had gone cold, so not even the food could cheer him up.

When he finally got back to his room and pushed open the door, he heard a soft slap, like a bare foot striking stone, and the "thump" of a body leaping hurriedly into bed, but when he looked around, both James and Ryan were in their beds, seemingly asleep, and Sam's bed was still vacant – the younger boy was likely still in class, even at this late hour. Still, there was that noise, so Tommy whispered, "Hey! You guys awake?"

When he got no answer, Tommy shrugged his shoulders. Maybe he'd imagined the noise, or maybe it was James turning over in his sleep – the larger boy was prone to flip-flop noisily in the middle of the night. Tommy got undressed, considered trying to study for a few minutes, and then gave up and went to bed.

Several days passed before Tommy heard from Micah again, and then everything happened very rapidly. One moment he was packing up his tray from lunch and heading to his next class, the next moment Chancellor Duvey was grabbing him by the arm and guiding him down a set of corridors that Tommy had not yet explored.

Tommy was about to object when Chancellor Duvey stopped walking and began speaking in his typical proper, clipped tone. "Lord Micah tells me that you are to go to the school of Lord Nence to demonstrate your spell in a knowledge transfer. Correct?"

"Uh... yeah. Yes, I mean." Tommy corrected himself at a narrow look from the Chancellor. Tommy had had some small interactions with the man, and he was always a stickler for proper speech.

"Very good. I will instruct you on what you need to know as we walk. Please try to keep up and pay attention." With that, the Chancellor set off at a brisk pace, and Tommy hurried to catch up. Tommy wasn't a small boy, but the Chancellors long legs ate up ground, and Tommy was suddenly grateful for all the exercise he'd been getting in his physical fitness classes. It would be embarrassing to get winded simply by walking, despite the brisk pace.

"The school that you are going to is very different from our school. Do you understand?" the Chancellor began, not waiting for Tommy's reply to the question. "Lord Micah believes in giving students freedom, and in trusting them to be responsible for their own studies. It is, I believe, a side effect of his strong association with the element of air." Here the Chancellor paused and gave Tommy a significant look, as if to say that he was not to repeat the information. That puzzled Tommy, since he would have assumed that Micah's affiliation with air was common knowledge. The archmage certainly made no secret of the fact. He didn't get long to think on the topic, though, because the Chancellor continued.

"The freedom Lord Micah gives students works well in part because the school is so prestigious. Few students who are given an opportunity to study here wish the squander the chance by failing to meet the requirements." Another pointed look from the Chancellor had Tommy thinking that maybe the man was suggesting that *he* was squandering his opportunities, an intimation that Tommy took offense to – he was leading his class in several areas of study, and was at least making the grade in all of them.

"Lord Nence, however, is not so discriminating in his choice of students," Chancellor Duvey continued. "Therefore, I think you will find the rules at his school extremely... stringent."

The Chancellor went on to detail a long list of rules. Tommy was not to speak unless spoken to by a teacher or school administrator. He was to use proper forms of address at all times, calling all teachers 'Lord' be they male or female. He was not to speak to the students of the school, and was particularly not to mention anything that went on at his own school. He was not to use magic in any way, including channeling, unless directed to do so by an instructor. The list went on and on, until Tommy began to regret getting himself into this position, and he started to wonder if he was visiting a school or a prison.

Finally, the Chancellor ran out of rules to explain, and concluded by admonishing Tommy. "Remember, above all, that you are a representative of the school, of Micah, and of myself. Do not embarrass us with poor behavior."

The tone of the Chancellor's voice caused Tommy to frown. "Wait, do you mean that no one is going with me?" he asked.

"No, indeed not. This is why it is so important for you to be on your very best behavior. None of us will be permitted to accompany you to the other school. We will meet at a neutral ground, you will go with Lord Nence, and he will return you to the same place at the agreed upon time."

Tommy's nervousness was increasing by the moment. "When is that? I mean, how long?"

The Chancellor favored him with an exaggerated sigh. "I do hope you remember to be on your best manners, since you cannot seem to remember them with me." That caused Tommy to blush. It was his nerves talking; he certainly would have remembered to at least be more polite if he wasn't so on edge. "And the answer to your question is, you will be returned to us after a period of six hours."

"SIX HOURS!?" Tommy burst out. "No one said anything about six hours!"

Chancellor Duvey stopped walking and turned to glare at Tommy. "DO try to control yourself, Mister Nelson!" he barked in a terse tone. "Six hours is the time frame agreed upon. It will be scarcely sufficient, I think, for us to learn all we require from Lord Nence's representative." His tone softened somewhat, then. If, that is, a stone could said to be somehow softer than something else, as it still had a gritty, commanding tone to it. "I understand that this is a difficult undertaking for you, Mister Nelson. But consider all that Lord Micah has done for you. Do you not believe that you owe this to him, no matter what the difficulty?"

Abashed, Tommy said, "I suppose" rather sullenly. He still wasn't so sure about doing this, anymore. Six hours seemed like a huge amount of time, and the task seemed to be getting more and more difficult by the minute.

Chancellor Duvey stood regarding Tommy for a long moment before nodding to himself and turning away. Tommy followed with much less enthusiasm that he'd shown previously.

Finally, they arrived at a door, which the Chancellor opened without knocking. Tommy followed him inside, and found himself in a small, extremely neat office. There was a small desk of dark wood with a thinly upholstered chair behind it. The walls were covered with pictures and framed documents, each of them arranged in precise order to compliment the others. The whole was such that the eye took in all the art without actually focusing on any single picture. Tommy wondered if that was intentional, or a side effect of what was clearly a mind obsessed with order. Clearly, this was the Chancellor's office; the room practically oozed order and proper behavior. There were two chairs in front of the desk, both of them upholstered as thinly as the chair behind the desk, and lounging in one of the chairs was Micah. Tommy wondered how the man managed to do that – the chairs looked horribly uncomfortable, like the throne he had been sitting in during Tommy's test, yet Micah managed to make it look like an easy chair.

Micah rose from the chair as Tommy and Chancellor Duvey entered and stepped over to clap Tommy on the shoulder. "Are you ready?" he asked.

Tommy nodded and swallowed over a lump in his throat. "Ready as I'll ever be," he said with a nervous chuckle.

"Great!" Micah quipped with a grin, laying his hand on

Tommy's shoulder. To Chancellor Duvey he said, "Meet you there?"

When the Chancellor nodded, Tommy felt a brief rush of magical energy into Micah, who still had his hand on Tommy's shoulder. Suddenly, the world blurred around him, and a moment later when he managed to blink his vision clear, he found himself standing next to Micah in a small, clean alleyway between two buildings. The buildings both had an architecture style that made them look old to Tommy – there were a lot of fancy carvings and friezes. The sun was high in the sky, but the air was brisk and cool with a tiny bit of bite in it. Tommy found himself grinning and taking a deep breath in spite of his nervousness.

Suddenly, Tommy realized that the Chancellor was there. Micah nodded to the other man, and the two of them set off down the alley. Tommy had no choice but to follow after them; he jogged a few steps and caught up to Micah so that he could walk next to the man.

The three of them came to the mouth of the alley, and Chancellor Duvey turned right onto the sidewalk of a busy city street. There was something odd about the whole street – the cars seemed slightly different than the ones that Tommy was used to, and they all seemed much older and battered. Suddenly, Tommy's eyes found the signs over the various stores along the street. He leaned over and whispered "Micah! Pssst, Micah! The signs are all in Russian!"

Micah merely laughed and shook his head. "No, Tommy. The alphabet is Cyrillic, but the language is Hungarian."

"Hungarian?"

Micah gave another chuckle. "Yeap, Hungarian.

Welcome to Budapesht, Tommy."

Tommy furrowed his brow. "Isn't it pronounced Buda-pest?"

Micah shook his head. "Actually, only if you are a foreigner. See, the city is made up of two large towns that grew together. Buda, and Pesht. Hence... Budapesht."

"Oh." Was all Tommy could say. He'd never really learned about this part of the world in school. He'd half expected there to be mosques and sand and lots of buildings with pointed domed roofs, but this city looked like pictures he'd scene of New York City in the 1920's, albeit with a lot more cars. "Why here?"

"Beg pardon?" Micah replied.

"I mean, why are we here?"

"Ah," Micah said, nodding. "There is an unusual... a conflux, it's called, in this area. It makes magic extremely difficult to control and manipulate, almost as if it's somehow more wild here. This means that novice mages cannot use magic at all, and even highly skilled mages have trouble with any kind of sustained magical feat. This makes it very hard for mages to actually fight here, since casting spells is so difficult, so we use it as a kind of meeting place. Like a safe zone, if you will."

"Why do you need a meeting place? I mean, I thought this guy was your friend."

Micah took a long, appraising look at Tommy as they walked. It went on so long, that Tommy started to feel uncomfortable, and he was just about to apologize when Micah spoke.

"Tommy... There is a problem with men who have great power. They are always on guard for other men who want to take it away. Even worse, most of the time, they are right – there are always other men out there who want to take their power, or who want to see them brought low. Sometimes just for the sake of seeing the mighty fall. Men like this, powerful men, have been on their guard so long, watching for every possible threat, that they forget what it's like to trust someone. Suspicion becomes part of their nature."

"But... you aren't suspicious!"

Micah laughed at that. "Am I not? Are you so sure? Do you think I fully trust... say, Lord Kalish? Or any of the other instructors?"

Tommy frowned, remembering Lord Kalish's warning not to place his full trust in Micah. Could the man's warning have just stemmed from an innate mistrust? Something that all powerful people had? "I don't know," replied Tommy uncertainly. "It seems like you trust him. You trust him to teach, anyway. And you trust Chancellor Duvey."

The Chancellor snorted a laugh at that comment, and Micah grinned. "Well, I trust him... and I don't, if that makes any kind of sense. I trust him fully, but I also keep an eye on him... just to be sure."

Chancellor Duvey snorted again. "Mister Nelson, if you had seen the number of hours Lord Micah has spent pouring over my records and books, scrutinizing every detail, you would not be so quick to speak of trust."

Micah grinned and clapped Duvey on the shoulder companionably. "You know I trust you, old friend. Besides, you'd be offended if I didn't stick my nose in your business every now and again."

The Chancellor snorted a third time and shook his head, and Tommy felt like he was privy to some sort of private bond between the two men.

Micah turned back to Tommy. "So, you see, Nence and I are old friends. I even used to call him 'Nancy' as a joke," Micah whispered conspiratorially. "He knows I have no desire to take over his school, and I know he has no desire to take over mine. But there's always that lingering seed of doubt; the possibility that, if given too much of a chance, if there is too much of an opening, each of us might find the opportunity too great not to seize. So... we trust, but with caution. It is always this way, with powerful men." Then, with a wink, he added, "And please don't say a WORD to him about the Nancy thing. He wouldn't find it funny, coming from you, understand?"

Tommy nodded his understanding and pondered on Micah's words while he stared around at the city around him. He was still staring at the unusual buildings and cars when Chancellor Duvey and Micah stopped, and Tommy took a few more steps beyond them before he'd realized.

"Here we are," said Micah, gesturing to a small shop in front of them. It was obviously a coffee shop; if the picture of a steaming cup of coffee over the door didn't tip him off, Tommy would have recognized it anyway. It looked just like every other coffee shop he'd even seen, with large, plate–glass windows in the front, a large seating area with round tables and low chairs, and a broad counter with numerous brewing implements.

"Best coffee in Budapesht," Micah said, and with a sweeping gesture, he led the three of them inside.

CHAPTER
TWENTY-FIVE

The inside of the shop was shockingly warm after the brisk wind outside, and the air smelled overwhelmingly of roasting coffee beans. Micah took a deep breath as he stepped inside, and Tommy followed suit. Although he'd never developed a taste for the stuff, he still found the smell of coffee simply divine. If only it tasted as good as it smelled, instead of being bitter and acidic.

It was then that Tommy noticed the other occupants of the shop. Besides a young woman standing behind the counter, the only other people there were two men and a woman sitting around a single table. All three of the customers were garbed alike, in a set of robes so dark brown that they were almost black, unrelieved except for a small emblem sewn over the left breast. All three were middle-aged, with one of them clearly older than the others by at least a decade. All of them bore dour expressions that seemed to be fixed on their faces, like they had been so serious and so severe for so long that their faces had frozen in that position. The oldest of the three stood, and the other two immediately followed suit.

"Nence," Micah said, stepped forward and addressing the eldest of the three. Tommy could almost hear the implied 'Nancy' in Micah's words, and could it be that the older man's severe face tightened a bit more? Tommy had to work very hard to suppress a grin.

"Micah," the older man replied, the lack of any sort of title made somehow significant by the man's tone of voice. The two men stared sternly into one another eyes for several moments as the tension rose palpably in the air. Everyone seemed to be nervously glancing back and forth between the two men and each other, and Tommy noticed Chancellor Duvey's hand start to stray toward his belt. Just when it seemed that violence was about to erupt, Micah grinned and shook his head. "I never could beat you at being serious. You've got the look down pat."

Lord Nence smiled back, and with a collective sigh, everyone seemed to relax. "Come, enroll in the school, Micah. We'll teach you how to be serious. For once."

Micah chuckled at that. "I tried, once, remember? You turned me away."

Lord Nence shook his head. "You were not serious then, just like you aren't serious now. Someday your sense of humor will be the death of you, I swear it."

Micah spread his hands in a helpless gesture. "If there is a better way to die, I don't know of it."

"There are no good ways to die, my friend. There is only dead, and not-dead."

"Ah, that's where you and I disagree. The 'how' is almost as important as the 'why'. You'll figure it out, some day. When you are older."

Lord Nence made a small, annoyed noise at that, and Tommy could see why – the man was clearly older than Micah, quite possibly old enough to be his father.

"Are we here to banter all day, or shall we make good on our agreement?" Lord Nence replied, clearly tired of the reparte'.

Micah nodded, and Lord Nence began with introductions. "Allow me to present Katerine, the artificer from my school who will be coming with you, and Sir Duffington, my sergeant at arms." Each of them bowed deeply at the waist when introduced, so, as Micah introduced Tommy and the Chancellor, Tommy made sure to give his best bow, as well. Tommy got the impression that, by and large, the introductions were for his benefit. All of the adults seemed to already know one another.

After the introductions, Chancellor Duvey extended his hand to Katerine. "My lady, if you would please come with me?" The woman took the Chancellor's hand, and the two of them turned and left the shop without another word. Micah watched them leave, shaking his head.

"Always the charmer, Duvey." He murmured once the man was out of earshot.

"He would be mortified to hear you say it." Lord Nence quipped, and Micah barked a laugh.

"True story," Micah added, and turned to Tommy. "Sir Duffington will be escorting you to the school. Obey his instructions as if they were mine, understand? Lord Nence and I have much to discuss. We will be waiting here for your return."

Tommy nodded his understanding, and Sir Duffington placed a hand on his shoulder, steering him toward the door. As they left, Micah called after him, "Don't forget everything I've taught you!" Tommy turned to reply that he wouldn't, but Micah and Lord Nence had stepped up to the counter and were placing their order, and Sir Duffington was holding the door open and looking expectantly at Tommy, so Tommy swallowed the words and stepped back out into the brisk Hungarian air.

Sir Duffington followed him out into the street but didn't speak; he merely gestured with an open hand down the street, and then started walking. Tommy was forced to follow the sergeant or stand there in front of the coffee shop looking foolish, so he followed, thinking that he'd been spending entirely too much time trotting after adults. After a couple hundred feet, the sergeant turned crisply on one heel and entered a narrow alleyway – Far too narrow for cars, yet still large enough that the two of them could walk abreast. A hundred feet down the alley, he stopped, nodded to Tommy, and extended his hand. Tommy took the man's rough, calloused hand, and felt the spinning, dizzying feeling that he'd come to recognize as them moving between two places.

As usual, it took Tommy a few moments of blinking rapidly and shaking his head to clear his vision and shake off a bit of vertigo. When his vision finally cleared, Tommy found himself in a small room. The floors and ceiling appeared to be wooden, but the walls looked like they were made of earth – not stone, like in his school, but compressed dirt, complete with bits of rock and such. As he steadied himself with a hand against the wall, Tommy found that they were cool to the touch and as smooth as glass. Despite that, the room looked for all the world like a coat room – there were wooden pegs set straight into the earthen walls, and a few of them had grey robes hanging on them. Still without speaking, Sir Duffington held up a single finger to Tommy, clearly asking him to wait one moment, and left the room. Although he was now alone, Tommy was somewhat glad; He was beginning to find Sir Duffington's refusal to speak eerie and somewhat unnerving.

However, no sooner had the door closed behind Sir Duffington then it opened again, and a young man much closer to Tommy's age stepped through. He was dressed in the same dark brown robes identical to everyone else Tommy had met from this school, but unlike everyone else, he quickly flashed Tommy a smile and extended his hand. "Hello, I'm Nick," the boy said through his grin.

Tommy took the boys hand and shook it, refreshed to find someone friendly. "I'm Tommy," he replied. "I think I'm here to teach a spell?"

Nick nodded. "Yes, so I've been told. I hope I'm allowed to sit in on the demonstration. I'm very interested to learn."

"I could show you now, if you wanted?"

Nick shook his head emphatically. "I'm not an instructor, so we can't channel magic, just you and me." He paused for a moment. "Didn't anyone explain the rules?"

"Oh, yes," Tommy flushed with embarrassment. He wasn't even here five minutes and already he'd messed up. "They told me, I just... I guess I just didn't think."

Nick grinned. "It's ok. We have a lot of rules, here, but... well, it's better than the alternative, isn't it?" Before Tommy could ponder the boy's strange comment, Nick began gathering one of the grey robes hanging on the wall.

"Here, you'll need to put this on and wear it during your stay. Just hang your outside clothes on a peg, you won't need them, and no one will bother them in here. Here, I think this robe will fit you. I'll step outside while you change."

With that, the boy opened the door and left, so Tommy began getting undressed. He considered the robe, and how much it would cover, and decided to leave his socks, shoes, and underwear on, but to shuck off his shirt and jeans. He paused briefly to consider the spell binder that Micah had given him. He always carried it in his pockets, and never let it out of his sight, but there didn't seem to be any pockets on the robe large enough to carry it. Reluctantly, he concluded that he'd have to leave it here. He'd feel less safe without the thing, but there really was no place to carry it, and Micah had been very emphatic about not letting other people see it. Not wanting it to be discovered, he rolled it up in his shirt, then stuffed the shirt down one of the legs of his jeans, and then hung the jeans on the peg. The robe was a bit dusty smelling when he put it on, and it felt almost like wearing a dress, but it wasn't particularly uncomfortable, so after a last check of himself, Tommy tapped on the door, took a deep breath, steeled himself, and stepped through.

CHAPTER
TWENTY-SIX

The hall that Tommy stepped into looked very similar to the room he had been in – heavy wooden ceilings and floors, walls made of the same compressed looking earth and polished to a glassy shine. Nick was standing there, next to the wall but not touching it, waiting for him. The other boy looked Tommy over, then nodded at what he saw; Tommy guessed that he was dressed acceptably.

"We're going to be walking down the center of the halls, because we're on a special assignment, okay? We don't want to interfere or get caught up in the normal class changes. Just be sure to make way if an instructor comes the other way, okay?"

Tommy nodded his acknowledgment, wondering what he'd got himself into, but he didn't have much time to wonder and Nick set off down the hallway at a brisk pace. Following, Tommy was quickly lost as the small, deserted hallways joined other corridors that were much larger, and much, much more crowded. The new hallways were wide enough that 3 people could easily walk abreast, and it was a good thing – groups of students of all ages in identical grey robes lined both the walls, each group walking in an ordered single file behind an adult in fancier robes. The center of the hallway was clear, and it was down this open pathway that Nick and Tommy walked.

"We're on a special errand, of course, and unescorted by an instructor, so we have to walk down the center, you see," Nick explained, glancing back over his shoulder at Tommy as they walked and evidently misinterpreting Tommy's confusion and uncertainty. "Just please remember that we have to step aside and let an instructor pass," Nick grinned. "I'm sure I don't need to tell YOU, of all people, not to get in the way of faculty."

Once again, Tommy furrowed his brow at the strange remark; the boy talked as if he should know something he certainly didn't. Sure, back at Micah's school, he might get out of someone's way if he was walking slowly, but it was just courtesy; Someone else might just as readily step around him. What kind of place was he in that they needed rules for *walking*?

Finally, after a good deal of walking – the school must be huge, almost as large as Micah's school – they came to a room designed like a small auditorium. There was a traditional-looking blackboard behind a table at one end of the room, and a set of risers on which long wooden desks sat in front of chairs arranged in groups, three to a desk. Each set of three desks was behind and about half a foot above the desks in front of it, so that the back row of desks and chairs, maybe 20 rows back, ended up being quite high above the base of the floor and the blackboard. As Nick ushered Tommy to the front of the room and then hurried out of the room, Tommy noticed that every single chair in the room was filled.

That left Tommy standing alone in front of what looked to be about two hundred people, all in identical, matching robes, all of them even with matching, or at least very similar, haircuts. And every single one of them sitting quietly and staring at Tommy. The effect was rather eerie – there was none of the soft conversation that Tommy would expect at his school, and everyone just sat silently and stared at him. Soon, Tommy began to fidget, shifting from one foot to the other and glancing around the room, anxious for someone to give him some sort of clue as to what he should be doing.

Finally, just when Tommy was about to clear his throat and ask the assemblage if he was supposed to be doing or saying something, an older man with slightly fancier robes swept into the room. The man dumped a sack full of small rocks that'd he'd been carrying onto the table, and Tommy gulped in apprehension – there were a LOT of rocks there, and if they intended Tommy to cast the spell that many times... well, he probably COULD do it, but he was certainly going to be tired by the end of it.

The older man then went on to explain to the assembled students about what they were about to witness today, and how the "esteemed visitor from the school of the august Archmage Micah" would be teaching them a new technique, and many other flowery words that basically amounted to, "Pay attention." After his speech, which droned on way longer than Tommy would have guess possible, he turned to Tommy and said simply, "Embrace."

Tommy frowned, unsure about the command. He thought it might mean that he should prepare to channel, but he also didn't want to commit a serious faux pas and embarrass himself and his school by doing something he was expressly forbidden to do. Micah, Chancellor Duvey, and Nick had all been very adamant about that. Tommy looked up at the older man, back to the class, and back again in confusion.

"Well?" the older man said impatiently. "Prepare to demonstrate!"

That, at least, was a command that Tommy could

understand, so, with a modicum of effort, he relaxed his mind and prepared to channel magical energy.

"Very good," the instructor said. "Now, demonstrate!"

Tommy cast the spell, being very thorough and deliberate with each of the steps – if he was going to teach them how to do this, he wanted to be sure to teach them right. He decided to start small, and selected a stone off the table. He... "spun" the stone, like wool on a spinning wheel – that was the only way he could think of to describe it – and stretched it out as he did so, eventually coaxing it into its final form, a small, thick ring, which he then laid back down on the table. There was some muttering among the students of the class, but the instructor slapped his hand down on the table and barked, "Silence!", cutting off the noise abruptly.

Turning to Tommy, the man said, "Yes, well done, except how is anyone supposed to follow that?" He stared at Tommy as if he honestly expected an answer to what seemed to be a rhetorical question. After several long moments, Tommy shrugged helplessly.

"No matter," the man finally continued. "Do it again. But this time, do it slowly. Step at a time. And please, explain what you are doing at every step, and why."

Tommy groaned inwardly. Casting a spell slowly was very, very difficult – it took a lot more energy and concentration to keep the entire thing from collapsing while you worked. Steeling himself, Tommy prepared, and began stepping through the spell one piece at a time, laboriously explaining what he was doing to the class.

CHAPTER
TWENTY-SEVEN

It was several hours later, several changes of the students in the class, and dozens of crafted rings later that the instructor finally told Tommy, "Well done, you may rest." Tommy slumped into a nearby chair, totally exhausted. He'd been making smaller and smaller rings as time went on, trying to conserve as much of his energy as he could, and he was glad that he'd decided to start with something small instead of trying to show off. There was a clock on the wall, and Tommy glanced at it – it felt like he'd been at this all day, without a break, but now he saw that it was lunch time and he'd barely been at it for a few hours.

"As our honored guest, you may go to the head of the line," the instructor said soothingly, and it took Tommy a moment to realize that the man was talking to him. The other students had already formed a line and were waiting to leave the classroom, with the instructor at the head of the line and a small gap behind him that was obviously for Tommy. "No rest for the weary, I guess," Tommy muttered to himself as he hoisted his body out of the chair and onto his feet. He couldn't help that his feet dragged a little as he joined the line.

"Right, off to lunch, then," the instructor barked, and set off with a steady stride. Tommy knew that the man had told him his name, but he couldn't remember it – there had been a different instructor with every class of students, and he'd long since stopped trying to remember everyone's names and titles. The line of students, with Tommy and the instructor at its head, flowed smoothly into the hallway where it joined other lines of other students. The almost clockwork precision of it all surprised and amazed Tommy, even as he found it slightly scary and intimidating – sure, it was impressive, but Tommy shuddered to think at the level of control and organization that went into such an arrangement. Still, it was rather efficient, he guessed, and this school seemed to be a lot more crowded than what he was accustomed to. They flowed through the hallways, sometimes pausing to let another group pass, sometimes moving on as another group let them pass, with no rhyme or reason that Tommy could discern on who went first. Finally, the group arrived at a room Tommy did recognize – a large kitchen and dining room. It was smaller and much more cramped than what he was used to, but it was still a dining hall, and Tommy found that he was ravenous.

The whole getting food process was much quicker and simpler than what Tommy was used to. There were no choices, no different options – he simply walked up to the kitchen counter and was handed a tray full of food, already put together, complete with a drink. It looked to be fairly simple fare – slices of chicken covered with some sort of sauce, cooked carrots, a scoop of macaroni and cheese, a tiny slice of pecan pie for dessert, and a small glass of milk and a larger one of water to drink. Tommy frowned at the tray but didn't have any time to voice any objection – he was quickly swept aside by the tide of other students waiting to gather their trays.

The seating was as methodical as everything else in the school. The students all took seats in order, each student in line grabbing the next available seat, with no space empty or wasted; Nothing at all like the random and diverse clumps of students that Tommy was accustomed to. There was another difference, too – although the room was filled with the low hum of soft conversation, it was quiet and muted; Nothing like the sometimes loud and boisterous noise that he was used to during mealtimes. Tommy took his seat, feeling cramped and crowded. His elbows brushed up against his neighbors on either side, and it was rather uncomfortable, but Tommy was hungry enough that he didn't care. He sat down and began to eat.

"Psssst. Hey, 'honored guest'," a boy across the table hissed to Tommy in a loud whisper. When Tommy looked up, the boy continued. "Yeah, you. Hey, what's it like at your school?"

Tommy couldn't quite decide how to answer. The question was so broad, and he'd been warned not to share any information about his school. Still, he felt that the questioner deserved some sort of answer, especially since it was the first time anyone had bothered to speak to him about anything other than the business at hand. His first instinct was to reply that his school was so much nicer and better than this one, but he instantly discarded that idea – it would be very rude to come to the school and speak poorly of it. After a few moments of stammering, Tommy finally came up with, "Well... it's... very different."

A young woman a few seats down from Tommy chimed in. "I heard that they make everyone learn how to use a sword at his school."

Tommy was a little surprised at that. "Well, yes," he agreed. "Just as a method of self defense, in case that you are ever not able to use..."

The woman didn't give him time to finish. In fact, she seemed horrified as she broke in with, "I don't think I could handle that, having to use a sword. Who wants to learn that, anyway?"

Tommy frowned. "You don't learn how to use a sword, here?"

"Only as an elective, of course," the original boy that had called for Tommy's attention chimed in. "But almost nobody takes it. Why bother with a stupid sword, anyway?" The other students at the table muttered their agreement, and Tommy kept his mouth shut. He didn't really want to try arguing against so many people who had clearly already made up their mind.

A silence that was decidedly uncomfortable for Tommy stretched for several long moments before another boy across the table finally broke it. "I heard that they make you refine energy for the school's use, in order to pay your way, and that they won't give you food or clothes if you don't do it."

The young woman who expressed such disdain for the sword slapped the boy on the shoulder. "You know that's just nonsense. Why are you talking such garbage in front of our guest?"

Tommy shook his head, though. "No, it's true, kind of." An audible gasp went around the table, and the boy who had mentioned it looked smug. Tommy went on, "You don't have to channel to get food, of course, but we do channel to help pay for our classes and instruction. It's a good thing, it helps us stretch our 'magical muscles' and get stronger. I know I've gotten much stronger since I started doing it. Just like learning the sword, it's good exercise."

Everyone around him seemed stunned into silence, and Tommy didn't know what else to say. Finally, another girl from much farther down the table chimed in in a hoarse whisper. "I heard that it's pure chaos there, no organization at all. Someone told me that they don't even take you from class to class, that you have to get there on your own, and that you get in a lot of trouble if you are late."

Again, Tommy was baffled. He could never recall getting in trouble for being late for a class... but then, he could also never recall actually being late for a class. He couldn't imagine Micah actually getting upset over something like that, but... it was a two minute walk from class to class, and even counting a trip to the bathroom and a stop back at his room to change clothes, he'd still never felt rushed or pressed for time when changing classes. All he could say was, "Well, yeah, but it's not a bad thing, it's..."

He was cut off by a sharp "Hsssst!" sound from down near the end of the table. The instructor that had escorted them there was staring down at their end of the table, specifically at Tommy, and glowering. Tommy cast his eyes down and quieted, realizing that he'd spoken out loud instead of whispering. He felt his face flushing bright red in embarrassment, and everyone in the area began studying their food in earnest. After several long moments, Tommy saw the instructor sit back down out of the corner of his eye, and he relaxed just a little.

"I... I'm so sorry," said the boy who had originally spoken to Tommy. "I didn't know. I didn't meant to embarrass you." A young girl sitting next to Tommy actually patted him comfortingly on the back, her eyes full of sadness and pity.

"No, it's okay, really," Tommy whispered back. "I love it there. It's... challenging. I've grown up a ton."

The other students merely shook their heads in bewilderment and commiseration, which was not the reaction that Tommy expected. He didn't know how to explain to them, to make them understand. He wanted to stand up and shout at them, to tell them that they were being oppressed, here. That things would be better if they were free, if they could rely on themselves. Did they think they were going to spend their entire lives in the shelter of this school? What would they do when they were done, when they had to go out into the real world, where no one was going to hold their hands and escort them everywhere they needed to be? Their entire lives were being lived for them, every action scripted and every moment controlled, and Tommy could only feel sorry for them. But he couldn't think of a way to make them see that they were basically prisoners, here, so he kept his mouth shut and ate the rest of the meal in silence, trying not to notice the occasional sympathetic stare directed his way by the other students.

After lunch, another instructor came and escorted Tommy to another classroom, while his lunch mates went off to another class with their instructor. Arriving at the classroom, Tommy saw that it was full of adults instead of children, all of them in the fancier robes that Tommy had come to understand denoted an instructor. The routine, however, was the same; the same commands, the same demonstrations. The class of instructors, however, studied Tommy like he was some sort of interesting insect, and after he was done demonstrating the spell a few times, the questions began.

"What made you think to twist the Water energy on the third motion?" asked a scholarly looking older woman, her thick glasses perched on the very end of her nose.

"Well... I don't really know," replied Tommy. "I guess I thought that, since I needed to change the shape of the stone, I'd need water. Kind of like turning dirt into mud, I guess."

That was clearly not the right answer; The woman snorted in derision and said, "Mud! Mud indeed."

Tommy was given no reprieve, however. A younger instructor, who looked barely old enough to have graduated high school, asked, "Why did you decide to change the stone's form entirely? It looks like you were almost... spinning it. Like wool on a spinning wheel. Why not just drop away all the pieces of the stone that you didn't need? That's the traditional way it's done." Several other instructors in the room nodded in agreement.

"Well, ummm..." Tommy began, feeling like the room was growing hostile. "I wanted it to be very smooth, you know? Like polished metal would be. So I could make stone jewelry for people. I think if I did it your way, it would be very rough, wouldn't it?"

The young man snorted as well. Tommy was beginning to think these people all had nasal problems. "We'll ask the questions around here, thank you very much. Your way may be smoother, but dropping the extra stone away is *how it is done,*" the emphasis on the last four words seemed to indicate to Tommy like it was some sort of immutable rule.

The questions went on and on for quite some time. Some of them seemed to stem from genuine interest in Tommy's spell – Tommy found himself discoursing back and forth with an elderly gentleman for quite some time on the specific mechanics of the spell, and the man's questions gave Tommy some ideas about how he could change the spell, perhaps to make much larger objects. Other questions were less friendly, however – there were a lot of questions that began with "What were you thinking?", and usually centered around Tommy's gross breach of tradition, rules, or protocol.

It felt like several hours passed before the barrage of questions and criticism was interrupted by a knock at the door; it was the student Nick who had escorted Tommy previously. All eyes in the classroom turned to regard the newcomer, but Nick didn't seem fazed at all. He simply bowed and said, "Beg your pardon, Great Masters, but I've been sent to fetch your guest. It is time for him to return." There was a good deal of muttering and grumbling in the room, but Tommy felt like a rag run repeatedly through a wringer, and the words were like salvation to him. Tommy turned to leave but was stopped short when one of the instructors cleared his throat quite loudly, giving him pause. As a group, the entire assemblage rose and bowed slightly at the waist to Tommy. The man who had cleared his throat intoned, "We thank you for your instruction, honored guest. Depart as you came, in peace."

Not knowing what to say, but feeling like he should probably say something, Tommy bowed back and gave his best formal reply. "Thank you, It was my pleasure."

It seemed to be enough to satisfy the group, because they left their places and began to form small groups, speaking softly to one another, and Nick motioned for Tommy to join him. Gratefully, Tommy did so. "Come on," Nick said hurriedly, "We have to go."

"Let's do it," Tommy replied gratefully, and they were off.

CHAPTER
TWENTY-EIGHT

Nick led Tommy through more hallways that were all the same pressed-looking dirt and polished to a bright sheen. They could have been the same hallways that they'd gone through before, or perhaps they were different; Tommy still couldn't tell one from another. Nick kept glancing back at Tommy as they walked, and after the fourth or fifth time, it started to make Tommy nervous.

"What? What's wrong?" he finally asked.

Nick stopped walking and looked abashed. "I'm sorry. It's just that I talked to Nancy a little bit - she sat near you at lunch. She told me some things about your school. You must really be dreading going back, after seeing how things work here."

Tommy couldn't stop himself from barking a laugh at that. "No, Nick, it's... it's really good, at my school. It's... free. I wouldn't leave for anything."

Nick stared at Tommy for a long moment before shaking his head, shrugging, and setting off down the hallway again. "It just seems so... hard. Stressful. How do you deal with it?"

Tommy didn't know how to answer. It was clear Nick couldn't understand, so he just shook his head and kept walking. Finally, with no further words spoken, they arrived at the door to the cloak room where Tommy had changed earlier. Standing next to the door was the instructor that had escorted Tommy and the class to lunch, an anxious, furtive look on his face. As they approached, the man spoke.

"Mister... Thomas, is it?" he asked, and then continued without waiting for a response. "A brief word, if you please?"

Nick bowed to the man. "Beg pardon, Great Master, but Master Duffington is waiting for us. We need to hurry."

The instructor scoffed. "The mute can wait. I'll only be a moment. Mister Thomas?"

Tommy shrugged and joined the man, who guided him a dozen steps down the hallway – not far, but enough that Nick would no longer be able to hear them if they whispered, which is exactly what the man did.

"You are quite the impressive young man," he began. "You could do very well under our instruction. You know that our founder is the greatest earth mage who has ever lived, right?"

Tommy nodded that he knew that; He remembered hearing something about that before. The instructor continued to whisper, while looking around furtively as if to ensure that no one would see them speaking. "You've seen our school, you've seen how well our students are treated, and how well organized we are. You would do very well here, indeed."

Tommy shook his head. "Thank you, sir, but no thank you. I'm happy at my school."

The older man made a 'tsk' sound. "No one is asking you to decide right now, of course. I'm sure you are probably anxious to get back to a more familiar place, right now, tired as you are. I... er, we, that is, we just wanted to let you know that you are welcome here, and that a young man of your potential always has options. We would even make special consideration based on your previous training." He looked around one more time before grabbing Tommy's hand and pressing an object into it. Tommy looked down at the object. It was a small, chipped marble stone with a single exotic rune carved in one side. He studied it a moment before turning a puzzled gaze back to the instructor.

"Just give it power – fill it with magic, as you would say – and it will call to us, and we will come get you. Someone will hear your call, and we will come save you." The man closed Tommy's fist around the stone. "Just hold onto it and... think about it, okay?"

With that, the instructor turned on his heel and strode confidently down the hall, as if he'd not just been whispering and acting sneakily. Tommy watch him go, almost too stunned to react. Why, he wondered, could these people not see that he was happy with his school? A tug at his sleeve jerked him out of his thoughts; It was the boy Nick.

"We really need to go. Please. Master Duffington is waiting, and he is not a patient master. You're going to get me in a lot of trouble!"

Tommy nodded and headed into the cloak room. His clothes were hanging right where he left them, and he dressed hurriedly. He was pleased to see that the spellbinder was still where he left it, rolled into his shirt and tucked into his jeans, and he quickly shucked the robe and began dressing as fast as he could. The last thing he wanted was to be responsible for getting Nick in trouble, especially after the boy was at least passing nice to him. After dressing, he stuffed the spellbinder into one pocket, and, after a moment's thought, put the rune-carved stone in another. He didn't know if the two magical objects could affect each other by rubbing together in his pockets, but he didn't want to take a chance; when he was much younger, he'd put a match and a stone together in one of his pockets, and he'd gotten quite an unpleasant surprise when the match had suddenly lit itself in his pocket. He didn't know if magic worked like that, but he was smart enough to admit to himself that he shouldn't take pointless chances with things he really didn't understand.

Emerging from the room, Nick led him off at a pace that had him jogging to keep up, and in short order they were almost running head-first into Sir Duffington, who was coming the other way in the hallway, evidently looking for them. The silent man pointed to Nick and made a gesture of dismissal, then pointed to Tommy, gestured for him to follow, and turned and began walking without bothering to see if Tommy was following. Tommy hurried after him, not wanting to be abandoned, get lost in these identical hallways, and miss his only chance at a ride out of here. The sergeant made an abrupt turn into a room, grabbed Tommy's arm when he followed, and suddenly Tommy found himself back in the dingy alley in Budapesht. A few moments later and he was back in the coffee shop, where Micah and Lord Nence were just shaking hands and preparing to depart.

Micah turned to smile at Tommy and gestured toward the door. "I'll be you are tired, and that you would enjoy finding your bed, eh Tommy?" Micah grinned. Tommy found himself both refreshed and comforted by the man's manner, and he grinned back. Tommy nodded, and Micah said, "Then let's go home."

As they left the shop and began walking down the street, Chancellor Duvey in the lead and Tommy walking a few paces behind him with Micah, the archmage turned his head to look at Tommy.

"So... what did you think about Lord Nence's school?"

Tommy didn't really know where to begin. "It's... okay, I guess," was all he could reply as he tried to organize his thoughts.

"What did they offer you to go join them?" Tommy jumped, and Micah laughed at his surprise. "You didn't think I'd know that they'd try to recruit you? They'd have been stupid not to. So, what did they offer you?"

"Ummm... they said they'd give me 'special consideration'. Is that an offer?"

Micah laughed again. "I'm sure Lord Nence thinks so. So, are you considering their offer? I won't stop you if you want to go, of course. You are free to leave at any time."

"What? NO!" Tommy was emphatic, shaking his head violently. Micah opened his mouth to speak, but Tommy spoke right over top of him. "I... I hated every single thing about the school! It was awful! I just said it was okay because I didn't know what else to say. I don't know how those people live like that!" Tommy ran down as he realized that he was speaking very loudly, and Chancellor Duvey was glaring daggers at him over his shoulder.

Micah, however, was chuckling. "People can get used to anything, Tommy. But more importantly, turning over control to someone else is the hardest thing to do, and the easiest thing to get accustomed to. Think about it. You have to get yourself up in the morning, get yourself showered, eat breakfast, and make sure you are at your first class on time. How easy would it be to have all of that laid out for you? To just follow the program like a robot? Of course, it comes with a downside, as you saw. Turning over control means turning over your freedom. It also means no opportunity to succeed."

Tommy considered that. "The man who spoke to me said that I'd do very well in his school."

"I'll bet he did. But what he meant was that he thought you'd fit into their mold. You see, Lord Nence is terrified of success. I've told you that powerful men are always afraid of losing their power. Nence lives in constant fear that one of his students will outstrip him. That's why all his students progress at the same rate. No one stands out. There are no superstars, there are no failures."

"That's.... terrible," was all Tommy could say.

"To people like you and me, it is. You have the will, the drive to be something more. But to people who lack the drive to be something more, it's comforting. It means they never have to try hard, they never have to work for anything, they just coast through life, expecting everything to be handled for them."

Tommy stopped walking for a moment as he considered that. They'd come to the alley that they had arrived in, and Chancellor Duvey turned and walked into it, with Micah a few steps behind him. Tommy stuck his hand into his pocket and dug out the rune carved stone that the man had given him. He regarded it for a long moment, and finally dropped it down into a sewer grate before turning and following Micah into the alley.

CHAPTER
TWENTY-NINE

When he'd returned home, it was still fairly early, and James, Ryan, and Sam had a ton of questions for him. Tommy was too exhausted, however. He was even too tired to go to dinner, he just went to his room, laid a soft, dry towel over his eyes, and went straight to sleep.

He awoke the next morning to the sounds of his roommates scurrying around. "What's going on?" Tommy asked, sitting up and taking the towel off his head. Glancing at the clock, he realized that he'd slept without moving for almost 14 hours and was feeling a little muddle-headed for it.

"It's testing day!" Sam exclaimed excitedly, bouncing up and down on his bed with an apple in his hand. "They brought us breakfast and told us we can't leave the room. We're all to be tested!"

Tommy leaned back against the wall while sitting on his bed and groaned. "Why'd they have to pick today?"

Ryan simply laughed and tossed him an orange from a tray. "You'll be fine, Tommy boy. You know you'll do great.

Besides, you just slept half a day. Must have needed your beauty rest. Looks like he could probably use a little more, eh, James?" he quipped, nudging the bigger boy with his elbow.

James, however, didn't laugh. Instead, he looked very pale, almost sickly. "I don't know. I... I think I need more time to prepare."

"Prepare?" Ryan scoffed. "How could you possibly prepare anymore? You've done the lessons just like the rest of us!"

"I just... I need... I... *urk*", James exclaimed, gaining a decidedly green pallor and dashing for the door. He ripped it open and plowed out, ignoring the protests of the older student outside. As the door slammed behind him, Tommy and Ryan met each other's eyes for a moment, and then began to laugh.

"He's got stage fright!" Ryan exclaimed, laughing all the harder.

Suddenly, Tommy recalled what Micah had told him about Lord Kalish's suspicions, and his laughter cut off abruptly. What if James was feeling sick because he'd been using dark magic? Or worse, what if the "preparations" he needed to make were some sort of evil ritual, or some other black spell that would increase his power and allow him to cheat enough to pass the tests?

Ryan noticed Tommy's silence, and his laughed trailed off, as well.

"It's not as bad as all that, is it?" Sam asked from where he sat on his bed.

Tommy was shaking his head. "Nah, it's really just..."

"We can't say anything about it!" Ryan interjected loudly over top of Tommy. Favoring Tommy with a significant glance, he said again, "We are sworn to say nothing about it, *remember?*"

Tommy did remember, and flushed scarlet at his near mistake. Sometimes Tommy felt like he was the worst person in the world for keeping secrets. He just wanted to be helpful to his friends! He didn't get very much time to be embarrassed, however – there was a knock at the door, and two older students entered and told Tommy and Sam that it was their turn to test. Ryan favored him with a encouraging smile as Tommy got to his feet, stretched, sighed, and followed the older student out the door. He'd only been awake for a few minutes, he hadn't had time to eat any breakfast, and he wasn't feeling very ready for this, but it was his turn and he certainly wasn't about give up without at least trying.

As he followed the older student, they passed James going the other way, obviously returning from the bathroom. James looked... better. His color was back, although his eyes still looked somewhat sunken and red-rimmed. He carried himself taller, not slumped over like he had been in the room, and as they passed, James reached out and gave Tommy a friendly punch on the arm. "Knock em' dead, Tom-Tom."

That puzzled Tommy and left him frowning. James had never called him Tom-Tom before, and the punch on the arm was a little bit hard. Tommy wondered again what was going on with James, and what truth there may be the suspicions that he was using dark magic. He certainly LOOKED better prepared for having gone to the bathroom, but could he have had time to cast a spell in there? Or, was it simply that voiding the contents of his stomach had refreshed him and brought him back into balance?

"Come on, hurry up!" the student that Tommy was

following hissed at him. Startled, Tommy realized that the older boy was now two-dozen steps ahead of him, and he hastened his pace to catch up.

The two of them wound their way through the extensive halls of the school. It reminded Tommy greatly of the following he'd done in the other school just yesterday, and he wondered if this was going to become a common thing for him, following another student down hallways. The difference, Tommy reflected, was that this felt like home. Although the grey walls were somewhat less interesting to look at than the pressed earth of the other school, the hallways were more spacious, less crowded, and, most importantly, felt more... free.

Finally, they came to a door, which his guide opened and beckoned for Tommy to enter. The room beyond was identical to the previous testing room he'd been in; dimly lit, with the only furnishing being a table in the center of the room and a darkened hallway stretching off opposite of the door they'd entered through.

"I assume you are familiar with the testing process?" his guide asked tersely.

Tommy nodded. "I passed the last test."

His guide simply nodded and gestured to the table in the center of the room, where a darkened lantern sat. "I assume you know what to do, then?"

Tommy wondered If the test was going to be the same as the last one, but he was confident that he knew what to do, so he answered, "Yeah, I got it."

The other boy nodded, turned, and vanished back through the doorway through which they'd come. After he'd gone, Tommy approached the table and picked up the lantern. He channeled energy into it, like he had before, and... nothing happened. Puzzled, Tommy turned the thing over in his hands, examining it. It looked to be the same as the one he'd used previously, for the last test, but when he tried to power it, it was almost as if there was no spell there to power; nothing absorbed the energy.

He cast the short spell to enchant his vision and allow him to see magical energies and looked the thing over again. As before, there seemed to be no spell or magical energy within the thing at all; it was an inert piece of metal. As he turned it over and over in his hands, studying it, Tommy happened to look at the bottom of the lantern, and there he found a series of markings – triangles, lines, and other glyphs that were clearly the directions for a spell. Grinning, Tommy realized that he could cast the spell without any difficulty, and once he did so, the lamp began to glow with a bright and steady light.

Pleased with himself, Tommy set off down the hallway.

The rest of the test was almost identical to the previous test, except that, at every gate and barrier, there was etched into the stone a series of markings that instructed Tommy on the spell that was to be cast to open the gate. One of them was a spell that pushed on the stone and opened the gate, another one made a loud clapping noise that startled Tommy even as it opened the passage, and another one shot, much to Tommy's surprise, a small arc of electricity that struck the stone and allowed the gate to open. That last one, Tommy reflected, might be useful someday, and he spent a little bit of time studying and memorizing the glyphs and the spell they formed, until he was sure he could reproduce it at will.

As he reached the end of the hallway, he came to the flat stone wall as before. Etched onto the wall were instructions for four different spells, and Tommy found it very tricky indeed to cast and maintain four different spells at once, but he managed it without too much difficulty, and the wall faded away and opened once again on the large open chamber that looked like a throne room. As with before, seated at the head of the room, lounging in an oversized throne, was Micah.

CHAPTER THIRTY

"Tommy!" Micah exclaimed, sitting up slightly in his chair so that he was in a more alert, less relaxed looking position.

Tommy approached, crossing the room while being sure to give wide berth to the open well with its endless sky and clouds below, which, Tommy noted to himself, Micah had apologized for before, but hadn't changed, either.

"Tommy!" Micah said, surprise and pleasure evident in his voice. "You made it! I didn't expect you so soon, given what you went through yesterday."

Tommy wanted to ask a question but didn't want to risk offending his mentor – the one person who seemed genuinely concerned for his welfare. He paused and bit his lip for a moment.

Micah noticed his obvious hesitation. "What is it, Tommy? You can tell me anything, you know that."

Taking a deep breath and steeling himself, Tommy asked, "Did you do it on purpose?"

Micah blinked confusedly for a moment before understanding dawned. Then, he laughed and said, "You mean, did I deliberately schedule you for the test first thing in the morning the day after you had an exhausting trial?"

Tommy could only nod; maybe he should have kept his mouth shut.

"Of course I did it on purpose. I've been watching your progress, along with the rest of your classmates, every single day now. I knew you could pass the test, but I wanted to see how difficult it would be for you if you weren't in an ideal frame of mine. Now, my question back to you – did YOU know you could pass the test while tired?"

Tommy thought about that for a moment. "No," he said finally, "I was really scared when they called me first. I don't want to fail. But it was actually fairly easy."

Micah nodded knowingly and shifted in his chair. "You have a great deal of talent, Tommy. I hope to someday be able to teach you just how much. In the meantime, consider this a lesson – you can do far more than you think you can, if only you put your mind to it. If your will is sufficient, there is no barrier you cannot overcome. And not just due to your talent, either, although that does certainly make it easier. Any person on this earth, with enough willpower, can achieve whatever they want to."

Tommy frowned in thought. "Not anything. I mean, I couldn't... say, move a mountain, no matter how much I wanted to."

"Couldn't you?" asked Micah. "If you had enough willpower, I bet you could. You could earn money to hire people and trucks to move it for you. Or you could just spend your entire life moving it one shovel at a time. Sure, you wouldn't be able to do anything else with your life, but that's not the question. The question is willpower. The only reason you can't move a mountain is you lack enough willpower to do it."

Tommy felt himself bristling slightly with umbrage. It wasn't very comfortable to hear that he lacked the willpower to do something. No matter what Micah said, Tommy felt, some things were impossible. Like... like flying to the moon. Although, Tommy thought, that was a bad example, because if he really wanted to, he could probably find some way to become an astronaut. But... well, surely there were impossible things out there. Tommy just couldn't think of any right now. In any case, what did it matter? He didn't WANT to move a mountain, anyway.

Perhaps Micah sensed Tommy's thoughts, or perhaps it was just that the silence had stretched between them for several moments, but the older man continued with a non-sequitur.

"So, how was your time in Lord Nence's school, other than terrifying? Do you think it was valuable?"

Tommy shook his head vigorously. "I must have demonstrated the spell a hundred times. Two hundred. The students watched me out of obligation, I think, but they seemed more interested in talking about how sad it was that I had to go to such a terrible and difficult school." Micah was chuckling as Tommy continued. "When I did the demonstration for the instructors, they all seemed to want to scold me for doing it wrong, or almost demand that I stop breaking tradition. None of them seemed to want to learn. What's so funny?" Tommy concluded as Micah's laughter intensified.

"I could have told you all of that," Micah replied, still chuckling. "You see, Tommy, you don't get that level of control and governance without a corresponding level of rigidity. Like I told you yesterday, Nence doesn't encourage independent thought. Anything that is new or different is a threat to his established order. Why, I would guess that in a month or two, most of the students and faculty there will have forgotten that you were ever even there... and those that haven't will be trying to figure out how to do what you did by using the same techniques they've always used. And, of course, they will fail. You can't bake a cake using a pie recipe, after all."

"But... then why do it? Why make the trade? Why put me through all that? Was it all just another test?"

"Certainly not! Nence never would have parted with the knowledge of his discovery without feeling he was gaining an equal trade." Micah grinned, and there was a sparkle in his eyes. "But you know me. You know I would never make an even trade. We gave Nence something he will never use. He gave us something we will absolutely use. So, we come out ahead, you got some valuable experience, and I got to spend a day drinking coffee. Everyone wins!"

Something occurred to Tommy. "Hey, do I get to learn the spell we traded for?"

Micah studied Tommy for a second, as if evaluating him in some fashion. "Of course you get to learn it," he finally said. "But not now, I think. It's a difficult spell and it is a bit outside of your capabilities right now. Besides," he continued with a grin, "You are going to have your hands full for the next couple weeks."

"Why?" Tommy asked. "What's next?"

"Combat training, Tommy," Micah replied with a smile. "Introduction to combat training."

CHAPTER
THIRTY-ONE

Tommy practically skipped back to his room, full of nervous excitement. Combat training! He'd been wondering what it entailed since Mae and Stephen said they were learning so long ago. He was also pleased to be advancing so quickly. Stephen had been at the school for a long time before Tommy came – he'd had well over a year head start on Tommy, and here Tommy was, less than a full year into his stay and already beginning combat training. Plus, Mae and Stephen had moved rooms and dining facilities, so that Tommy hardly ever saw them anymore. He was looking forward to moving up himself, so he could have meals with Mae again. He missed her desperately.

When he got back to his room, no one else was there. Ryan and James must both have gone off to their tests, as well. Tommy hoped they were both doing well. Although he'd originally been at odds with Ryan and had felt a companionship with James (despite his wearing that stupid "Canadian bacon" T-shirt that Tommy hated so), recently things had shifted. James had become sullen and withdrawn and had a bit of a tendency to lash out at his roommates, where Ryan had become more relaxed and friendly. Sure, Ryan still had a bit of an acerbic wit from time to time, but these days he was just as likely to use self-deprecating humor as he was to make a joke at someone else's expense.

What was in the room, when Tommy returned, was a fresh tray of hot foot, covered with a large towel to keep it warm. The smell coming from underneath the towel was wonderful, and as Tommy felt his mouth salivating and his stomach growling, he was reminded that he'd skipped dinner the night before and had only had an orange for breakfast. Pulling back the cover, Tommy found slices of roast beef in gravy. It was leftovers from last night's dinner, but it smelled divine. To go with the roast beef was a massive bowl of fried peas. Tommy had never enjoyed eating peas – he found the taste and consistency difficult to choke down. However, the kitchen here took the peas, and, instead of boiling them, they fried them in a little bit of butter until they were just a tiny bit crispy. The results was extremely toothsome and downright tasty with a little bit of salt, and Tommy spooned himself up a generous portion, along with a couple slices of the beef.

He had just finished wolfing down his food and was settling back on his bed to relax when the door opened, and Sam entered the room. The younger boy looked a little tired and pinched around the eyes, but he had a huge grin on his face.

"I did it! I passed!" he cried to Tommy as he entered the room.

"Way to go! I knew you could do it." Tommy replied and gave him a high five. It was clear the younger boy had struggled with the test, and Tommy wanted to give him all the encouragement that he could.

"Oooh, is that fried peas? I'm starving," Sam said, moving over to inspect the tray, and leaving Tommy to settle back on his bed and wait. He wished Micah had shown him the enchantment spell that they'd traded his stone-working spell for; he would have liked to sit and practice it. He briefly considered practicing the electricity arc spell that he'd learned during the test, but with Sam there, he didn't dare; they were strictly forbidden from sharing information about the tests, and Tommy was sure that teaching someone a spell they would need to cast would fall under information sharing. Besides, he'd already almost committed that faux pas once today, he didn't want to chance it again.

A few minutes later, Ryan returned to the room, a triumphant smile on his face. "Easy as pie!" he exclaimed as he sat down on his bunk.

For the next several hours, Tommy and Ryan sat and talked about combat training, and what they thought they'd learn in the coming days. Both boys were rather excited about the prospect. It was quite some time later that James came in and plunked face-first onto his bed. Ryan and Tommy shared a worried look.

"James...?" Ryan ventured.

When James didn't respond, Tommy tried. "James... Did you pass?"

Several moments passed by, and Tommy shared another look with Ryan and was about to ask again when James finally spoke.

"Passed it. Took everything I had."

"Alright!" cried Tommy, pleased that his friend hadn't failed like he feared. "That means we all get to move on to combat training!"

"Combat training." James muttered into his pillow. "All I need. Lemme sleep, I'm tired," and with that he rolled over and pulled the covers up over his face.

Tommy looked at Ryan, who gave an exaggerated shrug, rolled his eyes, and then pantomimed a grumpy face. Tommy and Sam snickered at his display, but Ryan's antics were interrupted as an older student stuck his head in the room and told them that the testing was over, and they were once again free to move about the school. Immediately the three boys set off for the dining hall; they'd just eaten a few hours ago, but food already sounded like a good idea.

The dining hall was a diverse mix of celebration and commiseration. Several students sat alone, heads down, and barely picked at their foods. Watching them, Tommy reflected that they must have failed their tests. He knew that he wouldn't want company if he'd just failed; he would want to be alone with his misery for just a little while. As they sat down, Mary bounced up to the table. "I did it," she grinned at Tommy. "I passed the test this time! I'll be joining your class, now, Tommy!"

Tommy was about to congratulate her when Ryan scoffed. "Pfffft. I don't even know how you could fail that test even once. It was, like, the easiest test ever. You'd have to be stupid not to be able to pass it."

Mary cast a dark glare at Ryan. "It wasn't easy for me," she retorted. "That last part. Doing..." she gave a significant look to Sam before continuing "Doing all those things at once. I just couldn't keep track of them all, the first time. It felt like trying to juggle a half dozen balls. Nothing had prepared me for that."

"Bah," replied Ryan, "I still think that..."

"No, the problem is that you DON'T think at all, RYAN," Mary broke in, putting considerable acid on the pronunciation of the name. In a much nicer, almost sweet tone, she continued, "See you later, Tommy, Sam." With that, she turned and flounced out of the room.

Tommy watched her go for a moment, then turned to Ryan, shaking his head. "Man, you give me grief and say I'm flirting with them, but you will NEVER get a girlfriend like that."

Chapter Thirty-Two

Of all the things Tommy expected when he'd heard they were to begin Combat Training class, what he didn't expect was an extremely long and boring lecture from Micah on the dangers of trying spells out on one's fellow students, even willingly. Of course, Tommy would never try to actually harm his friends, that was just ridiculous. But then, he wondered, how they would actually get to practice the spells they'd be learning.

"We will give you ample time to practice the spells you will be learning in a facility in the school designed for just that purpose, once I decide that you are ready." Micah concluded.

"Oh," thought Tommy. "I guess that answers that question."

"Before you can learn how to attack, however," Micah continued, perking Tommy's interest. "You must learn how to defend yourself, and there are two ways to defend yourself. The first, and best, of these ways is to counter an opponent's spell before it even gets cast, or before it takes effect on you. You can do this several ways – either by casting the exact same spell as your opponent, but in reverse – Replace fire magic with water, earth with air, and so on, and when the two spells meet, the energies will cancel one another out. Another good way to stop an opponent's spell is to simply block it. Create a barrier of some sort between you that the spell will impact upon instead of yourself. Yet another way is to disrupt your opponent's concentration while he is casting the spell; even a small injury, a tickling or itching sensation, some dust in the eyes or in the nose, or a noise in your enemy's ears can cause him to lose focus and either delay the casting of his spell, or cause him to fumble it completely." Here,

Micah paused significantly, as he often did, and looked around the room for a long moment before continuing.

"But let's assume for the moment that all that is past us, it is now too late to disrupt your opponent. A bullet, a knife, or a deadly spell is already on its way to you, and you no longer have the time to cast any sort of spell to stop it. What do you do, then? The answer to this is a structured sheath of magical energy that stops or deflects attacks away from your body. Other schools will call it a barrier, or a protective field, or any other number of names. Here, we simply call it a shield. At first, you will likely find it very difficult to maintain a shield. You will have to keep it well away from your body, or you might run into it yourself – last year, we had a student who jumped into the air, hit his head on his own shield, and knocked himself unconscious," Micah said with a grin, and the entire class laughed.

After the laughter died down, he continued. "But with time, you'll be able to bring the shield closer to your own body, so that it moves with you. You'll also be able to keep the shield up all the time, with hardly any thought for it at all. This is extremely important. *Extremely* important. Because in our line of work, being what we are and who we are, you never know when shocking things are going to happen unexpectedly."

No sooner had Micah finished speaking than Tommy caught a flicker of motion out of the corner of his eye. A scruffy man with an unkempt beard and filthy, ragged clothes had stepped through the door to the room. His eyes wild, the scruffy man drew a pistol from his pocket and began to raise it, aiming it at Micah.

"No!" Tommy shouted, standing up. Some of his classmates had their eye on the scruffy man, but those who hadn't noticed the man yet had turned to look at Tommy due to his outburst.

Tommy began channeling magical energy as fast as he could. Remembering the electrical bolt spell from the testing the previous day, Tommy hurriedly tried to pull it together... And, in his haste and panic, completely fumbled the thing, causing it to fall apart without effect. He was too slow anyway, though, because before he could complete the spell, there was the tremendous clap of a large handgun firing indoors. Several of the students either hit the floor or fell out of their chairs in surprise – Tommy couldn't tell which – and it sounded like he wasn't the only one shouting.

Then, all at once, Tommy realized that Micah was still standing in front of the room, wearing his usual small smile, and not laying on the floor bleeding. The bullet that had struck him had encountered a barrier – his shield – and fallen useless to the table in front of him. Turning his gaze back to the filthy man with the gun, Tommy saw the man's image shift and flow for a moment, and there, instead of the scruffy, ragged man, Chancellor Duvey stood, still holding the handgun. Tommy rubbed his eyes in confusion for a moment.

"Ok, ok, calm down. Calm down everyone, it was just a demonstration. Chancellor Duvey, thank you for your assistance," Micah said in a soothing voice, and the chancellor bowed deeply at the waist before departing without a word.

Several of the students were picking themselves up off the ground and taking their seats from where they had risen. Tommy sat down, feeling his cheeks flush with embarrassment – not only that he had been the first one to cry out, but that he had tried to stop the demonstration and failed spectacularly. Tommy noticed Mary wiping some tears out of her eyes as she rose; apparently the demonstration had shaken the poor girl. Maybe she felt much more loyalty to Micah than Tommy had originally guessed, to be so scared for his life that she had started crying.

"Seriously, calm down everyone, everything is fine," Micah continued to try to soothe the class. "Now, think about what just happened. Tommy, I saw you start to cast a spell. Good eyes and reflexes. You, too, Mary." Tommy felt his face flushing again, and hated himself for it. He was embarrassed that he had failed, and it seemed that Mary had failed equally badly. Tommy gave her a commiserating glance and a wink. However, Micah was still speaking. "But, as you can see, there wasn't enough time, was there? You were too surprised, off guard, and not prepared enough to possibly avert the attack." Micah picked up the mushroomed bullet off the table and tossed it in his hand. "And, within the confines of our school, luckily, you don't have to. There are no hidden assassins lurking in the halls of the school. But I want to be very, *very* clear to each and every one of you. Once you leave the school, it's a different world. There *are* people out there who want to hurt you, simply because of who and what you are. You must be on your guard at all times when outside the school and being on your guard means learning how to shield yourself, to protect yourself fully, all the time, no matter what else might be on your mind. So, let's begin."

Micah launched into an extended description of the shield, and how it worked. He explained creating the magical sheath that would protect them, keeping both arcane and mundane attacks from harming them. By the end of the class, Micah had them walking through the steps to establish the shield, and Tommy tried to listen with interest. He tried and failed repeatedly to create the shield, but he was distracted – he constantly felt like there were eyes on him, and every time he looked up, he found Mary glancing away, right in the act of turning her head away from where she'd been staring at him. It unnerved Tommy and prevented him from concentrating. What could he have done to spark her anger so, Tommy wondered? Was it because he, too, had tried and failed to stop the 'assassin'? Or was it because Micah had given Tommy credit for it first, and Mary second? Whatever the reason, Tommy was extremely grateful when Micah pronounced that they'd tried enough for the day and dismissed the class.

CHAPTER
THIRTY-THREE

It was a little over a week later that Tommy found himself in a small, almost claustrophobic room. The room had a high ceiling and was very long – probably almost thirty feet long – but barely wide enough to accommodate Tommy's shoulders. When the door closed behind him, Tommy felt a little trapped, a sensation further complicated by a waist-high barrier with a table on top that was just a few feet down the room. All in all, the room reminded Tommy of a police firing range that he'd seen in the movies. It was a fairly accurate analogy, since firing practice was basically why Tommy was here.

There was a large stone sphere sitting on a pedestal down at the other end of the room. Surrounding the sphere was a strong magical shield, like the one Micah had spent the last week drilling them on over and over again. This shield was so strong Tommy could almost see it with his vision unenchanted – it created a small ripple in the air, almost like heat rising off of the stone. Once Tommy cast the spell to enhance his vision, however, he could see it quite plainly – the effect was so strong it glowed to his magical sight, although he could not determine what was causing the shield or where it was being cast from. Certainly, it was being created by someone very powerful. Regardless of who was making it, Tommy was here to knock it down.

They'd just begun learning different kinds of attack spells, and now the class was getting its first opportunity to test them out. Each of his fellow classmates was in a similar room, faced with a similar shielded stone sphere. Their goal was to break down the shield and have a spell affect the stone sphere. Micah had told them that, at first, they'd be lucky to nudge the sphere enough to make it roll off its place on the pedestal, but that, with enough practice, eventually they would be able to shatter the sphere completely. Then, Micah had said, they'd be ready to move on. Tommy was determined to do well on his first try – he didn't think he'd be able to break the stone, but maybe he could crack it just a little.

"Get ready..." Micah's voice crackled from a speaker in the ceiling, causing Tommy to jump in surprise. He hadn't noticed the speaker before, and somehow it seemed odd to him that, in a place so full of magic, Micah would resort to using something as mundane as electric speakers.

"Begin!" Micah said again over the speakers.

It took Tommy a moment to recover from his initial surprise and gather his thoughts, but once he did, he set to attacking the sphere with gusto.

Tommy started out by using the electrical arc spell that he'd learned in the testing just over a week ago. He cast the spell and shot the bolt at the sphere five or six times before pausing. The spell took Tommy a little while to cast, and it was not having an appreciable effect; The shield was too strong, and Tommy felt immediately like he was trying to chip away at a mountain with a toothpick. After a brief consideration, Tommy decided to try a different tactic, and he summoned a small but intense blaze of fire around the sphere, figuring that, instead of casting a spell over and over again, he could cast one spell that would wear down the shield over time. Peering down the range at his handiwork, Tommy frowned. It looked like the shield was repairing itself and replacing lost energy over time; the damage from his fire spell was not even keeping up with the repairs on the shield, and he was quickly losing what little ground he'd gained with the electricity spells.

Frustrated, Tommy poured more and more energy into the fire spell. The flames grew brighter and more intense, and as he flooded the spell with even more magical energy, he saw the shield begin to start weakening ever so gradually. At least now, he was beating the repairs, and he would eventually wear the shield down.

But Tommy knew that he couldn't keep this pace up forever. He felt the energy draining through his body, and knew that he'd collapse from exhaustion long before his fire spell broke through the shield. He decided to help it along a bit and used a fairly simple spell to pull water out of the air, freeze it, and slam the ice shards into the sphere. This turned out to be a mistake, however – the cold and water sapped energy from his fire spell, and Tommy almost lost control of both of them. Quickly, he abandoned the ice tactic.

Frowning, Tommy regarded the sphere and its surrounding shield. The fire spell he'd cast was very bright, both with magical energy to his enchanted sight, and with the more mundane brightness that any fire generates, and it made his eyes water a bit trying to look past it. Gritting his teeth, Tommy tried to pour his full strength into the fire spell. The blaze intensified for a brief moment, and then vanished with brief thud of displaced, super-heated air. Tommy grunted in surprise – he hadn't expected that to happen, but he thought he understood why. He'd just put too much energy into the spell, and it hadn't been designed to handle the problems that arose when he gave it that much energy. The spell had, essentially, collapsed under its own weight. Tommy thought he could see a way that he could modify the spell so it could get hotter, but he had no time to try to figure it out now. Modifications like that would take him hours to work out, and the shield was once again repairing itself.

For the next twenty minutes, Tommy tried everything he could think of. He hit the sphere with arcs of electricity, smashed it with ice, burned it with fire, and pummeled it with blasts of pure energy. Nothing he tried made any kind of significant progress, and for a brief moment, Tommy considered vaulting over the desk and beating on the thing with his bare hands. He even tried pulling chunks of rock out of the walls of the range, so that he could smash them into the sphere, but the walls must have been shielded somehow – none of his spells affected the walls, floor, or ceiling at all. In fact, Tommy peered at the pedestal – his fire had been so hot that it should have at least scorched the rock, but the stone remained unblemished and whole, and showed no sign of Tommy's attack. So much, then, for his idea to damage the pedestal so that it became uneven and let the sphere just roll off of it.

Tommy sighed and had just started to steel himself to launch another attack on the shield when Micah's voice crackled again over the speakers. "Time's up everyone – leave your room and we'll meet in the common area."

Tommy left his room with a heavy heart – he thought he would at least be able to touch the sphere, but he hadn't even come close. He wondered who or what had been powering the shield that it was so tough to breech. Out in the larger room that connected all the small firing-range type rooms that the rest of his classmates had been in, Tommy saw that he wasn't the only one who was frustrated. By the look on Ryan's face, he was ready to spit thunderbolts with frustration, and the rest of the class displayed signs of varying levels of anger and fatigue.

Micah, however, grinned at the assembled students. "Not as easy as you thought, it is?" The instructor chuckled for a moment before continuing in a more serious tone. "This lesson was to prove a point. A strong, well maintained shield can deflect even the strongest attack. The shields you encountered were not created by any kind of senior mage at the school. They were created by the next class of students ahead of you." Tommy blanched at this. There was a chance that Mae had been powering the shield that he'd failed to breach, and he was suddenly afraid that she had seen his abysmal failure. Micah, however, was continuing. "It is easier to defend because you do not need to absorb the full energy of the attack – you only need to deflect or absorb what would actually hit your body." Seeing the confusion on the classes faces, Micah gave an example. "Think of a large explosion next to a brick wall. The wall does not need to contain the explosion. It does not absorb all the energy. The wall only needs to resist the portion of the explosion that hits it – the rest of it goes harmlessly in other directions."

There were some nods from the assembled students at that. Tommy thought he got it, but was too tired to really comprehend.

"What you should take away from the lesson is this – you will never, ever win a fight by defending. But it is far, far easier to defend than it is to attack. When faced by a superior opponent, in a fight you know you cannot win, you will find it far easier to protect yourself than to try to overcome your foe. Protect yourself. Flee. Call for help. Focus your energy on defense and do whatever you can to get away, to get out of the situation. There's no shame in living to fight another day." Micah paused, and then continued with a wry grin. "The old adage has lied to you – the best defense is not always a good offense."

CHAPTER
THIRTY-FOUR

Tommy was still tired from his ordeal with attacking the shielded stone when he made it to his physical fitness class. He was attacking a wooden dummy with a real, albeit dulled, metal sword. Normally, the students fought each other with padded wooden weapons, but during the last several weeks, Lord Kalish had set them to practice with the metal ones. The difference was not something Tommy cared for – the metal sword was much heavier, and quickly tired his arm after he'd been swinging it for even a short while. Further, when he struck the dummy, it send a jarring sensation up his arm and into his shoulder. In short order, Tommy found himself struggling to lift the sword on Lord Kalish's command to strike, and letting the weight of the sword hit the dummy instead of putting any of his own force behind it. Glancing to his left and right, everyone else seemed to be having a similar problem. Only Ryan continued to strike his target with any sort of vigor, and he seemed to be taking out his earlier frustration on the wooden dummy. Tommy shuddered for a moment and felt glad that they weren't fighting each other today. He had no desire to be bruised and battered on top of the other problems he was facing.

"Halt!" Lord Kalish called to the class unexpectedly. There was still quite a bit of time left in the class, and it was very unusual that he would end early. "Halt, weapons down!" he called again, then, "Gather round, class."

The students moved to form a semicircle around Kalish, taking off gloves and removing helmets as they went. Tommy actually let the point of his sword drag on the ground for a few brief steps before he caught himself; Lord Kalish was very unforgiving to students who mistreated their weapons, even the mock weapons they were using today.

"Today, Lord Kalish has a question for you," he began. "The question is this. Suppose that a man tells you he is your friend forever, and that he would fight and die with you. Is he your friend?"

Several members of the class exchanged glances, while others looked puzzled. Lord Kalish sighed and began again. "You know Lord Kalish. If Lord Kalish said to you, 'I am your friend, I will protect you', would you believe Lord Kalish?"

The answer seemed obvious to Tommy, and he said, "Yes" with several other members of the class. The whole thing smacked to Tommy of some sort of test. Maybe a test of loyalty. To Tommy's surprise, however, there was also a resounding "NO!" from a couple members of the class – both Ryan and James in particular. Tommy looked at them in surprise, expecting a reaction out of Lord Kalish.

But the instructor only smiled. "Very good answers from everyone." Now the class looked very puzzled, and glanced at each other in confusion again. Lord Kalish turned to address Sam, who was standing near Tommy. "You spoke yes. Why did you speak so?"

Sam shifted nervously on his feet and scratched his chin for a moment before answering. "Well, I guess if you said you were my friend and would protect me, it would be pretty obvious pretty soon if you were lying, right?"

"Just so. And you, Mister Thorton. You spoke no, why did you speak so?"

James looked exhausted. He always did, these days. But his voice was clear and strong when he spoke. "Uh, I don't know you at all. I mean, we have class together, but I don't really know you. Why would you say you are my friend when we don't know each other? Obviously, you want me to think you are my friend so I'll let my guard down around you."

"Well said," Lord Kalish replied, "But instead of let your guard down, say instead that I want you to trust me, yes?"

James thought about that for a moment, then nodded in agreement.

Lord Kalish continued. "So. Those who spoke yes, do you know Lord Kalish?" The students who had spoken up shrugged or shook their heads. "You know some about Lord Kalish, but you do not know all, to be sure, yes? If Lord Kalish was your friend... he would not have to tell you so, yes? You would know Lord Kalish was your friend, because you would know the heart of Lord Kalish." Many of the members of the class who had said yes looked abashed at being wrong.

But Lord Kalish was not done. "To those who spoke no. You are suspicious of Lord Kalish, yes? You do not know what is in his heart. Yet, perhaps, Lord Kalish shows you his heart with his statement of friendship, yes? You can accept Lord Kalish's offer of friendship without closing your eyes with trust. So long as your eyes are open, you lose nothing by accepting, but should you spurn Lord Kalish, you will surely make an enemy of him, yes?"

The arms instructor paused there and stood for several long moments regarding the class. Finally, Tommy stuck his hand in the air, and Lord Kalish acknowledged him.

"So... who was right?" Tommy asked.

Lord Kalish grinned, as if this was exactly the question he wanted to here.

"All were right," he said, "All were wrong. The answer depends on what is in Lord Kalish's heart when he speaks, and since Lord Kalish does not open his heart to you, none will ever know the truth."

Ryan interjected from the far side of the circle. "So what was the point of this, then?"

"The point," Lord Kalish lectured, "is that you must look past the words that a man says. If you wish to know the truth of a man, then you must know his heart. If you do not know the heart of the man, then you do not know the truth of him. Look to what a man does, not what he says, and you will know his heart." The entire speech was given as an answer to Ryan, and as a lecture to the class, but Lord Kalish's eyes rested on Tommy the entire time he spoke, and Tommy couldn't help but feel that the entire lesson was intended for him, and him alone.

"No more teaching for today. Class is dismissed," Lord Kalish said, breaking the silence and turning away from Tommy. Why had Lord Kalish stared so intently at him? Tommy had never been so grateful to head the changing rooms.

CHAPTER
THIRTY-FIVE

The days trickled by and settled into a sort of a routine. Micah had them practicing shielding themselves in every class – the only lesson he would teach, apart from how to protect themselves, was the frequent and repetitive lecture on how vitally important it was that they learn to create a strong and enduring barrier around their body. One day, he even brought a bucket of rocks to the class and threw them at the students while they shielded themselves. If the students flinched or lost control of the shield, the rocks hit them in the head.

"The point of this," Micah lectured that day, "Is that you gain faith in your protections. Do not flinch from the rocks. Do not fear that they will hit you, and they won't. Have faith in your shield, stand and face the attack, and allow it to hit you and be absorbed."

It was over a week of repetitive shield practice later that Micah began the class by telling them to gather their things. "We're taking a little walk. Come with me, everyone."

Micah led them through the halls and into an outdoor area. Tommy recognized it – it was a huge, sand-filled pit that

Lord Kalish often used to have them duel each other. "You must learn to fight on uneven ground, yes? You must not plan on only fighting on flat stone," Lord Kalish had told them the first time they used to pit. Tommy didn't care for it – the shifting sand fatigued his muscles much quicker than even ground, and even worse, the sand seemed to get everywhere – in his shoes, in his clothes, in his hair – he'd even found sand in his EARS after a particularly rough session.

"Tommy!" Micah barked, surprising Tommy out of his daydream. Tommy looked over, and Micah was gesturing to one side of the pit. "Over there, please?"

Tommy felt the heat rush to his face in embarrassment as he moved to take the indicated place. Micah had been pairing the class up, across from one another, while Tommy had been wool gathering, and Tommy was surprised to see that, this time, he was paired up with James instead of Ryan. Ryan was probably the most skilled member of the class, while Tommy was clearly the best at channeling, so they almost always got paired up together when it was time for partner activities.

Micah clapped his hands together loudly in his usual signal that instruction was about to begin.

"Today, we are going to put your shielding abilities to the test. You are going to attack one another. Now, this isn't some sort of brawl or contest. We are going to do this at a slow, measured pace, like civilized people. You are to use only the bolt of electricity spell that you learned in the testing chambers. That attack spell, and no others, understand? I trust that no one needs to be reminded of how the spell goes?"

All the students shook their heads, and Tommy felt suddenly stupid. He thought he was the only one that had committed that particular spell to memory, and he realized with a rueful grin to himself that he should have known better. All the students were hungry for knowledge, and he understood why everyone would want to remember that particular spell – it was the first attack spell that they'd really even been exposed to.

"I will call out the steps. You will attack only on my specific command, understand? The group on my left will attack first," Micah raised his left hand to demonstrate. "And the group on my right will attack second," again raising his head to demonstrate which group was which. Tommy was somewhat chagrined to find out that he was on Micah's right hand, which meant that he'd be on the defensive at first.

Tommy peered across the sand at James. *"Are you going to use dark magic against me?"* he thought to himself. *"No, not with Micah here, in front of everyone."* Besides, Micah said only one spell would be used. Still, who knew what James could do, using black magic? Tommy suspected that he'd used it to pass the last testing... although he had no actual proof of the matter. Tommy decided that he was probably pretty safe, here, out in the sun and the sand, with Micah and the whole class watching. He felt pretty confident that the shield he could construct would hold up against anything that James could throw at him with or without using forbidden spells.

"Very well, then," Micah continued. "Right hand group, prepare your defense."

Tommy concentrated, forming a shield all the way around his body. He poured more and more energy into it, strengthening it, and at last felt like it was just about as strong as he could make it without putting in a serious, lengthy effort. When Tommy looked up, Micah was studying the students on his right. Taking a chance, Tommy quickly cast the spell that allowed his eyes to perceive magical energy, and he quickly glanced around. With his vision enchanted, Tommy could see the shields of varying strengths that the students were building around themselves. He could also see the much, much stronger shield around Micah, and he could also see the broad dome of a shield covering the entire sand pit – clearly, Micah wasn't taking any chances with an errant spell from the novice mages, but what struck Tommy most strongly was the strength of the shields. Tommy couldn't imagine ever being able to breach the dome over all of them, even if he tried non-stop for years, even if the WHOLE CLASS had tried for years, and the fact that it was so huge as to cover the entire area was something that Tommy found simply staggering.

"Left hand group, prepare to attack," Micah said, raising his left hand, and when Tommy turned his eyes from the dome to look at the man, he saw that Micah was looking at him and smiling. Clearly, Micah realized that Tommy had seen his handiwork, and was pleased and amused that he was impressed. Tommy glanced around again and saw that all the other students on his side of the pit had established their shields.

"Left hand group, strike!" Micah cried loudly, bringing his left hand down in a chopping motion as he did so.

Tommy had never been subject to a magical attack, before, and the experience both intimidated and intrigued him. He could see James form the spell and hurl it at him. The casting took place very quickly, almost instantly, but Tommy saw as James was casting the spell how he could counter the attack or disrupt it. He did neither of these things, of course, but let the spell hit his shield as instructed. Although the impact wasn't all that hard – it was certainly in no danger of breaching Tommy's defenses – he still let out an involuntary grunt as the bolt of electricity impacted on his shield. Tommy couldn't say where exactly that he felt the impact, but more that it seemed to echo through his entire being.

When all the students had made their attacks, Micah continued. "Very good, class. Right hand group, you may release your shields and relax. Left hand group, prepare your defenses!" They stepped through the entire process again. Tommy thought that James' shield might crumple under his attack, but no such thing happened – Tommy found that it was difficult to increase the energy on the spell they were using very much, which, after some thought, Tommy realized was probably why Micah had chosen that particular spell, as it was very limited and didn't really do all that much damage.

Back and forth they went for the rest of the afternoon, shielding and attacking each other. By the time the class ended, every member of the class was totally exhausted, Tommy included. He'd even had to let his vision enhancement spell lapse halfway through the class, as he just didn't have the strength and energy to keep it going. Finally, though, the class was over, and everyone sighed with relief – although the exercise had been fun and interesting at first, interest quickly faded as exhaustion set in.

As the students were trudging away, Micah ended the class by calling, "We'll meet here again tomorrow for another session, instead of meeting in the classroom", and Tommy wasn't alone in letting out an involuntary groan.

CHAPTER
THIRTY-SIX

The attack and defend practices went on for much longer than just the next day. They were at it every day, without fail, for what felt to Tommy like ages, but in reality was just a few weeks. Fortunately, Micah tried to make it more interesting for them, and occasionally gave them games to play. One day, he'd formed them into two lines on opposite sides of the sand pit, thrown a shielded ball into the center, and let them use magical spells to pound on the ball and try to drive it across the opposing side's line. Tommy thought that was grand fun, although most of the other student's didn't seem to like it. As the ball got closer and closer to your own line, it was easier for that team to strike the ball harder, and more difficult for the opposing line to attack with force at the longer distance, so the end result seemed to be a ceaseless back and forth, with no clear winner or loser. Tommy had a blast with that one.

Micah also introduced them to new attack spells, teaching the spell at the start of the class and then having them practice using it on one another as the class went on. Some of them were interesting, and Tommy occasionally thought he saw how they could be altered, improved, or changed, but by the end of the class he was always too exhausted and drained to ever act on his insight. In fact, most evenings the entire class went to dinner together, ate in exhausted silence, and then cleaned up and went to bed. No one had the energy left to do anything more than necessary.

The students got better at their shielding, too – by the end of the first week, Tommy's shield was several times stronger than it had been when he started, and even the slowest student in the class, James, had made incredible strides in improvement.

After several weeks of constant practice, Tommy showed up at the sand pit for yet another long and tiring session. Micah, however, had other plans.

"You've all been working very hard, and I'm proud of you. Today, you've earned a break. I want everyone to take the afternoon off, go relax, eat a good lunch and dinner. I do **not** want you practicing spells or shielding, or anything of the sort. Your bodies need some time to rest and recover, and I will not have you wasting this opportunity to rest. Remember, it might be a long time before you get another chance like this. And then, tonight, I've got a special surprise for everyone!"

The class perked up even further. This was a rare opportunity to get some relaxation time, and if there was a surprise on top of it, it promised to be really good.

"Tonight, after dinner..." Micah paused, somewhat maddeningly, drawing out their suspense. Tommy found himself leaning forward involuntarily, hanging on the man's every word.

"Tonight is the Mage Games, and we are all going to be there. I've reserved a special section near the front for the class to watch."

The students shared glances and exchanged grins.

Everyone had heard about the mysterious mage games, and speculation had been rampant on what they might entail.

"Alright. We'll meet in our normal classroom at six o'clock, tonight, and I will personally escort you down to the games. Deal?" Micah asked.

"DEAL!" the assembled students replied as a group. Tommy hadn't spoken up –he'd assumed their response was implied, since it wasn't like they could actually disobey their teacher, nor would any of them even dream of passing up the chance.

"Great, see you tonight."

Tommy ate a hearty lunch, as Micah had suggested, and went back to his room and tried to relax, but he found it impossible to concentrate. His thoughts were awhirl with excitement about what the mysterious mage games were, and what they might entail. He tried to read one of the books that his parents had brought on their last visit, but after finding himself reading the same paragraph a dozen times and still not comprehending it, he finally gave up and put the book away.

Ryan and James were still at lunch, and Sam was away at class, since the younger boy was in a much less advanced class than Tommy and the rest of his roommates and thus had not been given the day off. Tommy tried to entertain himself. He considered working on some of the spells that he had ideas for, but he abandoned the idea after remembering Micah's admonishment to rest. He tried going for a walk, he went to the dining hall and sat and sipped water to try to pass the time, but nothing seemed to help. He didn't even have anyone to talk to – Ryan and James had never put in an appearance after dinner, and everyone else outside of his class was hard at work in their own classes and studies. Any other time, Tommy would have been delighted by the prospect of nearly a whole day off, but today, the time seemed to drag on interminably.

Finally, though, it was dinner time. Tommy forced himself to eat slowly and thoroughly even though he wanted to bolt his food. He knew that rushing would just lead to more interminable waiting, and he'd had enough waiting for one day. So he took his time, tried to enjoy his food, and chatting amiably with his friends. No one wanted to let on, but he could tell that everyone was ready and anxious to get on with things.

Micah was waiting for them in the classroom when they arrived at the class in almost a single group – most of them had been at dinner together, and they gathered in a few stragglers as they walked from the dining hall to the classroom. "I've been waiting for you," the man quipped, "I'd have thought you'd be a little more excited."

The class chuckled at the obvious joke, but Micah didn't pause. "Alright, this looks like everyone. Let's go!" he exclaimed, and then set off walking at his normal brisk pace. Tommy wondered briefly how the man could be sure everyone was there – it looked like it to him, but he couldn't really be sure, and in any case, it was too late – they were already on their way.

Micah lead them down a series of hallways and stairs into a part of the school that Tommy had never been into before. Although he loved exploring and finding new parts of the school, the passages and stairwells quickly became labyrinthine, and Tommy had gotten very lost a few times, making him somewhat reluctant to attempt exploring too much. Finally, after a great deal of walking, they pushed through a set of large, wooden double doors and into bedlam.

They were standing at the top of what Tommy could only describe as an underground football stadium. There was a large, packed earthen pit in the center of the room, perhaps two hundred feet across, and surrounding it were rows upon rows of seats on risers, each row of seats set high enough above the one in front that even the shortest viewers could see over the heads of the row in front of them. The seats were much nicer than any football stadium Tommy had seen – admittedly, he'd only seen the stadium at his school and some professional stadiums on television – but the seats here were plushly padded and well-spaced, with cloth-padded armrests that didn't come near to touching the adjacent seats. The steep rise in the seats meant that Tommy was quite high up above the earthen pit at the center - a hundred feet or more – and the combination of the vaulted ceiling, height, and the steepness of the slope gave him a bit of vertigo.

Many of the seats were already full and more people were arriving by the minute, with the latecomers dismayed to find that they had to pick the seats higher up. Tommy boggled at the sheer number of people in the room. There had to be several thousand people already seated, and with more still arriving, Tommy had to reassess his opinion of the size of the school and the number of its inhabitants. He knew that the building was vast, and that there were dozens of out-buildings on the campus, but this was the size of a small city. With the inhabitants of the room all laughing and talking with their neighbors, the noise level in the enclosed space was enormous, and Tommy had to fight a brief instinct to cover his ears. How had he managed to be in the same building as all this noise and never know that this was here?

Micah lead them down the steps to the very front row of seats, in the middle of the arena, where there was a large, conspicuously vacant group of seats. They weren't marked in any way, but as Tommy's class filled in to occupy them, Tommy saw that there were exactly enough seats for every member of the class except Micah. Tommy got a seat right on the end of one of the rows, right on the aisle, two rows from the very edge of the pit, where he could see the entire room very clearly. This close, he could see that there were two stone pillars in the pit, one on either side, with what looked to be a large crystal sitting on top.

Micah spoke to them in a hushed tone that somehow carried over the incredible din around them; Tommy realized he must be using magic to send his voice to them.

"I have to go officially start the games, so I'll be brief. Tonight's games are a one on one competition. Sometimes, we do competitions with groups of mages, but not tonight. You'll see them soon enough, anyway. Each contestant will stand on one side of the arena. The crystals you see on top of the pedestals, there, provide an almost impenetrable shield around each competitor; we call that the emergency shield, and it is there to prevent any injuries. The competition will be just like what we've been doing in class, albeit unstructured. Each competitor will shield themselves while attempting to use magical attacks to bring down his opponent's shields. The first competitor to breach his opponent's defenses and strike the emergency shield wins. Got that?"

There were some nods and some shrugs from the class. Tommy thought it made a kind of sense, but he wanted to know more.

"Like I said, it's just like what we've been doing in class, except it's a competition. It'll make sense once you see it." Micah added. "Oh, and speaking of seeing it – don't forget to enchant your vision. Otherwise, you'll barely be able to see anything!"

With that, Micah swept away and took up a place midway around the arena, where a large empty stone chair sat amidst several other large chairs occupied by members of the school's faculty. Tommy could see Lord Kalish seated near Micah, and Chancellor Duvey immediately on the man's right.

Micah stood in front of the chair and raised his hands in the air. His voice carried throughout the room, easily heard over the noise.

"Let tonight's Mage Games begin!"

CHAPTER
THIRTY-SEVEN

Immediately, the noise in the room came to an abrupt halt as everyone stopped talking at the same time.

Two young adults stepped out of doors in the sides of the pit. Tommy hadn't previously noticed the doors – they were the same grey stone color as the rest of the walls, and, when closed, they blended in almost seamlessly. The two people – one male, one female – wore matching ceremonial looking robes. Long and flowing but grey in color and trimmed with black, the robes seemed to accentuate their movements, making them appear to almost flow across the floor toward one another. Tommy noticed that each of them bore a similar design etched in gold thread on the shoulders of the robes, but he couldn't figure out any meaning from the pattern.

Reaching the center of the room, the two stopped and drew swords from their sides. It no longer surprised Tommy to realize that he hadn't seen them wearing swords or scabbards at their belts – he'd seen Micah and Lord Kalish both perform a similar feat several times, and now he took it as a matter of course that it was something that more learned people could do. Holding their swords out to their sides with arms extended, the point of the sword facing the ground away from their bodies, both bowed smoothly to one another before standing and retreating next to their respective pedestal.

Tommy had been so caught up in studying the two's actions that he had totally missed the fact that Micah had been introducing the two to the assemblage. He thought he caught that the woman's name was Jennifer something, but he totally missed the man's name.   He looked toward Micah, and saw he was standing in front of his seat, his hand raised into the air.

"Ready!" Micah called, and two combatants in the pit adopted a ready stance with the sword.

Cursing himself, Tommy realized that he still hadn't enchanted his eyesight, and he quickly cast the spell that would allow him to see magical energies. Suddenly, things burst into view. He could see the strong shields surrounding the man and the woman in the pit, and even stronger shields inside those linked to and being provided by the crystals on the pedestals.

"BEGIN!" Micah cried and the stands erupted into cheers as the man and the woman began flowing across the bare earth toward one another.

The male combatant opened up with a spell that shot a dozen flaming arrows into the air. The arrows arced out in a fan, forming a huge semi-circle around the woman, before changing course and speeding in toward her from above and all sides. Tommy's breath caught – with the attack coming from all sides, it would be very difficult for the woman to defend against this assault. Tommy was surprised to see, then, that she didn't even attempt to deflect the attack, but simply allowed the flaming arrows to impact upon her shields. Instead, she flung her free hand out, and a brilliant arc of white-hot lightning lept from her hand to strike the man's shields. The lightning flashed once, twice, and three times, each time upon the exact same course through the air, leaving a glowing after-image in Tommy's eyes and causing his seat to vibrate with a huge, thunderous boom.

The man staggered from the attack, and Tommy suspected it was almost as much from the noise as the actual assault on his defenses. But he was not to be deterred. He regained his stride and continued moving toward the woman, casting a spell of his own that caused a giant ball of fire, at least two feet across, to appear behind the woman and streak toward her. She let out a yell as the fireball struck her shield from behind, the shock of the blast knocking her forward ever so slightly. But she wasn't beaten; she merely rolled forward from the blast, tumbled, and rolled back to her feet, continuing to move toward the man.

He paused for a second, evidently surprised at the lack of a retaliatory spell, and began casting another fireball identical to the one that had just worked so well, but this one forming off to the woman's right flank instead of behind her.

Both Tommy and the male combatant both were surprised, then, that the woman actually had cast a spell. She had used the impact of the fireball and her subsequent roll to disguise the casting. Large, jagged fingers of rock stabbed upward from the floor and around the man, scraping along his shields before closing tightly in a cage around him, crushing and draining the energy from his defenses. His fireball spell faltered and vanished, and the crowd went wild with cheers at the display. Tommy thought the young man was beaten, but he paused only momentarily before spinning rapidly to the side, using the force of his own shield to crack and shatter the rock prison.

And then the two were on each other, engaging with swords as they continued to batter one another with fire and lightning. The man was clearly the more aggressive of the two, and launched a wide, double-handed swing of his sword horizontally across the woman's chest, while flinging a fan of flames that sprung from nowhere and flew at the woman's face. The crowd cheered approval at the attack, but the woman simply rolled forward again, dodging the flames and rolling underneath the sword attack. As she rolled to her feet behind her opponent, she brought her sword up in a long, drawing attack that scraped along his shield from his feet to his shoulders. She turned back toward him and flung a spell at him, a freezing spell that caused the very air to freeze solid for just a second as it flowed toward the man, but he cast the exact opposite of the spell, performing all the motions backwards, and when the two met, they cancelled one another.

Now, the two circled one another, panting. Although they'd just been at it for a few short minutes, Tommy could see them both panting with exertion. The woman lunged forward at her opponent, but he danced to the side and dealt her shield a brutal cut across her waist. She returned with another bolt of lightning that he tried to counter, but was too slow, and Tommy saw him grimace in pain at the impact on his shield. The crowd roared, some screaming in encouragement, others crying in vexation, depending on which combatant they favored.

In and out they danced, attacking and parrying, launching spell and counter spell. Neither seemed to have an advantage, but then Tommy noticed something. The man was surreptitiously pouring a portion of energy out of his shield and into a fireball spell immediately behind the woman. He was merely using his sword and his other spells as a diversion to keep her attention while he crafted the fireball, which he was able to make much larger and more intense with the additional time and energy he siphoned off his shield.

Finally, the fireball spell was done, and the man launched himself toward the woman in an all-out attack, swinging his sword at the front of her shields while he let the fireball go and streak toward her back.

Shockingly, though, the woman slid her feet forward and fell flat on her back with a grunt, causing his sword attack to miss. The man had released control of his fireball spell, too, once he let it fly, but the woman had apparently been waiting for that – she took control of the abandoned spell, adding her own energy to the effect and increasing its speed, causing it to fly harmlessly over her body and strike him full in the body.

He shouted as his shields, already drained from the combat and from the energy he had pulled from them, cracked and faltered. The woman, still on the ground, launched one more, much smaller lightning bolt that passed the man's shattered defenses and impacted upon his emergency shield. As soon as the impact took place, all the magical energy in the arena ceased, and the man's shoulders slumped in defeat.

Micah stood again. "Jennifer Riley is the winner! Well fought, both of you."

The male combatant strode over and offered Jennifer a hand up, helping her back to her feet, and the two shook hands. She gave him a consolatory grip on the shoulder, and the two spoke to one another for a moment, although Tommy couldn't hear what was being said over the cheers of the crowd. The two then bowed to one another again, sheathed their swords (causing them to vanish again), and strode formally away, each returning through the door they'd come through.

There was only the briefest pause, and then Micah was announcing the next set of competitors.

The contests went on and on throughout the evening, and Tommy found himself getting swept up in the excitement. He began discussing the matches with the other students around him, arguing different opinions on what each competitor did right or wrong, and trying to pick favorite combatants or predict the winner. Some of the matches were between extremely skilled opponents – a few of them even more skilled than the first match– and the combatants fought each other with a barrage of magical spells and swordplay that Tommy found dazzling and almost difficult to follow. Other matches were between students who were much less skilled, some of whom Tommy thought he might be able to out match. However, the skill of the combatants didn't matter one lick. The crowd cheered the less skilled students just as hard as the one who were more proficient, and there was just as much discussion of a relatively unskilled match as there was of a battle between masters. One thing impressed Tommy about the whole thing, although it took him quite awhile to realize it – there was never any jeering or booing when a mistake was made, or when someone's favorite competitor took a bad fall. Instead, the whole thing was on a positive note, celebrating the successes of the competitors without dwelling on their failures.

Tommy's voice grew hoarse throughout the night from his shouting and cheering at the matches, but he didn't care. He was having too much fun. He'd never been into sports in school, but now he thought he saw the appeal – all that it took was being interested in and excited about the event you were watching.

It was late in the event when someone interrupted Tommy's cheers by tapping him on the shoulder. He looked up to see one of the school's workers – one of the huge cadre of personnel that were neither students nor teachers, but who lived and worked at the school and kept things running. Most of them were friends or family of the students and other mages that had taken refuge in the school. They wanted to be with their loved ones, so they found a spot to fit in and contribute to the school however they could. Everyone at the school contributed in some form or fashion.

The man bent down double to whisper in Tommy's ear. "Mr. Nelson? I've been asked to fetch you for the next competition."

"What? Me?" Tommy asked, befuddled.

"Yes, the Lord Archmage has asked that you compete in tonight's final event."

Tommy looked around frantically for support. His eyes fell upon Micah, clearly watching him from across the room. Their eyes locked for a moment, and then Micah nodded subtly.

"Ok, lead on," Tommy sighed.

CHAPTER
THIRTY-EIGHT

Tommy followed the man up the risers and back through the door that he'd come through. Instead of continuing back up into the school, however, they took an immediate right turn down a long, curved hallway. Tommy quickly recognized that the hallway curved around the entire arena. After a short walk, they came to a set of stairs that branched off and lead down even deeper. The workman led Tommy down these stairs, which turned out to be several flights of steps, broken only by brief, unadorned landings, and which lead much deeper into the ground. Finally, just as Tommy's legs were starting to complain about the abuse, the stairs ended in a set of double doors. The workman gestured for Tommy to enter before turning and starting the laborious climb back up the stairs.

Tommy pushed through the doors and found a small carpeted sitting room, with chairs arranged around small tables bearing lamps. It looked to Tommy like a doctor's waiting room. There was another set of double door across the room, and seated in one of the chairs, much to Tommy's surprise, was Ryan, who groaned when Tommy entered the room.

"You! Why'd it have to be you?" Ryan lamented.

Tommy chuckled at that, and went to take a seat next to the other boy. "Pffft. I could say the same thing about you."

Ryan grinned. "You and me again, eh? Looks like it's always you and me. Well, don't think I'm going to go soft on you."

"Right, like you've *ever* gone soft on me before, " Tommy laughed.

"Well, just don't expect it now. I was never into sports, you know? My family just didn't do that. We didn't play sports. I've never had someone cheer for me. You do think they'll cheer for us, don't you?"

"Of course they will, they cheered for everyone else! They'd better cheer for us, at least! I'm so nervous, I could..." Tommy was cut off short by Chancellor Duvey, who burst through the doors and into the room.

"Alright, time to get ready. There's one more match before you both are on. We've got to get you ready. Come with me, please," the Chancellor barked, not slowing as he crossed the room and not even looking to see if the boys were following. Both Tommy and Ryan glanced at one another before leaping to their feet and hurrying after the man.

Chancellor Duvey led them into the next room, which looked like a combination armory, cloak room, laundry room, and locker room to Tommy. There were sets of lockers with benches in front of them in the center of the room. Tommy recognized a couple of the competitors from previous games sitting on the benches and chatting while they changed clothes. One side of the room was filled with rows and rows of pegs containing the robes that Tommy had seen each competitor wear, in sizes ranging from diminutive to gigantic, and everywhere in between. Opposite the robes was a wall hung with swords of every size, shape, and length, from fencing foils to enormous two-handed broadswords much like the one Tommy had seen Lord Kalish wield.

Chancellor Duvey began busily pulling robes off the wall and holding them up against Tommy, Ryan, or both of them. While he was trying, and rejecting, various robes, the Chancellor explained the rules of the combat to both boys. Apart from the formalities that Tommy had already witnessed – bowing to one another before and after the match, how weapons were to be held during the bowing, and to always be honorable and courteous to one another – the only rules that Tommy could discern were that there WERE no rules. Any spell, any attack, any strike with a weapon, it was all legal and permissible. At one point, Ryan joked that it was even legal to pull dirty tricks, "like throwing sand in the other guy's face". Chancellor Duvey however, was not amused and simply replied that, if Ryan could find Sand in the pit, he was welcome to throw it, for all the good a handful of sand would do against an opponent's shields. Tommy thought, not for the first time, that the man was totally devoid of a sense of humor.

Finally, Chancellor Duvey had picked a robe for each of them that he felt satisfied with, and he took them across the room and allowed them each to pick a sword from the wall. Ryan selected an unusually long, straight bladed sword like he had favored in class. Although Tommy had spent a lot of time training with a similar sword, he found that he was most comfortable with something long but narrow, with a blade that came to a very sharp point but was only sharp on one side, the reverse side being thick and hard for blocking. Tommy tested the blade with his finger, and gasped as the razor-sharp blade drew blood.

Chancellor Duvey clicked his tongue in a vexed sound at

that, and grabbed Tommy's hand, casting a brief spell that caused the wound to disappear.

"Please be more careful. Try very hard not to injure yourself with the blade. It won't look good if you are bleeding before you even step on the field," the Chancellor chided before chivying them away from the swords and over to the benches. "Put on the robes. Leave on whatever you want. I suggest shoes, socks, and underwear, but the choice is up to you. You're going to be hot enough out there without all the extra clothes. The rest of your belongings can go in any locker you want."

Tommy decided to take the man's advice and shucked his clothes. The decision was easier because, without taking off his pants, Tommy had no way to stash the spellbinder that Micah had given him into the locker unseen, and with several people, including the Chancellor, around to watch, it was a sure thing he'd be noticed with something as obvious at that. When both boys were changed, the Chancellor took them to a set of double doors opposite the ones they entered through, and bade them wait for this return.

Wearing the robe felt odd to Tommy. This robe was lighter than the one he'd worn at Lord Nence's school. It was an unusual sensation, having air free to blow up his legs, and evidently Ryan was feeling the same way, because the other boy quipped, "I wonder if this is what girls feel like? In a dress, I mean?"

Tommy had to snort a laugh at that, and quickly both of the boys had dissolved into a bout of anxiety fueled laughter.

Once their laughter had died down, Tommy asked "Hey, big boy, take a girl on date? Is that a longsword in your hand or are you just glad to see me?", and that set them both off in a huge round of guffaws. Both boys were still laughing and snickering when Chancellor Duvey returned, quirking a single eyebrow at both of them.

"If comedy hour is over, we can proceed...?" the man said, and that dried up the laughter from both boys.

The Chancellor lead them through the doors and down a hallway, which ended in a T. Chancellor Duvey paused and turned to face the boys with his back to the T. Without a word, he pointed to Ryan and gestured down the left-hand hall, and then point to Tommy and down the right hand wall. Then, he simply turned and walked between the boys, back the way they had come. Tommy watched the man go for a minute, then revised his opinion – it wasn't that the man had no sense of humor. It was that he hated laughter and everything to do with it.

Tommy turned to head down the hallway that the Chancellor had indicated was his, aware that Ryan had turned down his own hallway.

"Hey, Good luck!" Tommy called over his shoulder.

Ryan made no reply, and just kept walking.

CHAPTER
THIRTY-NINE

The hallway was long and curved, just like Tommy expected it would be, given that it had to lead him around the arena and to one of the doors into the pit. After a short walk, Tommy's intuition turned out to be correct – the hallway ended looped around to a small room with some chairs, a large stone door in it, and one of the school's workmen sitting and waiting. Tommy noticed that the hallways continued its long journey on the other side of the room – probably continuing on to another locker type preparation room on the other side.

The workman gestured toward one of the chairs. "You've probably got about five minutes, so you might as well sit and rest." Tommy nodded and took the seat. He should probably be doing some stretching exercises or something like that – he knew Ryan probably would be – but it had been a long, stress-filled day, and he just wanted to sit and relax for a moment.

However, a moment was all Tommy got. He was just starting to settle in and relax when the stone door swung open, and a young woman a few years older than Tommy strode through. She smiled briefly at Tommy as the door swung shut behind her.

"Good luck, kid. Hope you have better luck than I did!" She said with a rueful but good-natured grin before continuing past Tommy and down the hallway he'd come through.

The workman jumped to his feet and approached the door, motioning Tommy to join him.

"Okay, this is it. They're about to announce you. Don't forget to bow when you go out there."

As he approached the door, Tommy was shocked to find that he could clearly hear what was going on in the arena. Sitting in the chair, just a few feet away, it was totally silent, but here, even with the door shut, he could hear the muttering of the crowd behind Micah's booming voice, which was announcing Ryan. Tommy was both surprised and impressed with the things that could be done with magic, then annoyed at his own surprise – he needed to start thinking more like a mage or his own lack of faith in the strength of magic would hold him back.

Ryan's introduction was done in short order, and the workman ushered Tommy through the door as Tommy's own, brief introduction began. Tommy stepped through the door and into the sound and light of the arena. He did his best to imitate the swaggering stride that he'd seen other contestants use, but he wasn't sure whether he pulled it off with any degree of success.

He walked to the center of the arena, where he stood facing Ryan. The other boy had a solemn, focused look on his face as they bowed to one another, then each retreated to his respective pedestal. Tommy began the process of shielding himself – he could get a weak shield up very quickly, but it still took him some work to strengthen it to withstand any sort of concerted attack. Micah clearly realized this, because he waited several long moments before he spoke up.

"Ready!" Micah's voice boomed across the arena, and Tommy raised his sword and turned his attention to Ryan, although he was still reinforcing his protections while he did it. Suddenly, Tommy felt a new shield spring to life around him – A strong, nigh impenetrable one, protecting and sheathing his body inside even his own shielding.

"BEGIN!" Micah cried.

Tommy took a half a step forward toward Ryan, suddenly unsure and hesitating for a moment. Ryan, however, didn't hesitate for even a second. He immediately began crafting two different spells at the same time – the electricity bolt that Tommy (and apparently everyone else) had learned in the testing weeks ago, and another spell that Tommy couldn't quite make out. Tommy remembered from experience just how weak the electrical spell had turned out to be, so he decided to ignore that one and began duplicating the other spell Ryan was casting, but in reverse. As he started the casting, Tommy saw how easy it was – he simply did the exact opposite of what Ryan was doing.

Sure enough, Tommy found he was right. Ryan's electrical bolt struck his shields almost harmlessly, and as Ryan flung his real attack at Tommy, Tommy's counter-spell unraveled and destroyed Ryan's attack even as it formed. Tommy felt a smug sense of satisfaction as the crowd screamed their approval.

But he wallowed in self-congratulations for too long. Ryan was immediately forming another set of attacks. He launched a huge ball of fire that Tommy was able to destroy with an ice spell, quickly followed up by a nasty spell that caused a fine rain of acid to fall from the air above Tommy. While Tommy was summoning a wash of water to get rid of the acid that was burning its way into his shield, Ryan came back with another quick series of sharp jabs, alternating fire and electricity.

"*This is impossible,*" thought Tommy. "*He's too good! He's too fast!*" It was true – Tommy was barely able to defend against Ryan's attacks, and was forced to let one in three of them impact on his shields. Ryan's spell crafting was much faster than anyone else in the class that Tommy had ever seen. He wondered, in between blows, how Ryan had gotten so good, and why he never chose to show it in their classes.

The rain of blows continued, and Tommy pumped more and more of his energy into his shield, but to no real effect – Ryan was slowly but steadily wearing him down, and Tommy could hear the spectators cheering at the show.

Tommy was at a loss for what to do. He was clearly stronger than Ryan, but it didn't matter because he couldn't bring his strength to bear; Ryan was too quick, and kept him on the defensive the entire time.

Finally, his shields on the verge of failing, Tommy got a desperate idea. He ignored the most recent round of Ryan's attacks, letting them impact on him, and instead gathered every ounce of strength he possessed. Tommy could feel the strain on his mind and body as he pulled into himself all the magical energy he could muster, and then he flung it all, raw and unformed, not trying to cast a spell, just pouring a deluge of energy directly at Ryan.

The blast caught Ryan completely off guard. The boy tried to handle the deluge, first attempting to form it into an attack spell, and then vainly flailing in an attempt to shunt it off to the side. But Ryan's efforts were in vain. His abilities were overwhelmed by the sheer enormity of Tommy's magical energy. Ryan's spells fizzled away as the torrent of magical power overloaded the construct of the spell, and his shields wavered and then dropped as his mind failed to adequately manage the energy it was being subjected to.   Tommy's deluge of power touched Ryan's inner shield that was being powered by the pedestal...

And then suddenly, all the magic disappeared.   Tommy gasped and fell to one knee as the power he was channeling literally vanished from his control.   He looked up to see Ryan reeling and staggering, as if the other boy was drunk.

There was a moment of complete and utter silence in the arena, and then the spectators roared in a cacophony of cheers louder than Tommy had heard them give for any previous match. Tommy had to clap his hands to his ears, the sound was so intense.

Suddenly, Micah's voice sounded across the din.

"An   incredible   first   match,   well   fought,   both contestants," then, "Tommy Nelson is the winner".

Tommy headed back through the stone door, but instead of heading down the passageway he'd come through, the worker there directed him to go the other way.

"Losers go back the way they came. Winners move on," was all the man would say.

Following the hallway to its end, Tommy came to a large, opulent sitting room. Lounging in the chairs, sipping drinks and picking at plates of fruits, meats, and cheeses, were all the winners of the matches that he'd seen previously.   They clapped and cheered as Tommy entered, several of them coming over to shake his hand or clap him on shoulder.

He'd only been in the room for a few moments, and was still shaking hands and trying to remember names from introductions when Micah entered the room.   Congratulations stopped as everyone fell silent at the archmage's entry.

"Well fought tonight, all of you. This was a great round of the games, tonight, and I'm looking forward to seeing more from each of you in the future. I'll be meeting with each of you individually very soon, you can be sure."

The assembled students seemed to take that as a sign, and began gathering their things to leave. Tommy wasn't really sure what to do; he couldn't remember how to get back to his room, although his bed was sounding better by the minute.

"Mister Nelson, come with me, please," Micah said, resolving Tommy's dilemma.

Tommy held up his sword, which he hadn't used but had been gripped in his hand this whole time. "Ummmmm... What should I do with this?"

Micah gestured casually to a nearby table. "Just leave it there. Someone will put it away. Come on," and with that, he set off walking, leaving Tommy with no choice but to follow.

"That was an incredible victory you pulled off tonight, Tommy. But I need to warn you. What you did tonight was dangerous. *Very* dangerous. If you hadn't surprised Ryan, he could have easily turned the tables on you, and used your own magic to form a spell to crush you."

Tommy nodded. He had realized what might happen in the seconds after he launched his attack, when Ryan was frantically trying to deal with the energy. "I was desperate. I didn't know what to do. He was so *fast*."

Micah frowned at that, and furrowed his eyebrows slightly. "Yes, I know. It is odd that I missed that in the classes.

It makes one wonder why he's kept his skill hidden, does it not?"

Tommy could only nod again.

They were approaching the part of the school that Tommy recognized when Micah went on. "Still, well fought, Tommy, we'll have to talk more, soon. We'll have an award ceremony for you and the rest of the winners, as well. For now, I trust you can find your own way back to your room?"

Tommy didn't even have time to nod again before Micah turned on his heel and swept back down the way they'd come. Tommy paused and watched the man's retreating back – he hadn't even gotten a chance to complain to Micah for springing the whole match on him unexpectedly, as the least he could have done was warn him.

Shaking his head, Tommy stumped exhaustedly the rest of the way back to his room. Tommy opened the door to his room, and was greeted by an intense and overwhelming stench of rotting plastic. All exhaustion fled as a cold chill of panic spread. "*Black Magic! That's the smell!*" Tommy thought. But when he looked around the room, it was empty. No one was there.

"James!" Tommy said out loud. The big lummox must have ambushed Ryan when he returned exhausted from the mage games. Ryan could even now be in grave danger. Looking around frantically, Tommy had a realization. He sniffed at the air, and found that he could clearly discern the path that the boys had taken, covered in dark magic.

"I'm coming, Ryan!" Tommy shouted to the empty room, and he turned and began dashing down the hallways as fast as he could, pausing only at intersections to sniff the air to follow the scent. At one point, Tommy thought he heard one of his friends shout out his name from down one of the hallways – Mary, he thought it was, but he didn't pause to check or to make a response, he just kept running.

"I'm coming, Ryan!" Tommy shouted again.

CHAPTER FORTY

Finally, Tommy caught up with the source of the smell. He had been running, and burst into the room at a headlong tilt, stopping short at what he saw.

The room was one of the large common rooms scattered throughout the school. They were intended for multiple uses, and students used them for group study sessions, coaching sessions, to gather to play cards or just socialize, and any other number of reasons. The walls were the same dark grey stone that made up the rest of the school, but here the floors were carpeted to provide a comfortable atmosphere and to help muffle sound. There were a few high tables surrounded by chairs, and several low coffee tables that were surrounded by plush couches. Two other doors led out to other hallways – Tommy had never been in this particular room before now.

Right now, the three occupants of the room were Ryan, James, and huge, terrifying being that sent a cold sweat breaking out across Tommy's brow.

James lay prostrate on the floor, his arms and legs splayed. Ryan was standing over the clearly unconscious James with a long, wicked looking knife in one hand and a foul, inky black cloud surrounding his other. But none of this was what caused Tommy's terror; that was caused by the abomination standing over both boys. It was tall – so tall that it had to hunch to fit under the ceiling, which was well over ten feet high, like most ceilings in the school. The thing wore shadows like they were long robes cloaking its body, but where the skin showed through at the thing's hands and face, the skin was alabaster pale and stretched taught across the bones. Long, cruel fingernails protruded from each finger, each one the size of a small knife. The thing's face was the most terrifying, however. Glowing red irises shone forth from two otherwise unrelieved pitch black eyes. There was only a socket where the thing's nose should be, like the nose had been sliced away, and the things mouth resembled nothing so much as an over-wide cat's mouth, with long, sharp, pointed teeth that stretched almost from ear to ear.

The thing raised its head and regarded Tommy as he skidded to a halt, then it let out a long hiss from between its disgustingly overlapping teeth.

Ryan looked up at the hiss, and sneered. "You shouldn't have come, Tommy. You should have minded your own business."

"It's you," Tommy shouted back in his shock and terror. "It's been you all along. It wasn't James that was practicing black magic; it's been you this whole time."

Ryan laughed at that. "Everyone thinks James has been practicing dark magic to keep up with the class, but I've been using it on him. I've been siphoning away his little rich-boy soul, draining his power. It's not like he deserves it, anyway."

Tommy shook his head. "Don't do this, Ryan. Please. Micah will..."

"Micah and the other teachers are all fools. We've been playing them like a fiddle the entire time."

"Well, perhaps that is not entirely true." Micah retorted, striding into the room through a side door. Tommy hadn't seen the door begin to open, and apparently neither had any other of the room's occupants.

The effect of Micah's entry was galvanic. Ryan shrank back slightly, and pulled closer to the demon-thing in the corner. The demon-thing, however, hissed again and raised its hands, flinging black shadows from around its body directly toward Micah. Micah didn't flinch, however. He simply raised his hand and said, "I think we've had just about enough of that." Suddenly, a brilliant but short-lived pulse of stunning, golden light shone forth from Micah's outstretched hands. When it struck the shadows, the creature, and the spell forming in Ryan's grasp, the darkness shredded and then evaporated like a morning mist before the high summer sun.

The giant creature was gone. Where it had been, a short woman stood in its place, her arms raised to shield her face from the brilliant glare. Although less impressive than the illusory creature had been, she was no less grotesque, with stiff, snowy white hair on her head, open sores on her face and hands, and dirt in her teeth and fingernails. The woman's appearance was made no less grotesque by the fact that Micah's blast of brilliant light had singed her exposed skin, raising blisters and causing the skin to look like it had been very badly sunburned. She shook her head for a moment, as if shaking something off, and the action caused some of her brittle hair to break away and fall to the floor.

"Ah, Ruth. I should have known," Micah said calmly.

The woman shrieked in response. "That's not my name! I shed that name. I SPIT on that name. I am REQUIEM now!" She shot her hand out toward Micah, and a long bar of flame shot out from her palm. Micah never moved, however, and the thickness of the bar of fire narrowed and grew thinner until it vanished entirely. Requiem shrieked again at that, and began striding toward Micah, flinging bolts of fire and shafts of darkness, all of which dissipated and vanished well short of the man.

Micah merely shook his head, reached to his side, and drew his sword. Tommy was no longer surprised by the appearance of the sword – He was sure the man hadn't been wearing one just a moment ago, but there it was in his hand, a trick he had seen the man perform before. He turned to grin and wink at Tommy for a moment, and murmured, "Watch closely, Tommy. Now you'll see why we learn the sword."

With that, Micah leapt forward, spinning in a circle and bringing the sword around in a wide arc to strike at the woman. A black shell appeared momentarily and stopped the sword in a shower of sparks just before it made contact, but Micah didn't pause and was spinning again, bringing the sword around for another strike which also met wet with another shell and another burst of sparks. Again and again Micah struck at the woman, and every time the dark shell appeared to block the blow, but Tommy noticed some things – first, the woman was no longer striding toward Micah, and instead was being driven slowly backwards. The second thing Tommy noticed was that the woman's attacks had ceased entirely – all her energy and efforts seemed to be focused on keeping Micah's spinning blade from reaching her body.

A glimpse of movement out of the corner of his eye caught Tommy's attention, and he turned in time to see Ryan draw the long knife he'd been holding back over his shoulder, and pitch it across the room toward Micah with a shout. Time seemed to slow down as Tommy watched the blade spin through the air, straight toward Micah's unprotected back. His mind raced, desperate to do something, to warn Micah somehow, but all he could do was shout wordlessly, too overcome with fear to do anything rational. Ryan's face took on a broad, sneering grin as both boys watched the knife tumble through the air.

In Tommy's science class, they had studied gravity, and how objects orbit planets. There was a whole lot of extremely difficult and rather dull math around it, but one time the instructor had used magic to lift several small models of planets, and had used rocks to show the class how asteroids and other objects can get caught in the planet's gravity, or can even slingshot around the planet. That is the only analogy Tommy could think of to describe what happened next. As the knife approached Micah's back, it started to turn to the side. The closer it got, the more it turned, until it was no longer flying toward Micah, but was flying *around* him, and that is just what it did – the knife started orbiting Micah, flying around and around in a circle a foot or two from his body. Tommy's jaw dropped in surprise, and he saw that the leer on Ryan's face had also been replaced by a look of shock and surprise.

For several seconds, the knife continued to orbit, flying faster as faster as it whipped itself around Micah's body. Then Micah spoke very softly but clearly, and said, "Do not hurl the arrow which may return against you." Suddenly, the knife was flung out of its orbit and straight back at Ryan, flying much faster than Ryan had originally thrown it. The boy shrieked and tried to fling himself out of the way, but the knife cut a long score down the side of Ryan's cheek and ear before striking the stone wall behind him and shattering into several pieces.

Getting to his feet, Ryan put a hand to his cheek and felt the blood welling there. He looked at Micah still battering away at Requiem, gave a howl of despair, and turned and fled the room from the door opposite to the one Tommy had come in.

Tommy did nothing for a moment, then Micah's voice snapped him out of his reverie. "After him, Tommy! Don't let him get away!"

Tommy shook his head and dashed across the room for the door, vaulting over the back of a large couch as he did so. As he rushed out the door and into the hallway, Micah's voice followed him for one last piece of advice.

"Don't forget everything I've taught you."

CHAPTER FORTY-ONE

Tommy dashed through the school's hallways after Ryan. Fortunately, this section of the school was lightly populated, since most of the usual inhabitants were still off at the games, and after a few moments of not encountering anyone else, Tommy began to run recklessly, charging down hallways and through rooms. Although Ryan had a head start on Tommy, it seemed that Tommy was the faster runner; he was rapidly gaining on Ryan. He chased Ryan up several flights of stairs, taking them two and three at a time, and although he was beginning to feel winded, Tommy could hear Ryan's labored breathing ahead of him.

Suddenly, an immense arc of electricity flew down the corridor. Tommy tried to flatten himself against the wall, but he was too slow – the bolt grazed his leg, causing it to lock up in a violent spasm. Tommy fell to the floor, gritting his teeth in pain. The spasm lasted only an instant, but the pain lingered on as Tommy got back to his feet and renewed the pursuit, biting back some choice curse words as he did so – he had lost all the ground he'd gained on Ryan, and more.

The pain in his leg was lesson enough for Tommy,

however. As he ran, channeled magic and enchanted his vision so there would be no more nasty surprises, and just to be on the safe side, he prepared a defensive spell to shield himself from the next inevitable attack. As he ran, Tommy had a moment to reflect on how far he'd come. Less than a year ago, he hadn't even known what magic was, and had struggled mightily to even be able to sense it. Now, here he was, casting multiple spells while running.

He didn't have long to ponder his progress, though, because Ryan ducked around a corner and through a door. Tommy raced to the door and flung it open, the followed more cautiously. Sure enough, Ryan was waiting on the other side with what Tommy recognized as a particularly nasty spell designed to poison his blood. Ryan hurled the spell, but Tommy was ready, and deflected it with his shielding spell, causing the foul poison to strike the floor nearby, where it dissipated.

The two boys eyed each other across the room – it was another small, seldom used sitting room high up in the school, with a dusty couch and a small table with a darkened lamp sitting on it. The only other exit was an archway on the other side of the room that led to yet another set of stairs. Ryan was clutching his side, likely from a stitch, and had probably decided it was better to stand and fight than attempt yet another long stairwell.

Suddenly, both boys flew into action, and began in earnest the combat dance that they had practiced in training. Tommy cast a spell that caused the ground at Ryan's feet to protrude in spikes, but Ryan countered the spell and returned the floor to its flattened shape before hurling another bolt of electricity at Tommy. Tommy used his shield spell to deflect the electricity, and Ryan followed up with another spell that caused a small ball of fire to shoot toward Tommy's face. This, Tommy countered by channeling pure water at the spell, causing it to unravel and vanish.

Back and forth the two went, attack and counter-attack, thrust and riposte. As before, Ryan was clearly more skilled at spellcraft, and although Tommy felt like he should be much stronger at channeling than Ryan, something was wrong – a dark strength was behind all of Ryan's attacks, and Tommy began to understand with a rising panic that he was outmatched. His study of dark magic had given Ryan an edge that Tommy could not hope to match.

Soon, the battle became increasingly one sided, as Tommy was forced to focus less and less on attack, and more on defense. He thought for a moment that his battle began to parallel the one taking place between Micah and the woman Requiem, below, except that in this case, it was the dark side that was winning and Tommy who was forced on the pure defensive.

Suddenly, Tommy realized he had made a second critical mistake – he had let his thoughts wander too far, and hadn't been concentrating enough on the battle. With a cry of victory, Ryan slammed a spell home on Tommy, causing bands of thick, black smoke to wrap around his limbs and his torso. Tommy had a moment to stare at it in puzzlement before it began to constrict extremely tightly, and with a scream of agony, Tommy fell to the floor. The smoke was crushing his lungs, cutting off the flow of blood to his limbs, and slowly beginning to break his bones. Through his pain and panic, Tommy realized that he was going to die unless he did something.

He could only think of one thing to do. Gathering all the strength he could muster, Tommy channeled directly at Ryan, intending to overwhelm the other boy with power just like he had done in the practice battle arena. This time, however, Ryan was unsurprised.

"Not this time, Tommy boy. I'm ready for you this time,"

Ryan sneered nastily as he soaked up all the energy Tommy could hurl at him, and began working with it, using it to craft a dark and terrible spell.

Tommy could only stare in horror as Ryan worked. The bands crushing him were so tight he couldn't even scream, and black spots started to swim before his eyes. The pain caused him to lose touch with the magic, probably fortunately, since it stopped him from fueling the dark magic spell that Ryan was crafting.

Just as Tommy was about to black out completely, the pressure suddenly abated. A golden warmed spread through his body, and he sucked in deep breath and opened his eyes. Ryan was still standing over him, still working on the spell, and Tommy realized that, although it had seemed longer to him, mere seconds had passed. However, now there was a pulsing shield around him, pushing the bands of black smoke away from his body. Tommy wasted no time wondering about the source of both the shield and the magical energy filling him; he reached out and began channeling magical energy of his own, forming a small blade of pure magic that he used to slice through both the spells around him, and whatever dark spell Ryan was building.

Ryan grunted, and took an involuntary step backwards as his spell vanished, causing him to lose his hold on the energy, which dissipated into the air around him. Tommy gave him no time to recover, however. He thought back to the words Micah had shouted at him as he left, "Don't forget everything I've taught you." Tommy now realized what his mentor had meant, and he reached into his pocket and withdrew the large, golden needle that Micah had given him and named a "spell binder". Micah had said the device would create a spell that was effective against dark magic, so Tommy pointed it at Ryan and summoned every scrap of magical energy he could muster, both from his own skill and from the energy that was filling him from the nameless source.

Ryan had just recovered and was about to work another spell when Tommy let the energy go, pushing it into the spell binder. A massive, golden-white beam of energy shot forth from the tip of the spell binder and slammed into Ryan. The force of the blow lifted Ryan off the floor and hurled him across the room, where it held him pinned against the wall. Gritting his teeth, Tommy channeled harder, trying to force more and more energy into the spell binder. The beam of energy got brighter, until it seemed it would sear Tommy's eyes.

Suddenly, the spell binder let out a loud, high pitched whine, like that of a jet turbine, and with a final flash of light, it exploded.

Tommy instinctively threw his free arm up to protect his face as tiny bits of half-melted gold spattered him. He gave a small yelp of pain as the gold struck, burning his skin and putting small pinhole burns in his clothes. Tommy cursed as he dropped the remains of the spell binder, which now ended several inches shorter in a small bit of twisted, blacked metal, and used both his hands to bat away the bits of hot metal. He felt a burn on his head, and caught the stench of burning as he realized that a chunk of hot metal was smoldering in his hair.

It wasn't until the last bit of hot metal was gone that Tommy realized Ryan was screaming, lolling back and forth against the wall and scratching vainly with clawed hands at a glowing white sphere that was on his shoulder.

"You bastard!" Ryan screamed. "It hurts! It's burning me away! It hurts so bad!"

Tommy could only stand and stare. He hadn't known what was going to happen, and his instinct was to help his one time friend, but he was heavily conflicted; Ryan had been about to kill him just scant seconds ago, and would probably do so again if Tommy intervened. Then, the decision was made for him as Ryan uttered one more curse and, with a shriek, yanked open the door next to him and fled the room.

"Crap!" Tommy yelled as he dashed across the room. Micah had told him not to let Ryan get away, so Tommy ran as hard as he could, grabbing at the closing door and pounding down the hallway beyond after Ryan.

*   *   *

Mary pushed open the door she'd been peeking through, and entered the room. She took in the bits of metal, scattered around the floor, and hoped that Tommy hadn't been badly burned when the spell binder exploded. It would be a shame, after all, to ruin such a beautiful face.

She had been watching almost the entire fight, having followed Tommy after she caught sight of his mad dash through the school's hallways, and had wanted to intervene, but she'd been too intimidated. The energies both boys were wielding were staggering, and she had been afraid to get involved. However, when it looked like Ryan was about to seriously harm Tommy, she'd had to act, and had done what she could to lend him her strength and save him from the spell that threatened to choke off his life.

Suddenly, Mary heard footsteps approaching down one of the hallways. She gave one last, lingering look at the door Tommy had ran through, and whispered, "Good luck, my love," before she, too, fled the room in a different direction.

CHAPTER FORTY-TWO

Tommy dashed down the hallway, well behind Ryan, who he could see distantly due to the light cast from the golden sphere clinging to his shoulder and, seemingly, growing larger as time went on. Suddenly, the light vanished, and Tommy took a deep breath and ran all the harder. Arriving at a narrow spiral staircase, Tommy realized why the light had vanished – he could hear Ryan fleeing up the stairs, still cursing under his breath.

Steeling himself, Tommy started up the stairs. They were extremely narrow on the small side, and uncomfortably wide on the large side, so that Tommy found climbing them difficult and taxing. A stitch was beginning to form in his side, and after climbing what seemed to be at least a half dozen flights of steps, Tommy had to pause and catch his breath. He could still hear Ryan climbing, above him, and regardless there had been no doors, landings, or hallways down which the wounded boy could run.

Tommy heard the bang of a door slamming shut above him, and with a curse and a grumble he set off up the stairs again, wondering as he ran how Ryan found the strength to run up so many steps, wounded as he was.

He was panting and almost doubled over in pain by the time he'd run up the equivalent of about four more flights of stairs, although, like the previous steps, he had come across no exits from the stairwell, just more and more stairs that wrapped around and around. Finally, at the top, there was a small landing backed by large, solid wooden door. Taking a deep breath and trying to calm his pounding heart, Tommy yanked the door open.

A strong gust of wind blew into the room and howled down the stairs, nearly ripping the door out of Tommy's hands. Tommy readied himself as best he could while still trying to catch his breath, prepared to defend himself against magical attack, and stepped through the door...

...and onto a large, empty balcony. It was about ten feet long and half again as wide, formed into a semi-circle shape around the mountain, and made from the same grey stone as the rest of the school. A carved stone railing stood slightly over waist high, and a small pile of blackened ashes rested against the railing on one side, but of Ryan, there was no sign. Tommy peered back into the stairwell for a moment, sure he must have missed a door, but seeing none he made his way over to the railing and looked over. Tommy was grabbed by a sudden and intense feeling of vertigo as he looked down at the ground several hundred feet below him, with nothing in the intervening space; beneath the balcony there was only the wild wind whipping around the mountain.

Tommy backed slowly away from the railing, the profound sensation of vertigo making him afraid to move too quickly or to even turn around. He was still backing up, his eyes fixed on the ground in front of him, when he walked backwards into someone. His heart in his throat, Tommy spun around and almost feel to the floor in his panic, but it was only Micah, who grabbed Tommy by the arm and shoulder to steady him.

"You... you nearly scared the life out of me!" Tommy gasped.

Micah favored him with a smile. "It's just me, Tommy. No need to be afraid."

"I thought you were Ryan, sneaking up behind me."

Shaking his head, Micah looked around the balcony. "Where is the little demon, anyway? Did he get away from you?"

Tommy could only shrug. "I don't know. I saw him come up here, I heard the door close, but now... he's gone. We had been fighting, down below."

Micah nodded. "I noticed," he replied, holding out the shattered remains of the large golden needle that Tommy had dropped in the room below. "I see that you've broken my spell binder. You weren't supposed to put that much energy into it. You need to learn finesse, Tommy. You try to overcome every problem with pure brute force."

Tommy felt his face flush red. "I'm sorry. I didn't know what else to do. Ryan had hurt me so badly, I just... I wanted to hurt him back."

Micah laid a hand on Tommy's shoulder. "It's alright, Tommy. You did what you had to do to survive, and no one will ever fault you for that, understand?"

Tommy nodded. "Is there another way off the balcony? Could Ryan maybe have jumped over the side?"

Shaking his head again, Micah's voice took on the lecturing tone that he used in class. "Not if he wanted to live. Remember, Tommy, that flight is impossible. Every mage that has tried to figure out a way to fly using magic has died, eventually. There's no other way off the balcony, other than a long drop with a painful ending." He bounced the remains of the spell binder on his palm. "I really wish you hadn't broken this, though. They aren't easy to make, and this one in particular took quite a bit of time.

"I'm sorry," Tommy said, abashed. "I'll replace it for you."

Micah gave a chuckle at that. "I don't think I'll be able to replace it any time soon, if ever. You've got a long road ahead of you before you'll be ready to try making something like this. I am curious, though. It was only supposed to work against dark magic constructs, how were you able to use it against Ryan?"

"I don't know. I just put all the energy I could into it, and aimed it at Ryan. It left a kind of... white... ball... thingy on him."

"Hrm. Interesting," was all Micah replied.

"The ball stayed, though. Even after the spell binder was broken, I mean. Ryan said it was burning him up..." Tommy trailed off, the horror of sudden realization dawning on his face. His eyes went immediately to the pile of ashes resting against the thick stone railing. "He said... it was burning him up, and it looked like it was growing..."

Micah strode over to the ashes, and studied them for a moment. "Well, I guess we know what happened to Ryan, then."

"You mean... he's... gone? And I..." Tommy gulped past the lump in his throat. "I... killed him?" Tears were starting to form in Tommy's eyes as the full realization of what he'd done began to sink in. Ryan had been his friend.

Tommy hadn't realized he'd sunk to his knees until he felt Micah kneeling next to him, putting a comforting arm around his shoulders. "Hey, hey... don't be upset, Tommy. Ryan forced this on you, do you understand? He was bad. He was evil, rotted in his heart. He tried to kill James, and he tried to kill you. You did what you had to do to protect yourself, your friends, and the school, okay? Don't waste your tears crying over Ryan. He was a bad egg and he got just what he deserved."

Still sniffling, Tommy nodded. "What happened to the other one? The woman, I mean."

"Requiem?" Micah said with a grimace. "She got away. Fled. She teleported as soon as she knew the fight was lost." The scowl on Micah's face deepened. "I couldn't risk her doing something to the school, do you understand? I had to keep her busy defending herself so she didn't have the time to do anything. She could have done massive damage to the school and hurt a lot of people. Sure, I would have destroyed her, then, but at what cost?" Micah shook his head. "Sometimes, we have to do things we rather wouldn't, in order to protect those around us. That's what I did, Tommy. That's what YOU did, do you understand?"

Tommy nodded, and forced a smile. He wasn't convinced, but he didn't want to seem a coward in his mentor's eyes.

"'Attaboy," Micah smiled, clapped Tommy on the shoulder, and helped them both to their feet. "You'd better go clean up, now. You've almost missed dinner. We'll talk more, later, okay? I promise."

Tommy nodded and headed for the door. He cast one last look back at the pile of ash that had once been his friend, sighed, and began the long trudge down the stairs.

*   *   *

Micah stood on the balcony and watched Tommy leave, enjoying the feeling of the breeze in his hair. Tommy was a good kid, albeit a bit naive. Good in the heart, though, and that's what mattered right now. His naivety even worked out for the best, in this case.

After Tommy had gone and the door was closed, Micah walked over to the ash pile. He drug the toe of his boot through the pile, sending clouds of ash up into the air to be snatched away by the wind. There were a few small sticks buried in the pile; some of the senior students had come up here a few nights ago to camp out. They'd slept in sleeping bags and built a small fire in the lee of the railing so they could toast marshmallows. He cast a small spell that scooped up the entire mess and scattered it over the side; it wouldn't do to have Tommy come back and start poking around the ashes. It was doubtful that the boy would chance something he would regard as that macabre, but Micah was nothing if not meticulous, and he had invested too much time and energy to have everything fall apart now.

It was a shame to allow not only one, but two dark mages to escape proper justice, but Micah reminded himself that it was all for the greater good. Even now, he could feel the spell that he'd placed on the young boy Ryan. Requiem had taken the boy and retreated to a location somewhere outside of the city of Miami, in the United States, and from the vague impressions sent to him by the spying spell, Micah gathered that they were getting ready to move again. No matter, really. It was extremely unlikely that Requiem would think to check the boy over for such magicks;

overconfidence was always one of her weaknesses, and Micah felt that he'd been successful in giving both the boy and his vile teacher the impression that they'd fooled him, as if he didn't know exactly who had begun dabbling with dark magic the very minute the lad had attempted it in his school. No, it was unlikely that the spell would be found. Eventually, Requiem would retreat to her own home, in her own school. Micah would then gather the location from the spell placed on the boy and would settle with Requiem's entire coterie of dark mages and students at once. Micah smiled at the thought; oh, yes, the reckoning would come with the blade of a sword.

Micah stared down and back at the side of the mountain, as if he could see Tommy descending the steps inside. It was a pity to put the boy through this trauma unnecessarily, but he just wasn't ready to hear the unvarnished truth. Besides, in the long run, it would do him good to see what black magic could do to people that he cared about. Far too many people these days had taken a "live and let live" attitude, and he couldn't have Tommy giving in to his gentle side. Not when it came to tolerating that sort of foulness, anyway. He also didn't want Tommy worrying about Ryan. Worrying about where the boy might be, or worried that he might come back to trouble Tommy. No, far better to let Tommy think his friend was gone. At least for now.

A small smile crossed Micah's face. Yes, things were starting to come together. Years of work and planning were starting to bear fruit, and the future was starting to look bright indeed.

The smile was still on his lips when Micah arched his back slightly, cast a short spell, and smoothly leapt straight up into the sky, where he soared among the clouds, his laughter echoing off the mountains as he flew higher and eventually vanished into the distance.

EPILOGUE

A Walk in the Night

Tommy walked alone through the darkened town. It was well after midnight, and a light, soft mist was falling from the sky, and Tommy had his hands thrust into his pockets to keep them warm.

This was his hometown, the place where he'd been born and lived for his entire life, before everything went topsy-turvy. He used to sneak out of his parents house fairly often and just walk around the town late at night. It calmed him, feeling like he was the only person in the world, and gave him time to think. And that was what he needed, right now – quiet time, alone, to think. He and Micah had just had a very long conversation about Ryan. Micah always had a way of explaining things that made sense to Tommy, and their conversation had given Tommy plenty to think on. So, Tommy had asked to be sent here, alone. Just for a few hours, to clear his head.

Micah had explained to Tommy that Ryan had gotten the reward that he'd earned, and that Tommy should not spare him a second thought; that, if Micah himself had caught Ryan in the act of dabbling with dark magic, he would have personally destroyed him, and that, eventually, Micah WOULD have found Ryan out. That all made sense to Tommy, of course; still, it was one thing to know that a criminal had to be brought to justice, and another thing entirely to be the person that meted out such justice. Above and beyond even that... Ryan had been Tommy's friend. One of the best friends he'd ever had, if truth be told. Tommy had never hurt another human being in his life, and he didn't know if he'd ever get over the knowledge that he'd destroyed his friend.

"Heyyyyyyyyyyy, lookit here!" a voice said with a thick, heavy accent.

Tommy looked up in surprise. He'd been lost in his thoughts, and he hadn't realized where his feet were carrying him. He found himself standing in a dark alleyway next to a schoolyard. The yard was lit, but the alley and its contents were still dark, and cast in heavy shadows, so it was no wonder that Tommy didn't see the speaker – one of several young toughs sitting on cement blocks in the mouth of an open garage, drinking and smoking cigarettes.

"What do we have here, eh?" said the same speaker, as the toughs rose as a group and stepped into the light toward Tommy and forming a half-circle around him.

As the speaker came forward, Tommy found that he recognized him. "Poochie." He said in disgust. The older boy had been a constant torment to Tommy; he wasn't strong, or fast, and he certainly wasn't bright, but he always had a group of his friends around. Always. And that meant Tommy had never dared stand up to him, or even speak an impolite word. The danger was just too great. Poochie and his gang of thugs had taken Tommy's lunch money a couple times, and even once knocked him down and taken his brand new shoes – Tommy had been forced to lie to his parents about that. He'd told them that he'd taken them off to avoid getting them dirty, and misplaced them somehow. Tommy had always felt like his parents had seen through the lie – now, more than ever, he understood that they must have, but it had been the only thing he could think of to do at the time.

"Hey, Poochie, this little twerp knows you!" one of the goons laughed.

Poochie grinned. "Yeah, everyone knows the Poochie, eh?" He paused, studying Tommy's face. "Hey, I think I know this kid, too. He looks like the twerp that got kidnapped last year. The one all the cops were looking for. The one they said got taken by them mages. Is that true, twerp? You get hauled off and used by the mages?" Poochie sneered, and his companions gave a nasty laugh.

Suddenly, it was all more than Tommy could take. Ryan, Micah, the school, the evil man in the 'Canadian Bacon' T-shirt, it was all just too much. Tommy snapped. "Get away from me, Poochie. I mean it. I don't want to hurt you, but I will."

Poochie, however, didn't balk, and instead laughed again at Tommy. "Hey, guys, the twerp is gonna hurt me!" Poochie reached inside his pocket and pulled out a long, wicked looking knife. "Well, twerp, maybe *I* will hurt *you*, eh?"

Tommy's hands started to shake at the sight of the knife. He'd committed himself, now. There was no way this thug was going to let Tommy go now that Tommy had challenged him in front of his friends. Tommy could see the look in Poochie's eyes; The boy meant to hurt him, bad. Tommy did the only thing he could think of. He knew that was he was doing was wrong, he knew that he wasn't supposed to be using magic outside the school, but right now, he simply did not care. Tommy channeled and cast a spell, sending a strong arc of electricity into the hand

Poochie was using to hold the knife. Poochie's hand and arm convulsed, causing him to drop the knife to the ground, and with a cry of pain he stepped back away from Tommy, clutching his hand to his chest.

"He *is* a mage! Get him!" Poochie shouted.

The thugs took a threatening step toward Tommy, unsure about the magical display but determined not to look like cowards. Tommy called upon the magic again, and send a brilliant fan of flames into the goons' faces. It wasn't enough to really cause any damage – not like the arc he'd hit Poochie with – but it did burn off eyebrows and cause hair to smolder, and that was enough for the goons. "Screw this!" they shouted, and with that, they turned and fled down the alley, leaving Tommy alone with Poochie.

"Hey, man, I didn't mean nothing by it," Poochie said, backing away. "I didn't know you were some freaky mage!"

The comment vexed Tommy further. Even in his fear, Poochie couldn't help but be obnoxious and insulting. Tommy sneered at him, and sent another arc of electricity at Poochie, angling it this time so that it connected with Poochie's leg. Poochie screamed again as his leg spasmed, and he fell to the moist ground, leaving Tommy standing over him.

"I'm going to make you pay for every time you hurt me. You made me lie to my parents, you bastard!" Another arc of energy slammed into Poochie. And another, and another, as Tommy mercilessly pummeled the boy on the ground with his magical spells. A half dozen spells later, Tommy found himself panting as his rage and adrenaline drained out of him. Poochie was on the ground, crying and whimpering, his clothes stained from the damp ground and soaked through where he'd lost control of his bladder – whether from terror or due to the shocks Tommy

284

gave him, Tommy couldn't tell.

His rage gone, Tommy felt disgusted. Disgusted with himself for losing his temper and being such a bully, sure, but mostly disgusted with Poochie, and with Ryan, and with every other person who was so into themselves that they didn't care how they hurt others. These people were so small, so petty, that Tommy could only feel disdain for them. He didn't feel bad for hurting Poochie; Poochie had brought that, and more, on himself by years of abusing others. And suddenly, Tommy didn't feel quite so bad about Ryan, either. It was a shame that Ryan wouldn't be around to learn his lesson, but at least he wouldn't be bullying and hurting others, anymore.

Suddenly, Tommy felt deflated. He let out a sigh, and shook his head.

"I'm going home," Tommy said to no one in particular, and he turned and walked away from Poochie, back the way he had come. As he walked, Tommy realized that he was going home, but it wasn't to his parent's house. He was going back to school, to his new home, to learn how to be the kind of mage that stopped people from hurting other people.

THE END

THE CHANNELER

Book 1 of The Wind Lord's Gambit

Please enjoy this excerpt from the next book in the Wind Lord's Gambit, "The Guardian", available now

"Wh... what in the heck is THAT?!" Tommy's classmate John shrieked, and Tommy mentally echoed the boy's sentiment. Standing before them were what appeared to be four large animals, looking for all the world like a cross between an ape and a porcupine. They were an ugly, sallow grey in color, and, although they stood ready on their hind legs, they had a general slouched, drooping, ape-like posture in their stance. Thick fur covered their bodies, gradually becoming thicker and stiffer toward their forearms, lower legs, and backs, which were instead bristling with thick grey spikes. Their faces were furry and almost ursine, with a longish snout and a broad mouth, although there was a certain awareness or intelligence about their eyes that gave Tommy the impression that the creatures were possessed of, at least, a low form of cunning.

The largest of the bunch opened its mouth again and issued the same screeching-roar that had startled Tommy initially, and when it did, it revealed a double row of jagged, sharp teeth.

At the roar, John began backing away from the group, still shouting, "What IS it!?"

"Stay close!" Micah barked without turning his head. "Don't get separated from me."

John stopped his retreat, but didn't step forward back to the group. Tommy thought he was stupid – he didn't want to be any farther away from the Archmage than he had to be, and the only reason he wasn't crowding up behind the man is he didn't want to get in the way.

It was then that Tommy remembered he had a sword of his own. Chiding himself for being slow and stupid, he reached down and drew his sword, dropping into a ready stance with the sword held outstretched between him and the creatures.

As a group, the creatures bent down double, heads almost touching the ground between their feet in an impressive display of flexibility of which Tommy would not have believed them capable. Once they'd bent double, however, each creature shot a host of sharp, hair-like spikes off it's back at the party.

With a shout, Tommy threw his free arm up over his face to protect his eyes...

About the Author

Visit the author's website at www.williamhkline.com for news and updates.

William H. Kline was born in south central Pennsylvania in 1973. He is a highly decorated veteran of the U.S. Army and the Gulf War, and currently works in Information Technology and Cybersecurity.

Although he has lived and worked all over the globe —over 20 countries and almost all the states — William currently calls North Texas home, where he lives with his family of six.

William is an avid reader and gamer, including video games, role playing games, and board games. He enjoys watching and playing ice hockey, and normally plays right wing on the ice.

William enjoys writing Young Adult fiction. His first novel, "The Channeler", was released in December of 2018.

34008715R00173